LYING AWAKE

JESSE PULLINS

For my son, whose love for all things spooky has inspired me to create more terrible, unspeakable things.
Love you bud.

CONTENTS

*"The more you run, the deeper, more terrible it grows behind you,
its edges yawning at your heels."*
—Max Payne

CAR SALESMAN

I'm a car salesman.

Not necessarily by choice, it's something that just kind of fell into place. I work at a local dealer near the mall in town, one my dad's been running since before I was born. He loves cars and he loves to sell them; I guess that sums up why I work there. It's not a bad gig, and I've been doing it long enough to get pretty good at it. I've had some pretty good sales in the past. Some felt a little scummier than others, but hey, it's the way the trade works. I don't make much money if the cars don't sell, so it's in my best interest to do so.

I was sitting at my desk when it started. It was a decent but overall, slow day at the lot. The weather was nice, but I didn't get much of a chance to enjoy it because I hadn't had any sales all day. Not one. No young couple looking for a cheap ride, no bachelor looking for a lifted truck or sports car, no family scouting a replacement minivan. Nothing. So, I spent most of the day at my desk, twiddling my thumbs, listening to the radio, eyeing the lot in case someone happened to wander over. I was ready to get a sale, be productive instead of sitting around. My dad was out for the day, something about a golf outing with a competitor. He loved that stuff. Since I had the building to myself, I was hoping to put in some decent numbers, but on this particular day there was no one. I've had a lot on my mind recently and the business would help clear the chaos in my head. So there I sat, dicking around as the hours crept by.

That was until *he* showed up.

I watched him arrive by bus, getting off the shuttle at the stop through the window. I had nothing going on, so I watched him after he showed up. He got off the bus and looked straight at the dealership, a slow, almost limp of a walk starting as soon as he saw my building. My first thought of him was your stereotypical "boomer" dad—had to be pushing sixty. What was left of his wispy hair was gelled and combed across a colossal bald spot. His eyes were shielded by bronze aviator glasses and his outfit looked like it was ripped straight from an 80s business catalog. Khakis and old leather shoes, a floral print button up that barely contained a large beer belly, and a navy member's only jacket to tie it all together. He had his hands stuffed in the pockets of the jacket, and he was on a mission.

While he drew closer to the dealer I combed my hair, spit out my gum, and straightened my tie. It was evident he was coming this way, but he was heading straight to the lot, probably to browse. I just took that as my cue to meet him. I pushed through the door and into the sunlight, feeling the breeze for the first time today. He was just standing there now, scanning. He didn't linger on anything very long. I would have to do some digging to get this sale moving.

"How are we doing today?" I asked. "The name's Mark, I'll be your liaison today. Something I can help you find?"

He just stood there ignoring me for a second, looking at the cars at his own uninterrupted pace. With the aviators and the double chin, he looked like a grumpy frog. There was something unsettling about him from the get-go.

"I'm looking for a car," he said, "can't seem to find it. This is my third dealer today," he said plainly, very to the point.

I clapped my hands together, ready to start the routine I had done a hundred times.

"Well, this is your lucky day! We currently have an abundance of——"

"I'm not here for the sales pitch, kid," he cut me off, taking slow steps toward the shiny hatchbacks.

"Ah, well, certainly there's some way I can help. I know all the makes and models in this lot. We happen to be sitting on quite a bit—and let me tell you—*now* is a good time to be on the market." I started, turning around to face the luxury sedans.

"We looking for something sleek, for cruising, or maybe something a little sportier? Surely an old-top like yourself would—" I turned back to see he was already walking away. I felt a twinge of frustration. I'd have to work a little harder to get this guy to play ball. I scratched my head and caught up with him, then passed him up so I could lead.

"The mini-SUVs are one of our most popular items. Plenty of room for passengers, cargo in the back. All-wheel drive, too. I can't recommend that enough. You know how winter can be around here," I said. The man just looked ahead, chewing his lip a little. The wind blew at his combed strands, but he didn't seem to mind.

"Heated seats, Bluetooth, some of these even have TVs in them. They make the commute more enjoyable, *satisfying*. No interest on the first twelve months if you buy before the fall. We're at the tail end of our summer sale, but there's still time. Even if you need time to think something over, I'll get you taken care of. What do you do for a living if you don't mind me asking?"

Finally, he looked in my direction. His face was still blank, almost like stone.

"I was a car salesman. I'm retired now." He kept walking.

You've got to be fucking kidding me, I thought. This guy already knew the game. The tactics wouldn't work here. I'd have to follow him around like a lost dog and lap up whatever he fed if I wanted any kind of sale today. We could be here all day, and he still might not get anything.

"You don't say? Anywhere around here? Maybe you know my father?" I asked, keeping the enthusiasm going. The man had finally stopped at our little cluster of trade-ins from past transactions. The man looked them over one by one, the sun shining off the rims of his sunglasses as he panned slowly like an owl. He came to an old Buick and stopped, fumbling in the pockets of his windbreaker. He pulled out a pack of cigarettes and a zippo.

"Oh sir, I'm afraid I'm gonna have to ask you to put those away. We have a smoke-free premises," I said, but he continued anyway. He leisurely fished a cigarette out of the pack and lit it, taking a big drag before pointing to the Buick.

"The Lesabre. Get me the keys." He blew the smoke out at me, and I waved it away. I looked at the car, a creeping anxiety washing over me. It was a '98 Buick Lesabre Limited, silver with tinted windows. This car, of all things? Was this a game?

"Pardon? The trade-in? I assure you we can find something better to suit you. Walk with me, there's quite a bit I can show you."

"What's the deal with the price? Eight thousand? It blue-books for five tops. I know you heard me. Get the *fucking keys.*" He looked at me and took another drag. His tonal shift was alarming, and I found myself glancing around. We were still alone.

"Uh, y-yes. Right away, let me get those for you." I briskly returned to the office for the key. I was sweating a little, trying to wrap my head around the old man's choice. The Lesabre, of all cars. I thought about calling my dad, but decided against it. He would flip out, ask too many questions, want to know every little detail about what was going on.

When I came back he was peering through the windows of the car, his cigarette snubbed out on the pavement. I wanted to scowl at it, but I kept cool. I still wanted to get something out of this guy, I just had to figure out how.

"Looks clean. *Really* clean," he said as he peered through the driver's side window.

"They all are," I said, scratching the back of my head as I looked across the lot. The SUVs wouldn't do it. He was too old for a really smart car. I had a feeling the digital stuff would scare him away. Maybe the Lincolns?

The old man was looking at the paper that was taped to the inside of the windshield, the one below the large FOR SALE sign. It displayed the mileage and terms of sale. As is, no warranty, stuff like that. It was a trade-in, after all.

"Well, let's take a look shall we?" he was leaning on the car now, waiting for me to unlock it.

"Sure thing."

I smiled and worked the key, looking inside myself to make sure nothing was amiss. The front seat floors were still covered with paper shields to ward off shoe scuffs, and the back seat was nice and clean. Just as I hoped.

"Here she is." I reluctantly held the door for him, and he ducked his head in. It was hard to tell what he was thinking. It was those damn sunglasses. You couldn't see anything behind them. He chewed his lip as he looked up and down the dash, then his gaze held on the seats. They were tan leather, a clean shine still catching the light.

"Leather seats, very clean. Back in my day, these used to drive the girls *wild,*" he said under his breath, and I started to feel uncomfortable, "so many skirts in these back seats." He clicked his tongue and ran a finger down the clean leather. He looked at his fingertip and rubbed it against his thumb as if trying to feel dirt.

"Oh yeah? Is that so?" I played along, wiping sweat from my brow.

"Yes, of course," he continued, "you ever get a dame in the back seat of one of these, kid?" he asked, a grin forming on his wrinkled, stubbled chin. It gave me the chills.

"Ha, I'm afraid not." I gave a nervous laugh. "Say, a few rows down we have the Lincoln Town Car, a few of them actually, even in silver too."

Of course, he wasn't listening. With a labored wheeze, he leaned in and hit the button for the trunk. There was a soft clink when the trunk popped, and he immediately walked around me and headed toward the rear of the car. He stood in front of the trunk with it cracked a little, as if he didn't want to open it. He ran his thumb over the paint, then over the temporary license plate. When his thumb reached the dealership sticker, he stopped for a moment. The sticker was the silhouette of a diamond. He looked at me, still frowning.

"There it is, namesake of the business. You know, *Diamond Deals*. It was my dad's idea. I still think it's pretty cheesy, if I'm being honest," I said, unable to shake the feeling of nervousness. The old man seemed taken aback.

"Uh, yeah. There's that." He looked at the dealership sign, then lifted the lid of the trunk. As he stared into it, I found myself following and looking as well. The same silent stare. The trunk was empty, and there was a clear view to the little carpet hatch that led to the spare. The old man ran a finger over the carpet.

"Plenty of room in there, isn't there?" he asked. He was looking tired, perhaps the sun was getting to him.

"Yeah, I suppose there is. Good going-to-town car, I guess. Plenty of room for groceries."

"Or a woman," he spoke. It stood the hair up on the back of my neck.

"Excuse me?" I asked.

"You heard me." He looked at me, then slammed the trunk shut. It was loud, and I jumped a little.

"Sir, I think it's time I asked you to leave," I stammered, feeling a ball in my throat. I instinctively felt for my phone, and the old man stared and scratched at his stubbled chin.

"*Leave?* Who said I was leaving? I'm not finished here." He shoved past me and walked back to the driver's side. He dug in his pocket again, this time pulling a full half-pint of whiskey. He twisted the cap and broke the seal before taking a swig. I could only watch in disbelief.

"Hey, I don't know what the hell you think you're doing, but it's time for you to go. I'm calling the police." I pulled out my phone while he screwed the cap back on.

"Don't worry, I'll call them," he said, pocketing the whiskey and exchanging it for his own flip phone.

"*What?*" I asked.

"I said *I'll* call them. Don't worry about it, kid, I'll handle it." He flipped his phone open. I mulled it over in my head, sweating more and more as my confusion built.

"W-w-wait, that's not necessary. We can figure something out, I'm sure." I put mine away and held my hands up.

The old grumpy man looked at me for a moment before snapping the phone shut. He dug out another cigarette and lit it. I scratched my sweaty head and looked around, but it was still just us on the lot.

"When's the last time you drove this, kid?" he asked.

"What?"

"The Buick. You ever take her for a spin? After hours? When daddy's not lookin'?" he growled, his voice getting lower, like he was whispering.

"What? No, I've never driven this car before." I told him.

"Huh, that's funny. All these cars in the lot, and the only one without dust on the paint is this one. It's still got shine on the tires. Why spray that on there? Pretty it up? Why do that if it's overpriced? You only pretty up the front liners, kid." He was moving closer, the cigarette smoke dancing on the wind.

"I told you, I haven't really driven this car. Only around the lot, like the others."

"Another thing, kid. The paper on the window said it's got a hundred-thirty-thousand, seven-hundred and fifteen miles," he rasped.

"Yeah, and?" I demanded.

"Dash says seven-forty-seven." He took another drag.

"So what? The carFAX is off then. It's thirty-two miles. Who gives a shit? I'll print out a new one. I told you, the cars get moved around."

"Yeah, maybe a block or so, unless there's a maintenance issue. But you know what, there's a couple of bars in town, only a few miles away. You ever take her out for a spin, kid? Clean her up? Impress the girls?" he was taking another drink. My hands were starting to shake.

"I don't know what you're talking about," I said.

"Sure you don't. Let me tell you a story, kid, real quick. Like I said, I was a salesman too. I get it, I was there once. And I was *damn* good... But I tell you what else, I was a total piece of shit husband, and a worse father. I didn't give a damn about my kid, not really. They were just things that happened. The cars, on the other hand, I lived for those cars. That's what I loved—I got divorced a long time ago. Me and the wife never talk. My daughter, she must be a little younger than you." He was talking much faster now, raising his voice.

"Anyway, my ex calls me yesterday. We haven't spoken in years. She tells me our kid hasn't come home. She thinks she's missing. Said she called the cops. They didn't do shit, as far as I know."

"Yeah, so what? What's that got to do with me, huh?" I was getting loud, my voice echoing in the lot. I could feel the anxiety settling in.

"Thing is, her date picked her up that night. Like a gentleman. Car all done up, spick and span. Was the last time she saw her. Said he was driving an old silver Buick. Said there was a sticker on the bumper, like a symbol. She wasn't sure, it was dark out. But as it turns out, on the third dealer, I found it."

I looked at the large spinning sign, the glimmering letters: DIAMOND DEALS. I couldn't breathe.

"So, I think it's time to come clean." He took a last drag and snubbed it out.

"I don't know what you're talking about."

"Yeah, I think you do. Maybe your daddy ain't quite figured it out, but he will. He know you mark the price up on that car, to keep the eyes off of it?"

"*Fuck you.*" I clenched my fists.

"Sure, you only put a couple miles on. Bar's not that far. But I tell you what, you know what else isn't far away? The river. You could be there in ten minutes. So, what happened, kid? You push too far? She reject you?"

"You're wrong," I said, tears welling in my eyes.

"No, I'm not. This car's probably the cleanest on the lot. It's been vacuumed at least three times, and the outside's shiny and new. You don't wash the trade-ins kid, they're not worth the effort. How long till daddy finds out? You think he'll like that? You messing up that bad?"

"It was an accident," was all I said.

"Brat like yourself, maybe not used to hearing the word 'no'. She hurt your feelings, take you down a peg? Big man like yourself."

"I told you it was an accident." I felt my knees buckling, suddenly it was hard to stand.

"Sure thing, *kid*. I'm gonna cut to the chase. I'm calling the police either way. Either now, or when I'm on the way home on the next bus. They'll take everything I know and they'll find her—wherever she is. But it ain't gonna be quick. They'll drag you and your father through the mud through the whole process. You'll be finished," he said, and my legs could no longer hold the weight of the stress and guilt. I started sobbing, burying my face in my hands.

"What do you want me to do? I can't undo what I've done."

At some point he was standing next to me, getting one last thing from his pockets. Through tears and shame, I could see the pistol, a little .38 snub nose.

"I won't lie and tell you I was there for my daughter growing up. I wasn't, I know that. But she was still my daughter. I'm just doing what's right—it's the least I can do—but I'm no killer. You want to know what I want you to do? Atone for your mistake. Make sure it doesn't happen again. It seems like a better alternative to carrying the weight and rotting in prison, don't it? Either way, it's up to you. I did my part," he said and held the gun out.

I took it and cradled it in my trembling hands. The old man sighed and retrieved the whiskey, downing it in one large gulp. He winced behind his glasses and there was the glimmer of a tear behind the lens. He tossed the bottle into the parking lot and walked away, lighting a cigarette without another word. Through puffy eyes I watched him go, the same limp taking him back to the bus stop he arrived on. Without as much as a look back, he sat on the bench and waited for the next shuttle.

I climbed to my feet and went back to the office. I collected my things and locked up for the day, closing the dealership early. When I came back out, he was gone. The bus bench was empty.

Like he was never even there. The pistol in my pocket and the booze bottle in the parking lot reminded me of his visit; almost assuring me of what had to be done next. I got in the Buick and drove home.

It took me some time to process it all, but by the time I got home, I knew what I had to do. I sat down and wrote this, hopefully to clear up any questions for those that come looking for me. I know I'm a piece of shit and I did what I did. There's nothing I can do to fix that now. I'm sorry, really. I was in denial at first, and I tried my best to cover it up because I was scared. Scared of what I did, and the repercussions that would follow if it was discovered.

I've got a bunch of missed calls on my phone now. Too many to go through, and to be honest, there's no need. I've made my decision. There's a little bar on the outskirts of town called *The Sixth Shot*, with a little red neon sign. If you head east for eight miles or so, there's a small bridge with a river running underneath.

She's under the bridge.

I tried to use some rocks to weigh her down; I hope she's still there.

I'm sorry. She deserved much better.

Well, that's about all I have to say. I've learned from my mistake—I won't hurt anybody again. I got the pistol on the desk now and once I post this; I'm going to take the deal the old man gave me. At least that way I can try to set things right.

He did say he was a damn good salesman.

HUNTED FOR SPORT

A man once paid me to be hunted for sport.

I had stumbled across his post when I was browsing the web for work. I was looking for some sort of side-gig to pass the time. I was at a bit of a crossroads in my life; I had quit my previous job to break away from the redundancy it had sucked me into. It was a spontaneous decision with no real planning involved. Luckily in this day and age, the internet caters to people like me—people who don't care about chasing money or don't want to be tied down. It wasn't the money I was after, but the change it would provide. I felt like I couldn't enjoy anything in life, like I was just going through the motions.

That night I had been scrolling for quite some time, skimming over job posts, help-wanted here, short-handed there. I didn't think I would find anything to suit me. It all seemed like the same thing disguised under a different title. That was until I found this particular ad.

I thought it was a scam at first. Comical dollar signs on each side of the Craigslist title like a trap set for the elderly in search of credit card numbers. I clicked on it anyway, curiosity getting the better of me. In all caps the posting read:

$$$BIG MONEY FOR MANHUNT VOLUNTEER$$$

At least it was to the point.

The details below gave a brief introduction as to what the job entailed. I skimmed over them with amusement, half of me doubting it was true, the other half hoping it was. As ridiculous as the prospect was, I had to admit, it was exciting. There were some requirements for the job, however, and I was surprised to find that I fit the bill.

Must be male.

Must be young, and fit if possible.

Must not be afraid of the dark.

Must come alone.

No cellphones, no firearms, no police.

Must meet the night before to discuss.

The list went on for a while, but ultimately ended with a phone number and a typed signature as someone simply named Bob. I found myself thinking it over. I didn't exactly have anything to lose. No family, nor friends. I always lived alone; the idea of wanting to pack up at a moment's notice never seemed to sit well with any of the significant others I had in the past.

I don't know if it was stupidity or the need for adventure, but in the end I found myself grabbing my phone. I mean, how often do people get to say they were *hunted for sport?* The money wouldn't hurt, either. I gave him a ring.

The man who answered the call was tipsy but eager, and when I mentioned my interest in his post, he seemed to be ecstatic. Like I was calling to give him the lead role in a movie. The conversation was a little awkward considering the reasoning behind the call itself, but after a few minutes of cryptic back and forth we agreed on a meeting place. It was a few towns away—but he insisted I met him closer to his side of the woods.

The "hunt" would be at his estate, and I should stay in town so I was well rested for the event. We would meet at a local bar called *The Sixth Shot* to discuss terms and conditions. He seemed determined, like he had been waiting for someone for a while. He said he would understand if I was in no hurry, but with my current status of unemployment and lack of overall plans, I found myself matching his energy. I had to admit, the concept was a little exciting, if it was real at all. We decided to meet the next day.

The Sixth Shot was a bustling little place. A neon sign with a smoking gun made it easy to find. When I arrived, I found the guy immediately. He looked about how you'd expect a manhunter to look like, and he pulled it off well; a black polo and tan cargo pants, a shiny shaved head with a thick curled mustache, all worn on a very tan and muscular body. He was sitting at the bar alone, and he lit up like a Christmas tree when he saw me. Like he *knew* I was the one. He patted the stool next to him, almost like he was welcoming a long-lost friend.

When I crossed the bar, I was met with a firm handshake and a pat on the shoulder. He told me he was delighted to meet me, and drinks were on him. After a brief introduction, he got a glass of top shelf bourbon for himself while I sipped on an Irish red ale. I had acquired a taste for it recently.

Considering he was trying to hire me with the intent to murder me, he seemed like a pretty cool guy. We got to know each other a little before getting to the serious stuff, the people around enjoying their drinks none the wiser. The man known as Bob was actually Robert Callahan, a man born into a world of wealth and, as it seemed, perpetual boredom. His father ran a very successful chain of automotive stamping companies that he inherited from his grandfather. By the time his father passed there were so many buildings and people assigned to making the gears turn efficiently across the globe without his input he was able to live a life of leisure on a seven-figure income, all without as much as lifting a finger. The companies ran themselves as he grew older, and he filled his young adult years with seeking thrills across the globe. He tried anything that got his adrenaline pumping, from skydiving to white-water rafting. He took a liking to hunting—which he said had started an escapade of finding the world's most dangerous predators and killing them—no matter the cost. He said he had seen it all, but in all his years there was one thing he hadn't bagged: *a human.*

I laughed at his extraordinary lifestyle, feeling a bit mundane when it was my turn to share stories. Mine was far from exciting. I left the more boring bits out, but I told him I spent most of my twenties as a park ranger. It kept me close to nature and outdoors, but when it's all you look at, it tends to lose its luster. I left that to be a cab driver in the big city, something that kept me in transit and entertained for a while. Always moving, with so many people to observe in the busy city life. But in time I found myself too contained to the city itself, which was why I recently quit. Which brings me about to where I was now, discussing being hunted by another man. He was fascinated, jotting down notes in a little pocketbook while he sipped his bourbon. We conversed for a time. I finished a couple of beers, and he ordered another pour of bourbon. The conversation was nice. It had been a while since the last time I went out with "friends". Despite the fun I was having, we couldn't beat around the bush forever. When it came time to discuss the actual terms of our agreement, his face turned serious.

I would be paid five-thousand tonight, granted I still wanted to go through with it. He said this would help me "settle accounts" before the event. He said he owned a mansion outside of town, with over thirty acres of forest land. He was outside city-limits—his nearest neighbor was six miles away.

No one would hear screams or gunshots.

We would start tomorrow night; I was supposed to get to his estate at 10 p.m. After my arrival I would get fifteen minutes to head into the forest as a head start. He explained when the fifteen minutes were up, he would promptly signal with a flare. If I had any second thoughts, I needed to address them and withdraw from the woods before the signal. If I was still in the woods when the flare went off, I would be shot on sight.

He said I would be paid ten thousand an hour as I survived.

The hunt would go on until dawn, and *if* I was still alive come daybreak, I would be free to go. He would be armed with a hunting rifle and a combat knife, and I would be armed with my wits. It was evident it wasn't in his plans for me to survive, but that was something I had already come to terms with. He studied my face when he said these things, perhaps trying to gauge my reaction. I tried my best to play it cool, despite being a little nervous.

"Does any of this… bother you?" he eventually asked, downing the last of his drink.

"No. Not really. I've always just tried to go with the flow and doing that made me stumble upon your offer. Maybe if I get out and live a little, it'll encourage me to settle down for a bit more. That is, if I make it out alive." I winked, and we both had a laugh.

"Man, you're a *riot*. If I wasn't trying to kill you, I'd think we'd be pretty good friends."

After all the details were ironed out, he paid the tab, and it was time for us to take our leave. We shook on it before going our separate ways. He was excited for the next day, a pep in his step carrying him to his obnoxiously lifted truck. He burned out as he left, almost rear-ending a Buick as he left the parking lot.

I watched him go, feeling oddly serene in the cool night air. It was hard to describe. There was no one waiting for me to come back, no one to give me a courtesy call if I didn't turn up.

I don't know if it was the thrill of the challenge or just the drastic break in monotony. I spent my life trying to not be a creature of habit. Maybe this would be the last shift off course.

Or maybe tomorrow I would just die and not have to worry about it anymore.

With the moon shining bright and the cool breeze on my back, I decided I would take a walk before sleeping in my car for the night. It might be my last time to enjoy a night like this.

I woke the next day in the back seat of my car, feeling rejuvenated despite my choice of bed for the night. Through the blinding afternoon rays, I found my phone and checked my bank account.

He was a man of his word. The five thousand had been wired as promised.

I decided I would head into town and indulge in some of the local variety and find a place to shower before it was time to meet Robert at the estate. I climbed into the front seat and left the bar parking lot. On my way into town, I called my landlord and canceled my lease. I was already living in and out of boxes and my lease was month to month, so I wouldn't exactly be missed. After getting something to eat, I called and canceled all utility accounts for my apartment, electricity, internet, stuff like that. I had already put in my resignation at the cab company—there weren't really any ties to my life at my apartment. I would either survive till dawn and get the biggest payday of my life, or not have to worry about the next step if I failed. Either way, this was the end of the current chapter in my life.

After spending the day around town, I found myself driving to Robert's property, the sun already making its way into the horizon. His driveway was long and winding, leading to a gigantic house that looked like the surrounding forest was trying to swallow it. When I pulled up it was already almost dark. A butler greeted me at the mansion, an old man carrying a silver tray covered in a soft cloth. He opened the car door and let me out, introducing himself only as Charles.

"I'll be taking your belongings now. If you don't make it out, they will be destroyed at sunrise." He held out the tray.

"Of course," I said, handing over my phone, wallet, and keys. After placing them on the tray he offered a smile.

"Would you like a refreshment before heading in? Mr. Callahan said to accommodate you before heading into the forest. He truly appreciates you answering his ad," Charles said.

"I'm fine, thank you. I guess I'd rather just get to it," I said, wiping my sweaty palms on my jeans.

"Of course. If you will just follow me, it's right this way." He gestured for me to follow him.

Charles escorted me through the house. The inside was furnished top-to-bottom with luxurious wooden furniture. Bear skin rugs, chandeliers made of gold, paintings from the Renaissance era. The estate was definitely worth a fortune. We passed by a trophy room, filled wall-to-wall with mounts of animals from across the globe. They seemed to stare with their glass eyes, following us as we made our way through.

Charles made no effort to engage in conversation and neither did I.

The other end of the mansion consisted of a large patio. Waiting for us there was Robert, who seemed to be preparing for our little hunt. He was running a large combat knife over a whetstone, slowly and methodically sharpening the blade as we approached. Propped up next to him was his rifle. The bolt was pulled back, and several cartridges were laid out on a glass table. Next to it was the flare gun.

"The time is approaching," said Charles, and Robert nodded. He wiped the blade off and sheathed it on his belt.

I looked at his load out on the table, starting to feel sick to my stomach. This was seriously happening. Now that I was here and seeing him fully prepared, I couldn't help but feel like I was in over my head. Robert stood and grabbed his rifle. He picked up each .308 cartridge and loaded them slowly, one at a time until it was full. He racked the bolt forward and slung the rifle on his shoulder before grabbing the flare gun.

"Fifteen minutes. Then the flare. Having second thoughts?" he said, twirling the flare gun on his finger.

"No. Not really," I said, making my way off the patio. I wasn't exactly sure what to say in a situation such as this, so I figured it was best to just get it going.

"Excellent. I'll see you on the other side." He saluted me, and Charles gave me a nod. I turned and left the patio, making my way to the woods. Each step got heavier as I approached the trees, the darkness behind them getting eerier the closer I got. When I got to the tree line, I looked back at the mansion. Robert and Charles just watched expectantly. I swallowed and ducked in, feeling the full weight of my decision perhaps a little too late.

Once the mansion was no longer visible, I started jogging. I was mindful of my footsteps—a stray log or vine could trip me up. During my time as a park ranger, I spent dozens of hours hiking trails. I would survey the land weekly, picking up discarded things like trash and lost clothing.

This landscape was much different, however.

The ground was uneven, years of collected leaves burying fallen limbs and jutting rocks. I was wearing decent boots, but the terrain was unforgiving. One misplaced step and I could roll or break an ankle. I wouldn't be able to rush too much. If I could just maintain a steady pace, I would be able to put enough distance between us and maybe find a decent place to hide.

With the sun set and no light source, I couldn't see very far in front of me. I tried not to think about how much time had passed and focused on pushing forward. Ahead, the trees started to crowd, giant maples with lush branches blocking the moonlight that was trying to shine in. I ducked under them quickly. A twisted branch snagged my shirt, and I shook it loose. Birds screeched and rousted from their perch, flapping away in a panic at my presence. Their cries echoed into the night, sending a chill down my spine.

There's nothing to be afraid of, I thought to myself. *Not yet, at least.*

I came to a small clearing, and I took a second to catch my breath. I leaned on a tree, shaking clumps of mud and pine needles from my boots. The ground was wetter than I had anticipated. Off in the distance behind me there was an echoing 'pop'. I looked to see the flare reaching toward the sky, a little orange ball of fire. I pushed off the tree and continued. I had to keep moving. I ran across the clearing, each step squishing on the ground as I went. On my third stride my boot stepped on something awkward and hard. By the time I heard the clicking sound, I knew it was already too late—the sudden force clamping both sides of my ankle I couldn't help but cry out in pain. I stumbled awkwardly to the ground, agony shooting up my leg as I struggled to breathe.

I looked down at the bear trap, blood oozing from where the metal jaws were buried. I was frustrated by my foolishness. *Of course, he had trapped the woods. Why wouldn't he?*

I forced the jaws apart, the mechanism creaking, begging to bite down again. My hands shook holding the slippery metal and when my leg was barely free, I let it snap shut. The steel-on-steel bite clacked into the night, the sound so loud it bounced through the trees. A second later, there was an excited whooping noise.

He heard it. He would be coming.

I tried to see my ankle in the dark. There were nasty gashes on either side, but I didn't think it was broken. I got back up. It would hold weight, it just hurt like hell. I wanted to look back, but I pushed forward instead. Panic started to set in. Trying to regulate my breathing, I moved as quickly as I could—one strong step, one babied limp. I scanned the ground, looking out for more traps. There would be more, surely.

Branches whipped at my cheeks and pulled at my clothes. I tried to be more careful, but I just couldn't see them quick enough. My left foot squelched in its boot with every step, blood soaking through my sock and into the laces. I pressed on, hurdling over a large dead log. I had to find a spot to hide for a moment, catch my breath. My heart was racing. I was having trouble thinking rationally—as rationally as I could with the situation. An icy feeling of fear washed over me for the first time in a long time.

I had gotten what I wanted, a thrill to make me feel *alive*. But as I looked down at my mangled leg, I was starting to regret it.

Gunfire cracked in the distance. A branch next to my ear exploded, specks of bark and dust hitting my face from the racing bullet. I threw myself to the ground and started crawling, dragging my injured ankle. I drug myself to a large pine tree and I sat behind it, desperately trying to come up with a plan.

The gun went off again, closer this time. The round punched into the tree, shaking loose needles that fell from above. I squinted in the dark, attempting to see ahead. In front of me the ground started to slope, and I could faintly make out the sound of rushing water. It could be a creek or a small river. Keeping behind the large pine I slowly stood, trying to stay concealed until I was ready to make a run for it. I pushed off the tree and started to run for the slope, hearing the gunfire again as soon as I was in view. A fierce pain ripped through my shoulder and my arm went limp, but I couldn't stop. I started down the hill. I could see the shimmering surface of the creek below. There was something bobbing in the water—rotted logs from the looks of it. I needed to get there, get under the water and use the logs as cover.

I worked my way down the slope. The ground was wet. Each step threatened to slide out from under me. There were footsteps now, breaking sticks and brushing trees as they tried to catch up.

Another gunshot. The bullet whizzed over my head and missed. I tried to go faster and crouch down, but my feet were too unstable. I focused on the water, limping closer and closer like it was my salvation. I was almost there. Behind me I could hear the racking of the bolt action, and I shot a panic look behind me. I could barely see him working through the trees, twenty yards away. As I turned back to the creek, my good foot got caught on something and I fell forward.

I hit the ground hard and started to roll, painfully and awkwardly in the dark. I watched my descent in a swirl of moonlight and darkness, my elbows and knees clubbing the earth as I went. I came to a stop at the edge of the water, lying on my back, gasping for air. I could hardly move, my vision spinning as I looked at the sky. I could hear him coming down the hill slowly, carefully.

He knew he had won; he was taking his time.

Exhausted and defeated, I looked at the creek. It wasn't logs I had seen floating, but bodies. Several of them, bloated and rotting in the clear glow of the moon. The more I looked around, the more I saw.

Men. Women. Children.

I'm not sure what I expected. Robert was there now, boots squishing as he looked down at me. A pair of black goggles were over his eyes, a wicked grin on his face. He unslung his rifle and let it fall to the ground, then pulled the goggles off his face. He cast them aside like toys.

"Disappointing. Very disappointing. I thought with you being a park ranger and all, you'd make it further. But here we are, at the creek. They never make it past the creek."

Robert cracked his knuckles and pulled the knife from his belt. He held the knife in both hands and brought it down, aiming for my heart. I put up my hands to fight him, but it only delayed the inevitable. He worked free from my grasp and elbowed me in the temple, a blow that sent my vision blurring once more. My arms went slack, and he buried the knife in my chest, my lung collapsing as the blade went in. With a grunt he pulled the blade down, separating my torso down the middle in a nasty, gushing mess.

Satisfied, he got up and left me there to die.

I tried to talk, but it all came out as gurgled whispers.

"What? What was that?" he mocked, and he knelt to hear me. With the last of my breath, I spoke my last two words, just loud enough for him to hear.

"Thank you."

The involuntary screams came next. They were loud and shrill, broken vocal cords shouting in a mixture of barking and screeching. With both hands I pulled at the large incision, yanking the flesh apart in a spray of blood and disintegrating organs. His reaction was the same as all the others before him: a look of pure irrational fear.

My thin, inky black limbs burst from the gaping wound in my torso. I was on him in an instant, slashing the knife away and digging my nails into his flesh. I ripped his shirt like paper and separated his chest just like he did to me, my piercing screeches ringing into the night until I burrowed so deep they could no longer be heard. He thrashed and oozed from every orifice as he made room for me.

Just as the cab driver did, and the park ranger before him.

I ate and wriggled as he expired, worming and digging my tiny frame into each limb like a suit. When the fit was just right, I stood up and cracked my knuckles. I looked at my reflection in the water, running a hand over my face to feel the new fit. Better than the last one, for sure.

I took my time going back to the estate, making sure my walk was just right and everything was in place. The hours passed as I settled in, feeling more and more at home as I slowly worked the joints and muscles.

At daybreak, I emerged from the tree line to find Charles on the patio waiting. He came to greet me immediately.

"Sir! This one had you out *all night*. Was this one better than the others? Can I get you something to drink?" he said.

"Much better than the last. And bourbon, if you will."

PEEPING TOM

I'm a Peeping Tom. I've been peeping for years. I'm sure I'm not someone you want to hear from, but I don't have anyone else to talk to. If I can just get this off my chest, that'll be good enough for me. I'm not sure how much worse this is going to get. I'll start from the beginning, so I can try to answer as many questions as possible before it's too late. I don't think I have much time left.

I love to watch. I haven't always been this way. It's something that just sort of happened. It started innocently enough; I guess as innocent as peeping could be. It was curiosity at first, that and other people's inability to close their blinds. I've never hurt anybody. I've never stalked someone in the street, and I don't really use social media. Everything I've done has been done discreetly from the windows of my home. I don't take pictures or record, I'm just there in the moment, watching other people's moments.

I live in a nice condo on the second floor. My building runs parallel to the one across from me, with a little sidewalk courtyard deal filling the space between. It's a nice community, and I've lived there for a couple years now. I work remotely, freelance graphic design. I make pretty good money and it all gets done on my desktop PC. I don't really have friends, mostly just clients and colleagues from work. They mainly reach out when they need my opinion on a piece or want to do a collab, which is fine with me because I don't really like to go out. Almost everything I need can be bought online and delivered to my door. Before this started I was totally content with my boring introvert life. I never bothered anyone, and nobody bothered me. Plain and simple. That was until the Jeffersons moved across the courtyard.

Their name isn't really the Jeffersons, obviously. That's what I'll call them for simplicity's sake. The Jeffersons were your average young American family, hardworking husband and wife with a little girl. I'll call them Harry and Rebecca, and the little girl Julie. When they moved in, I watched from behind the blinds like your stereotypical nosey neighbor, just trying to see who exactly would be joining the community. Everyone does it. Before this the only thing I would gaze at out the window was a stray cat that would linger around, a little calico that had been there since before I started living there. I started calling him Cooper. I would've taken him in if I wasn't allergic.

At first, that's all it was. My time watching the Jeffersons changed slowly over. I wasn't just waiting there with my coffee creeping from day one. After they moved in, I would see them in passing; out the window, of course, because I never really left my home to begin with. The sliding door to their balcony was my dominant view most of the time, as they mostly keep their blinds open to let the natural sunlight in. This would let me see their whole living room. I was very discreet when I watched and I always watched the same way, on the right side of the window, in a crack at the very end of the blinds. I always kept my blinds closed, mostly to keep the light out. Once I started watching them more frequently, I decided it would indeed be problematic if I was caught, hence the discretion.

Harry was tall and handsome, with dirty blonde hair and fairly muscular. He worked construction or something like it, a regular nine-to-five kind of guy. His routine was mostly the same; go to work, come home and shower, help his wife with dinner and dishes, then spend time with the family until it was time for bed. Rebecca worked from home, some kind of online perfume trade, I think. She was a natural blonde like her husband and very fit; this I imagine came from the several at home workout regimes she practiced in front of the TV. I didn't watch for perversion; I watched because of admiration. I imagine I wasn't the only one watching her occasionally, but still probably the one watching the most. Julie would spend her days playing with toys and watching cartoons. It was amusing to see her on adventures, her imagination running wild. Sometimes when they came home from running errands in town, Julie would see Cooper trotting from the bushes, meowing as he went. She would stop and scratch him behind the ears before her parents called her into the house. Part of me wished they would adopt him. The three of them settled in nicely, like a little puzzle piece that was missing in the community.

Over time I grew fond of this family, and what started as a glance or two turned into checking daily. Outside my private routine of online design and clients, the Jeffersons provided a great distraction from the monotony. They seemed so alive to me. I was captivated by their existence; very real people in their day-to-day lives, something Hollywood tries so hard to replicate. There was no acting here, no script. Weeks of watching turned into months. I got to know them quite well. In time I would start to see patterns in the dinners they would make, in the TV shows they would watch. I would notice when one of them had a particularly bad day, and eventually I would be able to see an argument coming. But the Jeffersons were a pretty happy family from the outside view, and by the time I realized I was perhaps watching too much. I found myself unable to stop.

I watched them more and more. I would try to blaze through my work every day so I could get as much viewing time as I could. I would always break it up into segments; I wouldn't stand there all day, I would at least pretend I had interests of my own. I tried to get some other hobbies, video games, writing, knitting. I tried to binge TV series' online so I could get invested in another story, but I always found my way back to my bedroom window, peeking through the blinds. After all, I was already pulled into a story. And this one never ran out of content.

I watched all the time. I monitored Rebecca and her online perfume sales, and when she seemed to do better, I found myself sharing her excitement. To my surprise she started crocheting as well, and I got to watch her go from an amateur to building im-pressive skill. When Julie would play around the house, I would sometimes play along, and try to imagine what kind of story was unfolding. She started to draw, colorful pictures with crayons and markers. I bought a little monocular online, so I would be able to see the ones her parents put on the fridge. Harry picked up new hobbies as well. He started buying and indulging in more craft beers. At one point he picked up wood carving. I would chuckle at his crude starting sculptures, and I would wince and get saddened when he slipped and cut himself. When Julie got a little older, Harry and Rebecca started to have planned date nights, and Julie would stay the night with family. They would get all done up and go out all excited, then come home a little drunk and smiling. They would then pop bottles of wine or have one last beer, laughing and caressing as they made their way to the couch. Most of the time, they would close the blinds. Sometimes, they did not.

About two years went by as I enjoyed our little relationship. I was their little secret admirer. I know this sounds disturbing, and I do feel some guilt for seeing as much as I have. They never saw me, and I never tried to contact them. I never sent them gifts, I never tried to break the ice. Even though I knew enough about them, it would probably be easy to befriend them. I just wanted to continue my little watch from the bedroom window. This changed, however, the day I saw the moving truck parked in the lot.

I grieved the departure of the Jeffersons like the loss of a loved one. They packed quickly, and before I had time to come to terms with them leaving, they were gone as if they were never there. All I had were the memories of the Jeffersons. It pained me deeply when I looked through the slider and their presence was gone; the walls bare. As the maintenance crew came in and painted and cleaned the carpets, wiping their imprint from the place, I found myself drinking, lost in a slump in the shadows of my own home. They were gone, therefore my only hobby was gone, and I realized how truly alone I really was. Things were dark for a time, and for a few weeks the condo across the courtyard was empty. When I wasn't slugging through work, I was lying in bed, wasting the days away without drive or energy. I felt like a piece was missing, and I couldn't figure out how to fill the void.

One day another moving truck showed up, accompanied by what looked like a very expensive moving crew. For the first time in a while, I was back at the corner of my window, and I wondered if another tenant was moving out. The men in matching uniforms began unloading lots of exquisite furniture, much unlike what you would normally see around here. They carried it methodically to the empty condo where the Jeffersons lived and positioned the furnishings accordingly, even brought in decorators to make sure everything was positioned just right. It was a professional moving job, and as I lurked from my window, I wondered if maybe a movie star had rented the place out. They unloaded and set up in a matter of hours. Once the dishes were placed in the cabinets and the last painting was hung, they slammed the shutter on the loading truck and sped off into the night. It was very strange. I looked into the newly furnished dark condo with my monocular, trying to check out the stuff they had set up. I had never seen anything quite like it; grand leather couch and armchairs, ancient grandfather clock, paintings that must have been worth thousands. All set up and perfectly level. Truly immaculate.

I was so focused, looking over the possessions with my little monocular I jumped when someone turned the lights on. I pulled the monocular down and looked to see someone standing in the condo, almost like a statue. A young man stood by the light switch, looking around the room slowly at all of his possessions with a slight grimace of disgust. He was wearing all black, his skin pale, his eyes sunken. He moped around the condo painfully slowly, head cocked, looking at each furnishing one at a time. His face mostly void of emotion, he tucked his hands in his pockets and did this through every room. I watched with great interest, almost stunned to see a tenant so suddenly. I couldn't deny the excitement I felt, but something was off about the guy, something that made me uncomfortable. I couldn't explain it.

The incredibly odd fellow took twenty minutes to finish his rounds, and I watched in awe throughout the whole ordeal. When he finished, he stood in the living room once more, a quivering lip drooping into a frown. He was awkward and strange, but I still stood there staring. I'd felt so starved since the Jeffersons had left, I felt like I couldn't help myself. In silence I watched him from across the courtyard. With what looked like shaking hands, he got his phone out of his pocket and dialed, holding the phone to his ear. Whenever his call connected, he looked like he was mumbling at first. Small words, spoken slow. He started shaking his head frantically, blinking his eyes like he was trying to wake from a dream. Then, without warning, he was holding the phone in front of his mouth and screaming into it. Just raw anger, shouting into the mouthpiece of the phone, spit flying all over the screen. I could read his lips so clearly it was like I could hear him shouting in my head. Over and over again, he yelled at the person on the other end of the line.

I HATE IT. I HATE IT AND I HATE YOU.

Suddenly after another bout of screaming, he looked at the cell with pure rage and threw it into his television, sending it crashing through the flat screen. It had to be at least seventy inches, and now it was destroyed. I jumped again and decided I had watched enough for now. I didn't want him to see me, especially after an outburst like that. I left him to it and returned to work, hoping to get through a big project I was dragging my feet on. A local car dealership in town was going under, with new management already looking to take over once they threw in the towel. They wanted a design for the old lots spinning billboard, something sleek and new to scrub out the mom-and-pop look it had before it. There was talk of me doing the layout of their business cards as well if I delivered; all the more reason to climb out of my slump and get back to the grindstone. It would be nice to focus on something constructive. I sat at my computer and pushed the new neighbor from my mind, plugging away with into the night.

I worked into the late hours of the night. My mouse and keyboard clicked away as I found the right color scheme and layout on the billboard job. Time had been a blur; I had stopped eventually to brew a pot of coffee, getting up only to refill my mug and take a leak. I checked the time at the bottom corner of my screen: 2:23 a.m.

My progress had been pretty good, so I decided to call it for the night. I stretched and headed to my bedroom, sprawling out as soon as I was off my feet. I looked up at the ceiling in the dark, feeling the caress of sleep already luring me. My eyes grew heavy, but before I closed them I found them drifting to the blinds. I could just take a peek. What would it hurt? He probably wasn't even awake. There was no harm in checking after all. I sat up with a little excitement and creeped to the window and stood in the position I had done hundreds of times before. I cracked the blinds ever so slightly and leaned in. As soon as I looked at the condo across the street, goosebumps crawled across my skin.

The new tenant was sitting on the couch with the lights off, illuminated only by the glow of his broken TV. The flatscreen was a distorted mesh of colors, cracked black and white with rainbow streaks from his tantrum earlier. He just sat there in silence, arms at his sides as he blankly stared. The cellphone was still lodged in the screen. I rubbed my eyes with skepticism, thinking maybe I was hallucinating. I had been sitting in front of my computer for quite some time, surely I was just imagining it. I looked again, and he was still there, frozen on the couch. What the hell was this guy doing?

I watched for a while, going back and forth between his dead eyes and the destroyed screen. He didn't move a muscle, it almost looked like he wasn't breathing. It was hard to see with how dark it was. The seconds ticked by as neither of us moved, and a voice in the back of my mind started to nag at me. What if he actually *was* dead? I remembered the monocular in my desk, and I broke my gaze to go retrieve it. I shivered as I walked to my desk. The unsettling sight sent chills down my spine; I found myself rubbing my arms like the air conditioning had been blasting for too long. I got the monocular from the desk drawer and quickly returned to the window, discreetly angled it through the crack before looking through it. The looking glass exploded with color, and I realized I had it too far to the right. My entire view was the broken flatscreen. I started panning the monocular slowly toward the couch, carefully trying not to rustle the blinds. When I reached the couch, I saw nothing but shining leather; he was gone. I lowered my looking glass in confusion and nearly jumped out of my skin. Standing in front of the sliding door was the tenant, and he was looking right at me.

I gasped so loud and crouched in a panic, knocking my head on the windowsill. The blinds ruffled slightly, and I cursed at myself for being so stupid. I just *had* to look. I couldn't just leave him alone. And now he saw me.

I continued to crouch like a coward, not exactly sure what to do next. In my few years of people watching, I had never been seen, not once. This guy was full on staring at me; how he knew I was there in the first place I had no idea. There was no easy way out now. I had to deal with my situation. Maybe if I tried to play it cool he wouldn't call the cops, I guessed. I didn't really know.

After a deep breath, I peeked as slowly as I could. He was still there, standing in the dark. Staring at my window. Feeling like a piece of shit, I sighed and stood up. I pulled the drawstring for the blinds and held my hands up sheepishly, as if to say, "My bad." I held my breath and waited for a response, but he just stood there, awkwardly. We looked at each other for a time, neither of us breaking eye contact. I waited for him to get his phone and call the police or something, but then I remembered he threw it through his TV. I couldn't really make out the details from so far away, but I swore he was smiling. When the uneasiness reached its peak, I kind of shrugged and waved, as if to say "Alright, good night then," then I slowly grabbed the drawstring and let the blinds fall. It felt embarrassing, but I didn't know what else to do. I backed away from the window and scurried to the front door, making sure it was locked; it was. My living room is pretty bare, with a very basic couch and TV setup. The blinds on my balcony are always closed. I don't smoke, so I've never really had a reason to go out on it. With my lights off and door locked, I stood behind the blinds, wondering if he was still watching. I mulled it over for a while before deciding to look, and I held a breath before peeking. His living room was empty, and I breathed a sigh of relief. I wiped sweat from my brow, a bit surprised how worked up I had gotten. It was probably just an awkward misunderstanding. Feeling exhausted over the whole thing, I returned to my bedroom and collapsed on my bed.

I laid there for a time, tossing and turning restlessly in the dark. The silhouette of the man was still in my head, and I found myself picturing him every time I closed my eyes. Every time I would get close to drifting off, I thought of him. Eventually I rolled over, grabbed my phone, and started scrolling online for something to give me some peace of mind. I found a set of decently priced blackout curtains and purchased them, deciding I was tired of blinds, and tired of peeping altogether. I even paid a hefty amount to expedite the shipping. The site said they would arrive the next day, and I sincerely hoped that they would.

The next morning, I awoke disheveled. Throughout the night I had recurring nightmares of the man across the street. Just him and that damned broken TV with the distorted screen. I kept seeing his shadow in the corner, only to wake in an empty room. I felt ridiculous. After years of watching people, one person watches *me* and I can't sleep all night. The irony was not lost on me. The vulnerability changed me; I almost cowered around the windows. And when it came time to sit down for work, I found myself looking over my shoulder. There was no one there, of course. I was just psyching myself out. In time I started to focus on work, and I wrapped up the design of the dealership. After sending a preview to the client, I ended up scrolling online again, this time browsing for household self-defense. I didn't own a gun or anything for home protection really, not even a bat. It felt stupid, but I couldn't help myself. I still felt pretty rattled. I added one of those long flashlight baton things and a taser to the cart, and expedited the shipping once again. It would be better than nothing.

Later that night, I heard a knock at the door. I was on the couch playing on my phone when it happened; the sound nearly made me piss myself. I got up and tiptoed to the door, almost not wanting to check. Looking through the peephole, I saw the delivery driver, impatiently waiting for me to sign. I was still on edge, and the sight of him was a relief. I opened the door and signed for the package. The box was big and heavy, and I set it on the kitchen table. I opened it quickly and saw it was my blackout curtains. I guess this time the extra money was worth it.

A little excited I opened them up and carried them to my bedroom. They were thick black canvas, designed to block out direct sunlight. Hopefully they would block out everything along with it. I got a drill from the closet and started taking the old blinds down, drawing the screws out one at a time. It wasn't until I was pulling them down that I realized he was watching me.

I couldn't help but jump. I dropped the blinds in a fumbling mess at the sight of him, a grin visible on his face this time. He was standing in the living room in front of the slider with the lights on. Like he was waiting. How long had he been there? In the background the flatscreen still had the glitched spiderweb from his cellphone. I gave an awkward wave and tried to go about my business, but I couldn't help but notice he was holding something. Something white and rectangular. When he was sure he had my attention he showed it to me, holding it in front of him so I could see. It was a large poster board, a simple message drawn with big red letters.

I SAW YOU WATCHING ME.

I put my hands up and waved them, shaking my head, as if to say there was a misunderstanding. He shook his head slowly like I was wrong. I made some more hand gestures to try to convince him, but he started turning the poster board over, which made me stop. There was more writing on the other side.

I LIKE TO WATCH TOO.

I felt the knots in my stomach, and chills tingled down my neck. He was nodding slowly now, a big smile on his face. Panic started to wash over me, and I started to put up the blackout curtains with shaking hands. He saw me struggle and started to laugh, grabbing a marker while I tried to do my rushed install. He started scribbling with the cap in his mouth, and I started running screws above the window to speed the process up. I ran the screws through the curtains themselves and into the drywall, whirring the drill wildly while he scribbled. It was a hack job, but it would have to suffice. He put the poster board against the glass as I half-assedly draped the curtains on the screws, and I only saw a glimpse before shutting the view completely.

SEE YOU SOO—-

I backed away from the window and did the same as the night before. The door was locked, and I shut off all the lights. I didn't want him to see anything. I thought about calling the police, but decided against it. I thought back to all my times at the window watching the Jeffersons, dozens of times, hundreds. In a way, I felt I deserved this. I spent all night huddled in my bed; my desk chair propped in front of my bedroom door. I didn't sleep. Every creak in the building or gust of wind sounded sinister. I looked at the bedroom window throughout the night, wondering if he was watching behind it. The need to look nagged at me throughout the night, but I fought against it.

When daytime came, I was too tired to work and too anxious to eat. I laid on the couch for a while like a slug, unsure what to do. I moped around the house for a while, avoiding the windows. I tried to watch TV, but it couldn't hold my attention. I'm not sure how much time went by. The last thing I remember was checking the app for my online purchases, and there was an alert telling me my package was a few hours away from delivery. I snuggled up on the couch and decided to wait and ended up falling asleep.

It was nighttime when I awoke to a faint flashing light. I was in the dark on the couch, my lights still off from the morning. The light was blinking from under my front door, a repetitive flash that flashed into my dark living room. Disoriented, I shambled from the couch and turned on the lights. Against my judgement I looked in the peephole, only to see an empty hallway. I opened the door to see what the source of the light was. There was a small black trash bag on my doorstep, shining light shooting from small hole where it was tied off. I stared at it for a while, the light just blinking over and over again. I looked down the hallway. There was no one there. I picked up the bag. Whatever was in there was strangely shaped and stiff; there was no way to tell what it was by feeling it. I had to open it. I wish to god I didn't.

I brought it to the kitchen table and opened it with a knife. As soon as I punctured the plastic a foul smell filled my apartment, and the knife came back sticky and red. I didn't want to open it, my hands just did it, and the more I pulled apart the bag the worse it got. The overhead light illuminated the contents clearly, and I collapsed next to the kitchen table. Dry gagging first, then tears and uncontrollable sobbing. Stuffed in the bloody trash bag was Cooper the stray cat, his fanged jaws forced open into a petrified cry. The long flashlight baton was shoved down his throat, the lens strobing endlessly from his gaping mouth. The packaging receipt was stuffed in the bag too, a crude note scribbled in all caps.

WHY WON'T YOU LET ME WATCH?

I don't know what to do now. I left Cooper in the sink and I'm cowering in my room. I want to call the police, but I just can't. Part of me thinks this is a just punishment for all that I've done, the privacy of others I violated over the years. Maybe I do deserve whatever comes next. I thought I heard something on the balcony earlier. I wanted to look, but I was too scared. I ended up just staying in my room, and when things got quiet, I wrote this. It was a strange sound, now that I think about it. There was some shuffling, but it had to be the wind or something. I live on the second floor, there's no way. There was a loud snapping noise too, like crackling over and over again. Very weird.

It's been a couple of hours. The sun is starting to come up. I'm going to post this and get dressed. I decided I will come clean and go to the police. I'll tell them about the Jeffersons, the guy across the courtyard, Cooper, everything. I hope they can help me. The only thing that's bothering me is I haven't used my balcony in a long time. I can't remember the last time.

I hope it's still locked.

WATCH FOR DEER

The roads are different at night. It's something my mom used to say all the time. She said it when I was a child in the back seat, and she said it when she was teaching me how to drive. Every stretch of highway or backroad turn was different under the veil of darkness. I laughed at the concept at first, thinking maybe she was overreacting a little. I had just got my license, and I had driven many times before, but they had all been convenient, daylight drives in the past. I thought surely as long as I had a GPS and working headlights everything would be fine. In the end her words rang true, and it was something I learned the hard way.

My eighteenth birthday was two months ago. I was working a part-time day shift job as a dishwasher at a country club since I graduated high school. It wasn't a bad job, and it taught me the value of earning and appreciating your paycheck. I found that, despite my hate for school, I actually enjoyed working and making money to provide for myself instead of just hanging around and existing. My mom or my sister would pick me up after work in the family beater, an old Dodge Intrepid, so they could run errands and what not while I was at work. We didn't have a lot of money, and I was helping out around the house with what I made as a dishwasher. But that all changed when I ran into my cousin at the country club. He had offered me a job, making twice as much where he worked.

My cousin Scott was a steelworker. It sounded exciting to me at the time, a dangerous job, farther away from home than I was used to, lots of overtime, and bigger checks. I didn't have any plans for college, and I didn't have anything else lined up employment wise, so it seemed like a lifeline when he offered it to me. It would be my first Big Boy job, and I couldn't help but think of the dollar signs swirling through my head.

"It'll be good for you," he said. "You can get an early start, make some good money, try to get things on track. Make it through probation and you'll have a steady job to hunker down at for a bit."

After an application, a ride to a job interview, and a drug test, I was on my way to doing just that. I would start as a laborer doing grunt work, and when a bid came up, I might have a chance to move into something a little more concrete. I put in my notice at the dish pit, bought some steel-toe boots and some heavy cargos to wear until uniforms came in, and finished my two-weeks with impatience. I would start out on second shift, working three-to-eleven, and probably get forced into some overtime, but I was cool with it. Once my notice was up, I said goodbye to the friends I had made at the country club and got ready for bigger and better things.

With a new job starting, my mom said I would take the Intrepid myself, just in case I had to work way later than scheduled. She was worried about being out so late, and more importantly, driving at night. The mill was in a port twenty miles away, whereas my previous job was just down the road. There were only two ways to get there; the expressway that would get me there faster, or the backroad that went through the dunes that led to the port. My mother said the highway was out of the question, too many crazy people on the roads, and the fact I had never driven at night made her *very* uncomfortable. She said I would take the scenic route; it was covered in trees and traffic was light, and I would be fine as long as I watched for deer.

I was nervous and excited, but before I knew it, I was on my way to my first day. I plugged my phone into the aux cord. Since my phone was an old hand-me-down, I had to find a sweet spot for it to come in clearly. I set my GPS and put on some music and started the heavily wooded cruise. On my way to work, the drive was beautiful. The trees were tall and danced in the wind, rays of sunshine shining down all the way to the port. It was a more touristy route, I suppose, being so close to the lake. Gift shops and gas stations could be seen every couple miles, and there were several elderly men taking their project cars out for a Sunday drive on a Monday. At the halfway point in my drive, I caught a red light. The intersection was small, with an old train station next to it with a sign that read "Sandy Shores". There was a couple on a bench outside the station, cheesy smiles beaming as they posed for a selfie. It all seemed so serene, this beautiful drive, on the way to my much more profitable job, seeing these nice cars that maybe one day I would be able to afford. I looked forward to making this drive in the days to come. With my tunes playing on the stereo, a nice, easy speed limit, and lazily listing turns, I found my way to work and got to my first day.

The port itself was the farthest thing from beautiful. It seemed like a decaying hole in the land, nothing but dusty gravel, loud semi-trucks, and loud bangs echoing from the factories on every corner. I parked next to the other soot covered cars and headed in. After getting my own hard hat and being shown around, I was led to my station where I would spend the next eight hours putting bands on stacks of plate and verifying skid tickets. Some people were rougher than others, but the night crew seemed to be more populated with a younger crew, so I blended in just fine. I ended up with a guy named Terry, someone a few years older than me, who showed me the ropes and made sure I was out of people's way. He was a pretty cool guy, hard-working and priding himself on being an overtime hog. The job was a little stressful, but the banter in between packaged loads made it a little easier.

Despite the intimidation of the overhead cranes and loud percussion of the machines, I focused on the tasks at hand and doing the best I could. I wanted to impress management so I wouldn't get axed during my probation. The day seemed to fly by. Halfway through the shift, the supervisor let me know Terry and I were getting low-manned to stay over a few hours after the shift to pick up the warehouse. Something about cleaning up to install cameras for the line. Terry was pleased and said he would've volunteered anyway. It was seniority-based overtime, so if I wanted to keep my job, I didn't really have a choice. Even though the shift was extended, it went pretty quick; the labor was way less monotonous than doing dishes all day. I was told I could wrap it up for the day and head home. Terry said he would stay and try to milk it a little longer, and after a fist-bump I punched out and it was time to go home. I was feeling extremely accomplished and optimistic, that was until I got to the parking lot. It was dark outside. Very dark.

The parking lot was mostly empty, except for my car, Terry's, and the supervisor's. Out in the port, the air was chillier and more eerie than back home. It even *felt* darker, like I didn't belong there. Trying to maintain my high spirits, I walked to my car, which was now covered in the dust that blew around all day. I got in, started it up, and plugged my phone back into the aux so I could hear the GPS and music on my way home. I texted my mom that I was on my way, and after picking a song I was ready to go. *It shouldn't be too bad*, I told myself, and as I pulled out of the parking lot, I prepared to cross another milestone in the same day: driving home at night.

Leaving the port was just as different at night. Instead of the sun lighting everything up there was just a row of orange lamps lighting the way out. A few semis were shouldered for the night; drivers that were sleeping to get the jump on the next load first thing in the morning. It seemed so desolate compared to earlier this morning. As I drove through the exit and back on the scenic route that would take me back the way I came, I realized that the orange lights in the port would be the last of my light for a while. Once I left it was just me on the road, my old beater car chugging away into the night. It wasn't too bad; the visibility was a little worse than I thought, but at least I had the GPS and music. The drive was only a half hour. Before I knew it, I would be back home and showering after my first long day of work.

Entering the wooded portion of my drive felt like driving into a cave; the tall trees leaning over the road blocking out even the slightest hint of moonlight. I focused on the drive ahead, the worn aux input crackling over my music. Each bump in the road seemed rougher than before, each branch reaching just a little further in the headlights. I white knuckled the wheel as I drove, feeling silly for being as on edge as I was. It was just a short drive. What was the big deal? Everybody drove at night. People did it all the time.

Each winding curve seemed to turn into the same repetitive stretch of trees, like I was driving through the same segment over and over again. Time seemed to crawl as my car chugged down the road, the hi-beams reflecting off every sign as I made my way. Old, beat-up signs for no passing. Signs warning of a low shoulder. Signs for deer crossing. It looked at them all one by one, my eyes lingering long on the yellow square with the silhouette of a buck prancing.

Watch for deer.

To my surprise there wasn't much to watch out for, except for the trees. Just when I thought I wasn't making any progress, I found myself at the same intersection from earlier, caught at the same red-light. I slowed to the inevitable stop and sat waiting, my progressive rock drumming against long-blown speakers. My eyes drifted from the road in front of me to the train station, the sign for "Sandy Shores" not lit with a flickering neon. The bench with the couple I observed earlier now stood empty under a lamppost, littered with discarded trash from the commuters throughout the day. There wasn't a soul in sight. No other cars, nobody else making a trek somewhere in the middle of the night. It just felt so *dark.* I checked the GPS as I sat. I only had twelve minutes until I reached my destination. The drive was practically over already. As I looked down at my phone, I saw the green glow fill the cab as the light changed. I eased off the brake and continued.

I thought of the work I did prior, and how my muscles were sore in a way I had never felt before. My joints ached differently, like I had spent all day logrolling down a hill. I thought of a hot shower, and washing away the dirt and rust that circulated through the air of the plant as the production line ran. As fulfilled as it made me feel, in the back of my mind I wondered how people did something like that every day for work. I guessed I would just get used to it. Ahead, I saw a pothole in the headlight's glow, one I wouldn't be able to swerve away from in time. The passenger side tire hit it dead center, the impact rocking the entire car on its shot suspension. I winced at the crater in the pavement, and the crackling in the music got worse as the aux lost its sweet spot. The grinding distortion in the stood my hair up as I reached for the cord and found nothing but an empty seat. I felt for my phone in the dark, my fingers trying to trail the cord to the source.

"Come on," I said, fumbling in the dark. After several attempts I couldn't quite find the phone, like my hand wasn't making the connection to my brain about what it was supposed to be look—

I saw the eyes and the reflection of the fur too late, and I slammed on the brakes. The tires squealed as I flew toward the baby deer, my entire body seizing like a frozen statue. I could only squeeze the steering wheel and stomp my foot as hard as I could, unable to totally alter the momentum of the car. I stopped suddenly but not fast enough, the car screeching to a halt just late enough to smack the fawn with the front bumper. The hit was quick but solid, and I watched in denial as the young animal was tossed off its hooves and tumbled down the road in front of me.

I grit my teeth so hard they hurt. I looked at the body dumbfounded; it had happened so fast, there was no way it could just... come out of nowhere. I didn't have enough time. Even if I wasn't distracted, there was no way I could've... How was I supposed to—? The static was worse through the stereo. My phone lost somewhere in the abyss that was the passenger side floor. The cord had followed it, and it hung from the jack at a sharp angle like a tugged fishing line. I sat there with my jaw hanging, unsure of what to do, unsure of what to think. Before I had the time to even process what had happened, ahead of me another bright shape echoed in the headlights, another deer with big ears and a shiny coat had walked into the road slowly, like it couldn't believe what it was seeing. With hesitant steps it crossed the pavement, and as I painstakingly watched it nudge the motionless body with its snout, I came to the horrifying conclusion of what I was looking at.

Its mother.

Ahead of me, the majestic plump doe nudged the still corpse of its child, and as it registered what it had found, promptly erupted in the saddest cries of pain I have ever heard from an animal. With its head whipping around in desperation, it called to the woods surrounding us, its calls echoing through the trees and chilling me to the bone. Its loss, the emotion it felt, was brought on by me, and the guilt washed over me like a smothering plague.

I couldn't think, I could only watch. I watched helplessly, wanting to do something, but the cruel realization settled quickly. What could I possibly do? Other than run down its child, how could I *possibly* help the situation I had caused? From the passenger floor, my phone struggled against its lack of proper connection. The grinding static was worse and assaulted my ears, but I didn't dare look for my phone now. I could only look ahead at the grieving doe and the child I'd run down. I thought about calling someone, maybe calling my mom, but then what? She would be asleep, and when she woke up, there would be a cataclysmic uproar. And even then, I had the only car. It's not like she could come get me. I swallowed hard, and after what felt like an eternity of mulling it over, I decided the only thing my piece-of-shit self could do in a situation like this. I would try to go around them and drive away. I felt the tears welling in my eyes and my nose starting to run as I readjusted my grip. My foot was still stuck against the floor, so I started easing off the brake, committing to my decision to flee. Before I could let off, however, I heard a faint tap on my window. When I turned to my window, my blood went cold.

Staring at me was a giant set of glass-like eyes, belonging to a large eighteen-point buck.

With wide, bulky shoulders, it stood in the entirety of the on-coming lane, hunched down so it could look through my window. Its antlers reached far from the sides of its head, each pronounced point bulbous with velvet. After a deep inhale, it snorted into the chilly air, fogging the glass that seemed so thin under its size. The dark pupils were entrancing and terrifying, like the inside of the car was shrinking under their gaze.

"I-I'm sorry, I didn't mean, it just happened, I'm sorry," I mumbled to the large stag, my hands shaking on the wheel. The swirling fear pulled at my gut, and I felt like I was going to piss myself if I didn't look away. For only a second I looked at the doe and its child in front of me, my sense of flight wondering if I could chance it and take the shoulder off road and get past them. The groaning aux continued on the floor, the cord begging to be adjusted or pulled free altogether. I looked at the giant deer in desperation, wanting to apologize more but knowing it would be useless. Only when it raised its head did I realize it wasn't looking at me but past me, to the other side of the car. I followed its gaze and saw another of the herd had crept up, a younger male from the looks of it, two little velvet points sticking from its head. It investi-gated the car as it walked up, timidly observing the shape of the car before looking inside. It looked at me, then at the elder, exchang-ing their unsettling silent glare on opposite sides. As I was caught in the middle, the doe ahead let out another pained wail.

The great deer exhaled again, spreading the fog on the win-dow. It tipped its nose to the younger deer, and I watched as it fluttered its ears. The younger one started looking into the car, its head panning the interior as the older one watched. The static on the radio came in and out, like a radio station tuning. After a moment it paused and stared at something in the dimly lit cab. It didn't make sense to me. On my left the elder was looking at the same thing. At first I thought it was the dash, but they weren't looking quite at it. Slowly, I realized it wasn't the glow of the radio they were transfixed on.

They were looking at the keys.

In a fit of panic, I reached for the switch next to me, and locked the doors. A second later, the younger deer lowered its head and hooked one of its nubs on the door handle and jerked up, trying to work the latch. The loud knocks of the handle slapping were loud, and I jumped. The larger deer snorted angrily. It looked at the lock on the windowsill in a way that I could only explain as pure anger. I blindly felt for my phone again and was painfully reminded it was still on the floor. The radio cackled as I fumbled with the cord, and I could swear I could hear words over the frequency. It was barely audible, but I could swear it sounded like: "Let. Us. In."

The larger deer stared at me again, and without warning, smacked its antlers on the window. I jumped at the sound of it, and I prayed to God the glass would hold. I looked forward again, at any possible route to drive away. With them boxing me in, I would have no choice but to swipe one of them or run into the mother directly. The larger one smacked the window again, this time busting the velvet, leaving a gritty red splotch on the fogged glass. It drug it across the window, making a dark smear as the bony point scraped along. Ahead, the doe rested its head on its still offspring, its chest heaving with human-like crying. Tears streaked down its fur, and at the sight of it was like I could *hear* the sobbing inside the car, over the radio.

"Let. Us. In. Or. Let. Him. In."

I tried to reach for my phone again. I chanced a glance at the floor, and I could see the outline of it on the floor in the far corner. I gently pulled on the aux cord and the distortion worsened with every tugged, assaulting my ears. I tried to turn off the radio, but it wouldn't work; the volume and source buttons only yielded the same digital ERROR message on the display. The larger deer was rattling its rack against the window faster now, a bleeding mess trailing behind the shedding velvet. The younger deer pressed the side of its face against the passenger side window, its dark eyeball pressing against the glass as it tried to look in as close as it could. The mother deer's crying could be heard over the radio. There was a menacing chorus rising in the static, something that was trying to push through. The human crying was so loud it was like a woman sobbing in the backseat, sobbing in my ear. I looked at the window with the larger deer, with the array of bloody streaks, and as the streaks seemed to take shape, the crying and the chorus grew louder. The streaks weren't just random nudges; it was drawing something. It was drawing a pentacle.

With the last crude stroke that completed the crimson star and circle formation, there was a fog rising from the ditch on the side of the road. The mother buried her face into the lifeless fawn like it was trying to hide. Now that the crying had subsided, the chorus seemed clearer, and it hit me that it wasn't singing or anything like it.

It was screaming.

Horrible, tortured screams.

Through the billowing fog, a wicked amalgamation of antlers jutted from the damp leaves and grass. With bright red rays it tore through the earth, the sounds of a hundred screaming souls droning over the radio as the rack poked through. The volume on the radio kept turning up. I covered my ears to thwart the punishing sound. The deer on both sides of me just stared at my anguish, the sound rising a pitch so great I thought the windshield would shatter. As the deer stared, I could see their faces began to shake, like a movie stuck on fast forward. Their eyes rattled in their skulls as their faces blurred, the speakers in the car whining under the strain of hopeless cries and pleas.

The phalanx of antlers gave way to fur, wrapped around a skull bigger than a moose. Through the cold mud it steamed in its ascent, whether it was torn velvet or strips of flesh hanging from its points I wasn't sure. They dangled like drying strips of meat. Beside me the deer shook so fast their features distorted, some of them animal, others human. It matched the screams coming through the radio. As the full bust of shiny black fur was through the ground, the fog wisped away as if on fast forward as well. The head of the giant deer opened its eyelids to reveal two bleeding spheres the size of baseballs, its jet-black pupils narrowing in on me, cowering behind the steering wheel. I closed my eyes, wondering when I had started to scream. My scream blended with the others, one and the same.

The screaming stopped. I sat there with my hands over my ears, my eyes squeezed shut, afraid to open them again. I heard the snort once again, and it was a moment before I gave in and looked in its direction. The large deer was still there, but it wasn't looking at me anymore. The screaming was gone. The bloody pentagram was gone. The mysterious fog and the shadowy black deer were gone. I lowered my hands to see the younger buck was looking as well, its ears fluttering with excitement. Not only were they not looking at me, they were walking away.

Ahead of me the fawn I had hit just minutes ago was blinking awake, confused and disoriented. After a struggle it stumbled to its feet with the help of its mother, and weakly stood on its own after a few licks and prods with her nose. The large buck snorted and nodded at the baby, and after a moment of consideration, it nodded back. The large male gave an approving snort and turned to the mother, who nodded as well. I watched them in silence, not even sure what to do anymore. All at once they looked at me, a family of four, their many glassy eyes reflecting in the headlights. I put my hands up in defeat. I couldn't help but stare back, my hands shaking as they huddled closer together. With a snort the large male nodded, once at me, then once to the open road behind them. I didn't believe it. Slowly they moved together, giving me enough room to drive past them. I hesitated, but not for long. As soon as there was enough room, I let off the brake and started driving, creeping past the family herd as they watched me go.

I gave an apologetic look at the baby, who returned it with twinkling eyes. As soon as I was clear of them, my foot pressed the accelerator and I got the hell out of there. Even though I was clear, I couldn't help but look in the rear-view mirror behind me, to make sure they weren't chasing me.

I wish I would've just kept my eyes forward instead of behind me.

They watched me go in silence, their dead stares unblinking as my car got further and further away. Just as they were almost out of view, they stood up on their hind legs. One by one until they were all upright with their front legs at their sides. The mother and fawn walked away first, with the younger buck following close behind.

The father stayed, however. His stare followed until all I could see was an open stretch and trees behind me.

TAKE ONE

It happens the same every year. All the houses in the neighborhood don their yards with skeletons and spooky lighting, carved pumpkins, paper cutouts of bats. They dress the properties up with just as much enthusiasm as the kids and their costumes, all for the sole purpose of basking in the spirit of Halloween.

The house two doors down always goes all out; strobes, inflatables, artificial fog—the whole nine yards. It attracts kids from all across town, serving as some kind of meeting point for the trick or treaters. With pillowcases slung over their shoulders and plastic jack-o'-lanterns in their hands, they start their proud march, every princess and zombie trying to get the biggest haul of their life.

Every year I turn off the lights and pretend I'm not home, sitting in front of the TV with my dog for the annual marathon of slasher films. I'm a bit of a scrooge this time of year—I don't really decorate my house. I don't even pass out candy. The street bustles with the combination of laughter and screams, each child and teenager trying to make each year more memorable than the last. From the darkness of my home, I catch glimpses from the window on the commercial breaks. Everything seems festive and normal, all except the house across the street.

I didn't notice it at first. The house across the street is abandoned, almost derelict at this point. It was a modest loft house before it went unkempt, with a little garage and a big stretch of porch to walk up before you hit the front door. There's a rocking chair on one side of the door and a window on the other—I imagine it would've been a nice set up back in the day. A nice fall day, sip some cider on the covered porch in the rocker, hear the television from the open window. Now, the windows are boarded up.

The garage door sits lopsided on its hinges, and there's so many old twigs and leaves matted on the porch roof it looks like it'll cave at any second. The rocking chair sits empty, dust and mold collecting over the years. No one's lived there for a long time. I don't think it's even on the market. It remains its old, weathered self all year round and everything seems fine. But as trick-or-treating comes to a close, that changes.

I have it narrowed down to the last twenty minutes. Every year from five to seven, the kids go up and down the street raising hell—hopped up on sugar and the Halloween spirit. The old house stays dark and quiet most of the time, but at 6:40, that porch light kicks on. In the flickering light a little orange bowl appears in front of the door. A few feet away, the rocking chair is no longer empty. There's a clown sitting there. His get-up is crude and old, like an alcoholic uncle that threw on a cheap jester one-piece. The eyes are closed but the eyelids are painted, cartoonish eyes staring at you while it sits perfectly still. A rusty kitchen knife held in a frozen hand. A little paper sign is stuck to the door, and in big red letters it reads:

TAKE ONE.

I've never seen anybody physically set it up, it's just there. One minute it's dark and the next the light is on. It's almost like someone ran up when you weren't looking and propped the stuff up as a gag. But I've never caught anybody, never seen anybody in the act. It just *happens*. The thing is, that little orange bowl, it's loaded to the top. Not with dollar store candy either, King-Size Bars. The first time I thought maybe the property owner was trying to give back for having such an eyesore year-round. Or maybe a homeless guy was trying to have a little fun, scare the kids, that sort of thing. But it shows up every year, and it's exactly the same every time. The same scuzzy clown, the same candy bowl, the same written sign. The most unsettling thing is the window by the door. All year the windows in the house are boarded up. But when that light kicks on, the window by the door is open. No boards— nothing. The faded drapes on the inside sway in the night breeze, but that's all you can see. It's pitch black when you look in there. There's just that damn clown with his painted eyelids and the open window.

People started going missing. Articles in the paper would be shown the next day, some kid or teenager wouldn't make it home after going door-to-door looking for candy. Every year without fail, there would be a new face to look out for. I would think of the house across the street immediately. But the strange thing is, I seemed to be the only one to see it.

The porch light, the clown, the bowl of bars.

I talked to some of the neighbors—and everyone thinks I'm crazy. It got to the point where I called the police; I was sure they'd kick down that door, find a body, or at least some evidence. Maybe bones or clothing—something.

I've called them twice. Twice they came out, and they searched the whole damn house. They found nothing, absolutely nothing. No human remains, murder weapon, not even footprints. Like nobody has been there in ages. They tell me next time I cry wolf, I'll get a ticket.

This year, at 6:40, I watched from the window. The light kicks on and they're there. Clown, bowl, paper sign, open window. I see some kids coming down the street, both dressed as animatronics. They look tired and ready to go, but they see the light. They go to the door. They see the giant bars, they jump with excitement. They read the sign.

TAKE ONE.

They look at the clown, and they wait for the jump-scare. But he just sits there—with a knife held limp and blank-painted stare. Each of them picks one out, but there's a longing as they look at the bowl. It seems like their conscience got the better of them, and they leave without succumbing to greed. Heading off the porch, they pass a teen in a hoodie and skull face paint. He pushes past rudely, almost knocking over one of the kids. They seem upset but they don't look back; they don't notice the clown behind them. The painted lids rise, revealing staring, bloodshot eyes.

This year, I passed out candy. I turn on my light and I'm out with my own bowl, waving the kids over—waving them to safety. The eyes of the clown look at me menacingly, like a warning, but it doesn't last long.

The teenager is stuffing the bars in his pockets, as many as he can hold.

I show the kids my bowl of suckers, tell them the haul's over, to take as much as they want. They're ecstatic. Too happy and focused to look back at the slowly standing clown.

The teenager leaves, and arms of nothing but bone shoot through the open window. One grabs his arm, the other planting a stiff hand over his mouth to silence him. The clown is there in an instant, eyes wild, the knife digging deep, stabbing over and over.

The kids take handful after handful. I show them the silly paint I put on, and if I have to, I'll ask them about their costumes.

The teenager fights, but it's over just as soon as it started. The clown stabs and rips, the old blade eviscerating crudely. The arms are already pulling him in, his screams blend with others in the distance.

My eyes tear up and the kids get worried. I dump the candy in their bags, trying to stay joyous. My hands are shaking, but I play it off. I call my dog to the front door so they can see the silly spider costume I made him wear. Their laughter drones out what they don't want to hear.

The clown grabs the teenager by the ankles and helps the skeletal arms in the window, pushing him into the dark abandoned house. He leaves the knife sticking from the torso, arterial spray staining his ratty costume. When the feet are sucked in, he slams the window shut. For a moment, he looks at me. His stare is cold and terrifying, but I don't look long. I don't want to draw his attention.

Across the street, the porch light shuts off, and it's all gone. I still feel the eyes on me—but there's nothing there. Other houses seem to take it as their cue, and one by one, trick-or-treating comes to an end. The kids grin with their heavy bags and wave goodbye, going back the way they came. I'm left at the front door and the air is suddenly chillier. I look at the porch ahead and I almost swear I can see him still sitting there in the dark, but when a car passes the headlights show an empty chair. I take my empty bowl and *shoo* my dog inside, realizing I'll either have to do this again or move. At least I have some time to figure it out.

Happy Halloween. Until next year.

BRAXTON THE SNOWMAN

Everyone loves the holidays. The decorative lights go up, the bell ringers jingle outside the stores, and the cheerful music hits the radio a little earlier than the year before. The holiday season lifts the spirits of everyone around. The colorful pines, fake and real, are erected in living rooms, ornaments hanging from every branch with the shining star placed at the pinnacle. Carols are sung and gifts are bought, each wrapped in prints of reindeer and candy canes. Aside from the annual stress, everyone gets a little lift from the Christmas spirit, and just for a while, everything doesn't seem so bad.

That is, for everyone except me.

I hate the winter, and more than that, I hate Christmas.

Not in the sense of Ebenezer Scrooge, or the mischievous grinch. The disdain is imprinted in my mind, and no matter how hard I try to repress the memories they resurface from the moment the jolly tunes can be heard. From my window I watch the serenity of the first snowfall, that magical canvas of white drawing kids into the cold so they can throw snowballs or make angels. I watch them frolic in their little wonderland, laughing and giggling as they stick out their tongues to catch a dancing flake.

So much happiness, and yet the only thing I see… is his face.

The plopping of wet rocks, the creaking of broken branches, the clacking of fake teeth. When I watch them pack the snow, I get sick to my stomach. I dry heave in the toilet until the nausea passes and my hands stop shaking. Years of therapy. Medications. Drinking. No matter how hard I try I can't escape the horror of the past. Just when the walls start to repair, he's there. I close my eyes, but he haunts my dreams. Each time I start to drift away the grip of branched hands pulls me back.

I'm not allowed to move on. I'm not allowed to forget Braxton.

This story happened a long time ago. Twenty years ago, to be exact. Sometimes I think it was just a bad dream, that it never really happened. Growing up I blacked out the memories, drifting around like a shell. As I got older, however, the memories returned. Slowly at first. The winter wind, a broken branch, a pair of dentures. For a while I questioned whether it even happened or not, but when I go and look at the police reports, I am brutally reminded that it is forever etched in history. "The Tragedy of Cyprus Glen" that shook the small apartment complex in the early 2000s has long since been forgotten, as all the families impacted have moved away, or in some cases, were incapable of moving on. Nobody speaks of it, not even a little. But as I watch the first snow behind the fogging window, I find myself adding something stronger to my hot chocolate as the candy-caned shovels unearth the memory once more.

It happened in December 2001. I was eight years old. The winter seasons were much harsher then, in the days when "lake-effect" snow meant literally burying the town in several feet every time a storm hit. I was eagerly awaiting Christmas, my busy little mind full of thoughts of presents and the jolly old man. We were on the first week of winter break when the snow hit, and it showered relentlessly until it was drifting halfway up the patio doors. With so much white everywhere, it was just like the movies, watching it come down in the warm living room through the glow of festive lights.

My mom was a bartender at a bar at the edge of town. My dad was a marine and currently deployed. I didn't understand the significance of these things. I just remember wanting him to be home for Christmas, and not knowing why he wasn't. My mom worked a late shift at the end of the night, and she would leave me home alone for a few hours while she made cocktails until after I fell asleep. This was back when you could do something like that. I was a brave little kid, and it wasn't my first time hanging out in a blanket fort by the Christmas tree, hearing the same iconic lines from Rudolph and Frosty on the television. With fits of excitement, I watched the accumulation outside, knowing full well I would be begging my mom to go play in it as soon as I got up.

The next morning, I opened the blinds to find nearly a foot and a half, and the neighbor kids trouncing about. With squeals of delight I jumped on my mother's bed, waking her and begging her to let me out and play. After a few grumpy dismissals, she sighed and dug out my snowsuit and boots. They were wrinkled and beaten up from so much use and hours in the dryer, but they still fit. My gloves were too worn out, so my mom made do with several pairs of socks on each hand. I didn't care, as long as I could get out there before the other kids could hog all the snow. As she brewed coffee and started breakfast, I threw open the slider and dove headfirst, thrashing around to disturb as much as the untouched canvas as possible.

Feeling the snow melt on my face, I sat up in my cold coffin, taking a moment to admire the scene around me. Heavy flakes were still coming down, deafening the air with its muffling static. It always felt so calming, the way it blocked out all of the unnecessary noise. The sky was a gray and white marble. It was showing no signs of letting up. Ahead, the kids had noticed me and were starting to high-knee over.

There were five of them in total. The oldest was Robbie, who was ten. Tagging along with him was his little brother Christopher, who was messily taking a bite out of a snowball. He was four. Christopher would always gravitate toward his brother, and Robbie hated it. Behind them was Lucy. She was also 6, and was always easy to spot because she mostly wore pink. Even now she trudged behind them, pink hat, pink gloves, pink boots. Coming up last were the twins, Preston and Presley. They were inseparable, always traveling like they were conjoined at the hip. They both had long hair, Presley's done in cute little pigtails. Their gloves, hats, and coats alternated colors; it was something their mother did on purpose.

"Bout time you made it out here," Robbie said. Christopher smiled, mouth full of snow.

"How long have you been waiting?" I asked.

"Only five minutes," Lucy said. The twins said nothing, but waved at me together.

Behind us a plow was hulking through the snow, lowering its blade with an awful grinding sound. We all stopped to watch it, the metal dragging across the parking lot as it pushed the snow into a gigantic mound in the corner. We watched the pile build slowly, all of us knowing we would soon be climbing all over it. Robbie turned around suddenly, a big grin on his face. He was always the one to come up with ideas.

"You guys want to build a snowman?" We all exchanged looks; there was only one answer.

While we waited for the plow to finish the lot, we started building it. Robbie was the first to get the ball rolling, his bigger hands making for easier work. His would serve as the base.

"We'll make the head," the twins said together. And without another word, they started packing a decent ball together.

Lucy and I decided to make the body, and Christopher tried to jump in and help Robbie push as it got bigger. He was mostly laughing and falling down, but Robbie didn't seem to mind. He would watch and smile at his little brother, but only when we weren't looking. We worked diligently, and it didn't take long with the four of us. We huffed and puffed with rosy cheeks, the cold meaning nothing in the excitement. It wasn't long before Robbie was done with the bottom. The big boulder rolled to a stop, and wouldn't budge further. Robbie collapsed and sat next to it.

"Phew. I'm pooped," he said, taking deep breaths as he looked at the sky.

Me and Lucy had just finished the body piece, her pink gloves and my socked hands smoothing it out. We lifted it together, and placed in on the bottom, almost dropping it in the process. Christopher helped, giggling as he went. The twins came shortly after with a perfectly spherical ball they had packed together and placed it gently on top. It was an odd-looking snowman, but it was good enough. It was a little taller than Robbie and stood like a blank silhouette in front of my patio. Once it was done, we all sat and admired it. The snowplow drove away, leaving a freshly packed mountain of snow in its departure. We all caught our breath, large flakes hitting our faces.

"It's missing something," Lucy said.

"Duh, everything," Robbie said.

We all looked around for something to decorate it with, but there was nothing but white everywhere you looked. There was no fancy carrot, no top hot.

"How about this?" Robbie said, turning to us all. "Tomorrow, we all bring something from home to decorate him."

"Him? How do you know it's a 'he'?" I asked.

"It's too big to be a girl," said Lucy.

"Exactly," Robbie agreed. After a moment, we were all in agreement.

"But what do we name him?" Said Christopher.

Together we sat in silence, looking up at the blank sculpted face of our winter friend. With no eyes or mouth, it reminded me of the mannequins you would see at the store. Just when it seemed there wasn't an answer, the twins spoke up.

"Braxton," they said, and we all exchanged looks. We knew the name all too well, and just hearing it made even Robbie bite his lip nervously. Braxton was the school bully, and a nasty one at that. He was much older than all of us. Our town was small, and our school consisted of one building with all grades. It looked just like the shoe factory in *Jumanji*. Starting at kindergarten and ending with twelfth, it housed all students that lived around us, since the closest town was too far away. Braxton was a middle schooler, and he loved to pick on little kids. Whether it was in the hall, on the playground, or outside of school, we each had our run-ins with Braxton, and he didn't discriminate. He was awful to everyone.

"Are you sure? We can pick *any* other name," said Robbie.

The twins just shrugged; it was hard to tell what the reason was behind anything they did. I didn't have any ideas, and when I looked at Lucy, she just shook her head.

"We can name him Cookie!" Shouted Christopher.

"Braxton it is," sighed Robbie.

We agreed to come back to the snowman tomorrow and put on the finishing touches. We got up and played for a while, climbing the large pile of snow the plow had made. We climbed it and jumped off, rolling to the bottom until we got too dizzy. The hill was so big, the possibilities seemed endless. We burrowed a tunnel into the mound, big enough so one person could squeeze in at a time. When we were almost all the way through to the other side, my mom called to me that it was time to have breakfast. I wasn't ready to go in, but the socks on my hands were soaked and my fingers were starting to go numb.

The other kids seemed to be tired as well, so were dispersed on the promise we would return the next day with our own decorations for the snowman. We said our farewells, and I tired headed inside, passing Braxton on my way to the patio. He just stood there quietly, his smoothed-out head making it impossible to tell which way it was really facing. I warmed up inside, ate some breakfast, and contemplated what I was going to contribute. My mom told me we were going to my grandmother's house for a couple days for the holiday, and tomorrow morning would be my last day to play outside until next week. I was bummed but grandma's house meant sweets and presents, so it wasn't all bad. I would just have to make the most of it tomorrow.

That night, as my mom got me ready for bed, an idea popped into my head. My father was in the military, and he had all kinds of cool stuff that he brought home in his time away. He kept it in a box in the closet. As my mother tucked me in and headed off to work, I pretended to fall asleep so she wouldn't think I was up to anything. I watched her go out the door, and sneakily waited for her car to leave. Braxton stood in the dark outside silently, looking in all directions with his emotionless face. Even though it was nighttime, his stark appearance made him stand out.

Once the coast was clear, I bolted into my parents' room and turned on the light, determined to find something in the closet. The box was at the bottom of the closet, covered in some junk and a hamper of old clothes. I quickly got the box out and opened it, feasting my eyes on the exotic objects within. There were photos, little chains with tags on them, different sized bullet casings. Most of the stuff was cool, but none of it seemed right. That was until I saw the big red sticks. I picked one up and looked over it curiously, reading the side of it to myself.

FUSEE 10 MIN.

I didn't know what they were, and the words made no sense, but there was only one thought in my head. It would be perfect for a nose. It would look weird, but it reminded me of my dad, so I decided it would be perfect. I packed everything up and put it back as I had found it, then ran back to the living room. I tucked the big red stick under the couch cushion and hoped my mom wouldn't find it before it was time to go out and play. I spent the rest of the night watching cartoons, excited to go back out the next day. As my eyes grew heavy, I looked out through the slider and looked at Braxton. The snow had finally stopped, his round body standing in the calm night. I nuzzled into my covers and fell asleep, wondering what the other kids would bring.

The next day I woke up bright and early and immediately felt stricken by disaster. I looked at the slider to see Braxton where we left him, but he wasn't the same. He was shriveled and mangled, his head looking like it was about to roll off at any moment. The sight brought me to tears. I opened the glass door in a panic to feel it was warmer than the day before. The tracks we had left behind from rolling the snowballs were turned to grassy ruts, and the frivolous amount of snow we had the day before was now less than half. Everything looked wet and bogged down.

I woke up my mother crying, and she tried to calm me after I showed her the catastrophe. She assured me that it wasn't the end of the world, that there would be more snow and we could make another one. After some pouty back and forth, she suited me up so I could go play once more, and when she went to go make coffee, I got the red stick from the couch and stuffed it in my coat. I ran out with puffy eyes, slipping in slush as I approached the withered snowman. I was first outside this time, and I decided to wait until the others came out before I did anything.

The twins showed first, huddling next to each other like they always did. They saw the damage as they walked up, and their only emotion was a slight frown. Lucy was next, skipping on the shoveled sidewalk in a blur of pink. She stopped skipping when she noticed and promptly started crying as I had earlier. She plopped next to me, where we waited in sadness until the last two showed. Robbie and Christopher ran a little late, the older brother pulling the younger behind. When Robbie saw its poor condition, he came running, practically dragging Christopher.

"No! Nonononononono!" He cried in frustration. His face was red as he looked at it, his hands fumbling with something in his pockets. He asked what happened, but the weather was answer enough. We pouted for a while in defeat. Our snowman was ruined.

"Wait! We can fix him!" he exclaimed, and we perked up at the thought.

"We roll him, piece by piece. Build him back up with more snow," he said.

"But all this snow is melting. And it's too windy," said Lucy, kicking her feet.

"I know, that's why we roll him into the woods. There's not as much sun in there, and it's not as windy," he said, pointing to the trees that were in the distance, past the yards of the apartment complex. It was a steep incline to the trees, but we could see from here that there was plenty of snow in the clearings.

"We're not supposed to go in there. Our mother says so," the twins said.

"Nobody goes in there," I said.

"I know, I know. But it's either that or we lose him. We all brought our stuff, didn't we?" he asked. We all nodded. I felt the red stick in my pocket. Robbie was right. We had to try and help him.

Everyone was hesitant, but in the end we decided to do it. We would roll Braxton's pieces into the woods where the snow would be less disturbed and try to build him back into shape. I explained it was my last day to play for a while, and even though this saddened the kids, it made everyone get to it. We worked quickly and as a team, each of us assigned pieces we would ferry to the woods. The twins took the head and cradled it like a golden egg. Lucy and I detached the middle portion and moved so Robbie could start rolling the bottom. Robbie struggled at first, but once he got it to the hill gravity took over. It bounded down the incline, packing more snow as it went. The rest of us rolled our pieces down too and picked them up at the bottom.

Robbie and Christopher kept it rolling into the trees and over the untouched snow. It was tiring, but we kept going, cheering each other on as we went deeper into the woods. We started rolling the smaller pieces as well, packing the wet snow as they grew back to their former glory. I pushed and pushed with my sock covered hands, looking over my shoulder every once and a while to see how far we were going. It went slowly at first, but the more we focused, the faster it went. Eventually, the bottom piece was too wet and heavy, and Robbie couldn't move it anymore. We halted on our pieces and helped him, all of us pushing together as a team. The big snowball continued to roll, picking up wet leaves and grass as we pushed onward. The ground got muddier and uneven, and tall trees made it darker. I looked back at the apartment and could barely see it. We kept pushing. There was cracking and crunching under the massive ball, and we could see little twigs had been crushed under the weight. Some of them looked old, and they were covered in some kind of straw. We slipped on rocks, little gatherings of them that we couldn't see under the snow. We pushed until we couldn't push anymore, and when we looked back, we couldn't see the buildings through the trees.

Exhausted but driven, we doubled back for the other pieces. The wind picked up, hissing through the bare trees as we rolled the next one. We packed less so it would be smaller, but with the uneven ground it was difficult. Little feet stamped over the twisted sticks; our feet kicked around the loose rocks. When we got to the end, it took all of us to lift the body and pack it into place. We carried the headpiece the rest of the way, the twins packing and fixing it as we went. The snow out there was dirty, sticky, and it caked our gloves as we finished it up. We passed it to Robbie, and he stood on his tippy toes and placed it on top. Finally, he was ready for his face.

With him reconstructed, we all showed what we brought. With cold, tired hands, we held out our items. Robbie and Christopher each brought a dark smooth rock, ones they had found on the beach over the summer. Preston and Presley brought their grand-mothers old dentures, the jaws filled with worn artificial teeth. Lucy untied her pink scarf, and after some reluctance, held it out with a smile. I held out my red stick. We looked over each other's contributions, each just as unique as the last.

"Wow," said Robbie, "That's gonna be an ugly snowman."

We rounded up our belongings and handed them to Christo-pher, who we hoisted up to put them on. He stuck them all on softly, careful not to knock the head off. Two beach rocks for eyes. The big red stick for a nose. Dentures for a mouth. Christopher wrapped the pink scarf around its neck, and we lowered him down. We realized we were missing arms, so we gathered some of the broken sticks we saw when we rolled him over here. We gathered some of them from the path; some of them were still attached with thin strands of rope. There were notches and scratches in the old wood. We bundled them together and used them as arms. It was crude, but it went well with the rest of his decorations. We stepped back to admire the finished product, and in our exhaustion, ex-changed high-fives. Braxton was finished.

"Well I'll be," Robbie said.

"Wow," said the twins.

After all the hard work, it felt magical. It was short lived, however, as we finally got a moment to rest, I could hear my mother shouting from away. She sounded angry. I turned to my friends, sad that I had to go. They agreed they would take care of Braxton while I was away so we could play with him when I got back. We said our goodbyes and I went running along, trying to get to my mother before she got too mad.

My mother was furious that I was in the woods. She sat me down and explained it was against the apartment rules, and if we were caught in there, she would have to pay a fine. She was more in a hurry to go, so she cut the lecture short, and I got off easy. She had packed our bags while I was gone, so as soon as I got changed we loaded up the car and hit the road. I slept in the car on the way there, and we made it there in no time.

Waking at grandma's filled me with the Christmas spirit. Her house was a spectacle of lights. She made all kinds of desserts. I was having fun, but I thought of my friends and Braxton. I was looking forward to getting back to them. The night went on, filled with fun things my grandmother had planned that we do together. The snow started up again, the heaviest we had seen yet. It came down relentlessly through the night. The news talked of a snow-storm, the worst we had seen in a while.

The next day, that's when the calls started. I remember my mom on the phone while I watched cartoons, talking into her old Motorola with wide hand gestures. She seemed upset, worried. I went back to my cartoons, not knowing what was going on. A little later, there was another phone call. This one lasted longer than the previous. She started crying, saying she didn't know over and over again. The snow was getting worse outside, and something about it made me uncomfortable. I don't know if it was just my mom's sudden mood change, but there was something definitely wrong. She hung up the phone and talked to my grandmother in the other room. I couldn't hear what they were saying. Then her phone rang again. And again. There were only a few words I could make out. Things like "find" and "search". It didn't make any sense. Later that night, my mom told me the next day we were going to head home early, once there was a break in the storm. Something about having to help as much as we can.

It snowed all through the night, and most of the next after-noon. Around 6pm the next day it finally stopped, and once the road was plowed, we made our way back home. As we were halfway home, it started once more, thick slush and heavy flakes trying to rush us off the road.

When we got back, there were a lot of people around the apartments. It had snowed nearly two feet while we were gone; it didn't look anything like it did when I had left. They had to answer a lot of questions from police officers inside the apartment and away from the blizzard. Questions about my friends, the last time I had seen them. I told them about the snowman and how we played together. I asked if everything was alright. They told me every-thing was fine, that they would be back in the morning when the storm cleared up. It was late by the time everything was done, and my mother and I were tired from the drive and the company. Everybody left, and we decided to go to bed early. My mother told me I had to sleep in her bed, so she would feel better. I agreed, and after snuggling in some blankets, my mother was snoring, and I was drifting off.

I woke to the sound of tapping. I opened my eyes to find my mother still asleep, snoring softly into the night. I got out of bed to see what it was, not wanting to bother my mom after the long day she had. I went down the dark hall into the living room, and I could see a tall shadow behind the blinds of the sliding door. I watched the shadow reach up with a skinny arm and tap again.

I opened the blinds to see Braxton standing on the patio. He was moving.

He looked at me with his beach rock eyes and held a finger up to his denture mouth. The red stick was a little beat up, and there were a bunch of marks on his face. My guess was from hitting branches. Strange as it was, it felt like a Christmas miracle. With a big smile I opened the door quietly. Braxton knelt down to see me before he started to speak.

"Would you like to play with me? I've been waiting," he said. His voice was deeper than I thought, and it was off-putting. But Braxton was a big snowman, I guessed that's just how he talked.

"I can't, I'll get in trouble," I said, Braxton's stone eyes furrowed. His pink scarf blowing in the wind.

"But I have something to show you. You must see what we made for you. It will be quick, I promise. The others are waiting." It didn't make sense how he talked through the dentures, but they clacked and rasped through the snow.

"The others are waiting for me?" I asked.

"Yes. We better hurry."

That was all I needed. I dressed quickly and quietly, careful not to wake my mom. I would just be there and back, it wouldn't take any time at all. After suiting up I went outside and Braxton took my hand. The bundles of sticks had been rearranged into joints and fingers, and they gripped my hand tight. We headed into the woods silently. My boots crunching the deep snow, and Braxton scooting on his round base. I looked up at his animated face while we walked, and he looked down at me. It seemed like he was trying to smile, but the dentures wouldn't cooperate. I got a better look at the marks on his snowman face. They looked like little handprints, and some scratches. They must have tried to give him eyebrows or something. We walked into the dark woods, Braxton taking me by the hand.

"How are you alive?" I asked.

"I don't know," Braxton said.

"Where are you taking me?"

"To the others."

"They're waiting for us? This late?" I asked. We were all going to be in trouble if our parents found out.

"Yes. They are waiting."

I looked behind, and the building was getting further away. I could barely see the parking lot lights in the distance. The woods looked completely different from before, the large amount of snow blanketing everything. I couldn't see the ground like I did before. Suddenly we stopped, and I bumped into Braxton. He scooted aside so I could see. It was a hole. Looking in I could see it was a little opening for something bigger within.

"Where did this come from?" I asked.

"We dug it. So we could play." He put a twig hand on my shoulder and ushered me in.

I ducked into the tunnel, straining so I could see. The snow blended into dirt like it was a little cave. There was a flickering light inside, weakly illuminating the passage within. Something felt wrong. When I looked back at Braxton, he just nodded to keep going. I went further towards the light, so I could see better around me. When I got closer, I started to make out a dark shape on the floor of the snowy cave. It was close to the light, and when I got closer, I could see it was someone holding a flashlight.

Robbie was laying in the snow, the flashlight held in his outstretched hand. Christopher was next to him, huddled in a ball. Their gazes soft and hazy. As I drew closer, the sinking feeling of cold fire washed over my skin.

They were frozen solid.

I screamed and stumbled backward, my hand grazing something hard in the snow to my right. When I saw the pink coat, I knew it was Lucy, her face stone in the dark snowy cave. I looked from her to the boys in denial, my mind refusing to make sense of what was in front of me. The three of them laid there, their gloves torn to reveal black fingertips. Their skin was pale beneath their clothes, dark jagged marks across their skin on each of them. Bite marks.

I turned, ready to run, but Braxton was blocking my way out. He was hunched over, his twig arms holding him up. His dentured mouth was open unnaturally wide, and something was sliding out of his expanded tunnel of a throat. The frosted mass of dark blue and red slid out of his snowy gullet like a slug and landed on the dirt with a wet 'plop'. Two little figures embracing, frozen together.

The twins.

I started screaming. Braxton's throat closed, the deep groan echoing in through his warping inside. When his form returned to normal, he looked at me blankly, his snowman head cocking to the side in confusion.

"What's wrong?" he asked, scooting a little closer.

"Get away from me. Look at what you did!" I shouted, and Braxton flinched.

"I don't understand," he said, his words plain and sad.

"My friends. What did you do?" I sobbed, my hands shaking.

Braxton's eyes shifted for a moment in silence, looking from one body to the next.

"We wanted to play. We wanted to make a house we could play in."

He drew closer, his hands crackling as he flexed his fingers.

"They got tired and wanted to go home. But they couldn't go. We had to keep digging, *together*."

His fake teeth ground together, the flashlight flickering on his face.

"The grown-ups started looking, so I had to hide them. If they found them, we couldn't play anymore. So I hid them in the snow so they couldn't see. They'll be up soon, then we can all play together." He reached a wooden hand out and I flinched away from it. He recoiled, and his stone eyes narrowed on me. The guttural grind of vocals in his throat got deeper, the dentures opening slightly.

"You want to leave? You don't want to play with me?" he asked, his voice getting deeper with every syllable. I shook my head, tears streaming down my face.

"Don't leave. They'll wake up soon," he said, reaching his hands out. They were inches away.

Just as his fingers touched my coat, I broke away and ran. Braxton tried to catch me, but he moved awkwardly in the little hole, swiping wildly with his hands. As I ran out the exit a beastly roar erupted from the little cavern, echoing through the trees like a lion's roar. I heard him scooting after me, but I kept running.

The apartment building was far away, and the snow was coming down hard. The wind whipped through the trees. Behind me, Braxton was working his way out of the cave. The mass of his lower half made him struggle, and I got a head start.

I kept my focus on the building, getting closer and closer with each bounding step. Behind me, Braxton called after me, his voice more animalistic than human. I could hear his tree branch arms digging into the snow to pull himself along faster. I ran as hard as I could, blinking away snowflakes in the terrible weather. Behind Braxton cursed as one of his arms broke and he stumbled in the snow.

I broke through the tree line and started up the hill, my boots slipping with every step. I could hear him hissing through the fake teeth. His single arm raking to catch up. His scoots becoming more rapid. I pawed at the ground as I crawled up the hill, running across the yard. Ahead I saw the mound made by the snowplow. I thought of the tunnel we made days ago. It could make it there faster than home. I ran straight for it, the aggravated groans of Braxton echoing as he worked his way up the hill. With each high-kneed step I ran for snow mountain. When I got close enough I could barely see the opening, the crack of where the snow had almost completely covered it up. I decided it was worth a shot.

Behind me I felt the claws snatching for my snow suit. I ran and ran, Braxton's cold breath on my neck as we neared the hill. I dove headfirst into the tunnel, painfully jarring my neck as I punched through the open tunnel inside. I squirmed in, Braxton's single hand grabbing my ankle. I kicked at it and it broke its fingers, the loud growl sounding again. I backed into the tunnel, screaming as Braxton shoved his head in. The dentures clacked as he bit at my feet. They clamped down on my boot and I kicked his face, the big red stick knocking loose and rolling toward me. I grabbed it and held it out in defense, swinging the black capped end to hit him. With a snarl he bit down on the end, thrashing his head around to tear it from me. He crunched and the end and there was a fizzle and pop, and suddenly the stick erupted at the end.

Blinding red light exploded at the end of the stick, the searing heat melting Braxton's face in seconds. The heat scared me and I wanted to drop it, but once I saw the damage it did, I held onto it for dear life. Braxton snarled and his terrifying growl and I held the stick out like it was a magic wand. His features wilted under the heat, but he kept on chomping at me as he tried to squeeze his way in.

I could hear sirens in the distance on the howling wind. The blaring red light gave me energy, and I thrust it into Braxton's eye, knocking one of the stones loose. Like a blowtorch the searing ember melted the front of his face until the other eye slid away, the hole that once held his nose pooling into a waterfall. As he thrashed I worked my way backward, holding the red stick out to thwart him. The closer he got the more I melted. The flame charred the dentures, and they shriveled away, his gaping throat choking with rushing water. He tried to scream, but it only came out as gargling, spitting, and splashing as I crawled away. My head hit the end of the tunnel and I pushed, yelling as I tried to break through to the other side. It started to give and Braxton grabbed me, my entire foot getting sucked into the melting vortex. I stabbed the stick deep into his face and left it there, the bubbling burn eating through like a hot poker. I yanked my foot free and pushed as hard as I could.

I broke through the other end, rolling away in a mess of white. Braxton's cries echoed as he wormed into the tunnel, the dull burn of the stick silencing him slowly. The red and blue flashes of police cars flew into the parking lot as the snow mountain shook and caved in. Smoke whooshed and water gushed from both ends as it flattened, the heavy snowfall and wind already working to blend it in. As the officers approached, I folded in the parking lot and cried until they brought me to my mother.

I don't remember much after that. The police took a team through the storm and found the hole in the snow, and the little cave that my friends rested. It was already getting snowed in when they found it, like something was trying to bury it. The losses were devastating; they were my last true friends and I never really moved on from that. I didn't see much of their families after that, they moved far away from me and everything in Cyprus Glen.

The police combed through the mound that held the monster and found nothing but a charred scarf and burned plastic. The storm kept them from properly searching that night, and eventually they called it off. They acted sincere when they questioned me, but I know they never believed my snowman story. Nobody really did.

As time went on, people stopped talking about "The Tragedy of Cyprus Glen", a terrible night when four children disappeared after getting lost in the snow so close to home. I never really got any answers until I was older. I dug up the police report many years later to find it was mostly incomplete and hushed away. Nobody likes to speak of it, nobody wants to acknowledge it happened. Hypothermia, they said. Maybe it had made them delusional. Maybe that's why they were digging. But I know the truth, even if no one wants to talk about it.

Now as I look through the slider, my eyes rest on the freshly packed pile of plowed snow. It sits pushed in the same corner of the parking lot as it did years ago. I'm renting the same apartment my parents had a long time ago just in case it happens again. I own dozens of flares, flare guns, flashlights, the best winter coats and boots money can buy. I hope I'll never need them. I figured if I lived here, I'll be the first to know if it happens again. The neighbors call me a creep, but I check on the kids every time they're playing in the yard. Every winter I watch the snow fall and the kids get excited all over again, none of them knowing the horrors of Braxton the Snowman.

Sometimes when it snows, and the children erect a new winter statue, I watch it through the night, over and over again, until that bastard melts. And with the blowing snow and hissing wind, it stands there, watching me back.

NEON NIGHTMARE

Palm trees passed in a blur as Rodger leaned back in his seat, cigarette held tight in his lips. He flicked open his Zippo and tried to light it, shielding both sides as the flame burned erratically despite his best efforts. He got it going barely, scorching his beard in the process. I glanced in amusement as he sat up, dilated eyes peering over his aviators as he puffed the cherry to life. With a chuckle he tucked the lighter in the pocket of his white suit jacket and readjusted his glasses. I shifted up, feeling the car growl under the pedal as the needle climbed.

"I gotta say, Warren, this shit is *good,*" He said, taking a big drag and exhaling it to the wind.

"Yeah it is," I said as I gripped the steering wheel, admiring the glow of the setting sun ahead.

"No man, I'm serious, I mean look at this," he said, running his hands over the suit jacket and floral button up combo, the collar popped "This could be a new look for us. This is some next level shit. I could get used to this." He clapped a hand on my shoulder excitedly before reaching into his jacket. He pulled out a cassette tape, his eyebrows raising behind the glasses, cigarette held in a crooked grin. He popped the tape in and cranked up the volume before sinking back into his seat. A nostalgic 80s banger started playing, an electric tune to match the racing speed of the Corvette.

He was right. The glow hitting the sunglasses, the blazers and button-up shirts, the roaring 85 convertible on a stretch of road into the horizon. It felt better than anything else we had done before. It felt *right,* like we were meant to be here. It felt like vacation. I worked the pedals and shifted up again, letting my hand rest on the stick as I left it in fourth gear. The music got louder the faster we went, and I couldn't help but smile as the wind tossed my hair. It felt good to breathe, like my chest was getting lighter. It was a soothing feeling that stretched from my chin to my groin. Even at the increasing speed I was starting to loosen up. I looked at Rodger, who was slapping the door to the rhythm, cigarette burning brightly as he finished it off.

"Rodge? You good?" I asked.

He tossed the butt to the wind and nodded. Some of his hair had matted to his forehead, with the same cold sweat I felt through the desert air. He took off his shades and wiped his brow. His pupils were the size of olives. He unbuttoned the top two buttons of the Hawaiian shirt, the breeze lapping at his exposed chest hair.

"I'm good brother, I'm good. How about you?" he shouted over the wind. When he looked away from me, his eyes rested on the sun. I followed his gaze to the skyline and found myself lowering aviators as well. The setting orange rays that beamed across the desert highway started painting in a new light, the orange fading, no, bleeding, into pink. The colors melted to the brighter shade, casting a vibrant filter over every passing cactus and rock. The sun burned like a blazing neon star, the surrounding clouds echoing its incandescence across the sky. Down the ever-expanding stretch of road, the lines started to run together. Rodger put his sunglasses back on, the lenses now bright bronze. Through the ecstasy of controlling my own breathing, I mouthed the only words I could muster:

"Holy shit."

The world shifted before me, its bold clarity bringing a sense of heightened awareness. I looked at the head of a passing palm tree and watched its leaves dance frame by frame. It was like watching an old movie, and when I turned back to the wheel, I would once again hear the rumble of the Corvette eating the pavement. I was reminded of Rodger's presence by his laughter, his hair wild from the wind, his laughter booming with magnified pitches.

There was a rising commotion over the radio, and we were pulled from our vivid distraction of the passing environment. It was the high-pitched rev of a motor, and I looked in the rear view mirror to see a single headlight gaining on us. It was the iconic scream of a crotch-rocket motorcycle, and it was coming up fast. Rodger swiveled in his seat and watched the rider approach with fascination. The motorcycle caught up and matched our speed, tailgating us for a moment before swinging around to pass. Through the view of the side mirror I watched the rider advance, their jet-black bike revving until it was coasting parallel with us. Together we turned to look at who it was, Rodger lowering his glasses as I hid behind mine. They looked back, their helmet and visor matching the same gloss as the bike they leaned on as they kept up. They were garbed in full riding gear, skin-tight leather showing the undeniable curves of a feminine frame. Rodger and I exchanged looks and promptly shrugged before turning back to her. My first thought was that she wanted to race. I edged the gas pedal provocatively, and Rodger hooted and pumped his fist. As the slowly darkening pink landscape blurred around us, the rider only stared, their only expression my own animated reflection in their visor. When they did respond, they shook their head, strands of freshly permed hair tossed by the wind. She flicked her head backwards, nodding to the road behind us.

"Uh, Warren?" Rodger said cautiously, already looking before I had the chance. The rider turned ahead and, with the crank on the throttle, she sped off, leaving me to look at what was behind us. I watched in the rear-view mirror, and felt an unexplainable tightening in my gut, like an irrational fear was taking hold. My lack of comprehension of the pursuer made me incredibly anxious; just seeing it made me uncomfortable.

Behind us looked to be a man, but from the looks of it was made entirely of tar. It looked like he was running in place, but every step was connected to what looked like a pour of black paint. The way they moved was jerky and unnatural, like a mannequin. Every step was yanked from the oily substance, only to be sucked back into it over and over again. Even as the Corvette reached 100 it was not only keeping up, it was getting closer. I couldn't explain why, but just by seeing it I knew it was hostile. It wanted to hurt us. We could feel it.

"Don't let it get close!" I said, and Rodger nodded. Behind us the figure was getting closer, only two car lengths away. I looked in the mirror and saw it staring at me, bloodshot eyes locked on to me in the mirror's reflection. There was something else to it, even though its mouth wasn't moving we could hear it, like it was speaking to us. It was more like a silent scream, a muted whisper in our head that was beaming at us with its tired, unmoving eyes. One car length away. It was looking at Rodger now, its silent hostility growing as he reached behind the seat and pulled the sawed-off Mossberg pump. Holding the pistol grip to his hip, he repositioned in his seat and worked the slide, checking the breach to make sure it was loaded. Once it saw this, the pursuer got much louder, its silent screams clear enough to understand now. It just repeated the same phrase maliciously, and in all the glow and distortion of this neon world, my hair stood on end.

JUST A TASTE.

JUST A TASTE.

JUST A TASTE.

It looked at Rodger and without warning it dove at him, inky black strands keeping it tethered to the black slime pool it stood on. Rodger pulled the trigger. A ball of fire shot from the shotgun's muzzle, the blast of 00 buck tearing through its shoulder and neck. In an awkward tumble it fell to the blur of pavement, limbs breaking and shaving into the road as the tendrils pulled it back to the mass. Rodger ejected the spent shell to the wind and steadied himself against his seat, watching in disbelief as *more* emerged from the black streak. Some men, some women. They materialized already running, almost thrashing out of the streak competitively. They shoved and pushed off of each other, all the while keeping their gaze on me and Rodger. The same menacing chant echoing from their tired, dead eyes.

JUST A TASTE.

JUST A TASTE.

JUST GIVE US A TASTE.

"Get us out of here, Warren!" Shouted Rodger, the gun bucking in his hand as he fired at the closest one. The pellets tore through the crazed face of a female pursuer. She faltered, only to be elbowed out of the way so another could replace her.

The road ahead did nothing but stretch to the horizon, the neon sun dominating in the sky. The only way out was forward. With the scattered palms and cacti, going off road would only mean death. I buried the pedal to the floor, hoping we could outrun them. The rear end bounced as one pounced on the car, sharp liquid fingers puncturing the trunk. Rodger raised the twelve gauge and removed one of its arms, and it flailed to stay on. As its legs grated into asphalt, another tried climbing it like a ladder. The next blast went through both of them, my ears ringing from the gunfire. They tumbled off the car, several behind it tripping over their rolling bodies, immediately to be replaced by more. Despite their animosity, they worked together as one, each of them shouting and reaching for the car.

JUST A TASTE.

GIVE US A TASTE.

"They're not stopping!" yelled Rodger, and I looked to see the thrashing mob of them almost reaching the car, no matter how fast I tried to go. As the 80s banger rang from the speakers, Rodger cut them down as fast as he could, but there were always more. He worked the pump again to find his gun empty, and he tossed it away. He reached inside his suit jacket and pulled a pistol, then tried to aim against the beating wind. He looked down the sights only to see one leaping for him, its head reared back, inky strands separating as its mouth opened. He pulled the trigger and it spit in his face, a steamy burst of goo covering his aviators and forehead. He started screaming immediately, and I watched as his sunglasses started melding to his face.

"My eyes! My fucking eyes!" His gun clattered to the floor as he turned in his seat, fingers curled as he clawed at the mess that seemed to be spreading. The rear-end bucked again, this time a thumping slapping the wheel well. It sounded like a flat tire. It happened again, then on the other side. Trying to keep the car straight, I looked at them again and felt my stomach sinking away. They were throwing themselves into the wheels.

JUST A TASTE.

They dove headfirst into the tires, their bodies wrapping and liquifying in a self-sacrificial oil slick. I lost traction as the tires spun free, flinging wet bits of them like half-dried paint. I let off the gas and tried to slow down, but the tires smoked and spun freely. I could feel their bodies whipping around beneath us, wrapping around the drive shaft, bogging us down however they could.

"HANG ON!" I shouted, fighting to stay straight as the wheels failed me. We slid out of control, the wheels locking as they clogged the axles with their destroyed bodies. Rodger screamed and clawed at his face, and in the whirlwind of madness I could see his eyes melting, the black goo bubbling and eating away. We spun several times, tires squealing and smoking, the vibrant colors running together. I saw the incoming tree in slow motion, and everything went black.

"Warren? Warren, where are you? I hear them coming. I can't see."

I opened my eyes to hazy, double vision. Engine smoke and dust burned my sinuses, the steering wheel jammed horribly in my stomach. I could hardly breathe, my body felt bruised and broken from head to toe. I could see the palm tree, and the twisted metal of the Corvette wrapped around it. My vision recalibrated slowly, and I tried to move, but I was stuck. I could hear squirming, sizzling, groaning.

"Rodge? Rodge? Where you at?" I called, coughing against the smoke in my lungs. I moved one of my arms and felt the sting of cutting glass.

"I'm over here, pal! Help me! I hear them coming." I could see him now, the details coming in with the same slow frames. He was on the ground in front of us, his suit torn and a bloody mess. He had gone through the windshield. I saw them there, inching closer. I tried to feel for the gun, but I could hardly move. The only thing my hands could find was glass and pain. Ahead Rodger looked blindly, a corroded cavity serving as his eyes.

"I can't see you, Warren! I hear them coming. They're gonna get me, they're gonna——ah! AAAH! AAAAAAAH—" The shadowy figures descended on him, and I could only watch helplessly. They ripped at his legs, tearing at his skin and cutting him deep. They tore open his stomach, his screams getting louder and glitching as they pulled his entrails from his body. The horrible sounds seared my mind. I felt the sadness work up bile from my gut. They cut and slashed. Dark red splatters staining the sand. An inky hand ripped off his bottom jaw, and after tossing it away, put its hand together and startled to force its way down his throat. The horrible gurgling, the screams fading as it slithered in. As they consumed Rodger, some of the stragglers started looking at me, and decided it was my turn. Their bloodshot eyes were wild, their teeth jagged and broken. The first one leapt at me, claws outstretched, inky mouth opening.

JUST A TASTE.

With a deafening blast its head exploded, and its body writhed in the sand helplessly. With the sound of breaking glass and the whoosh of flame, the group feasting on Rodger were engulfed by fire, orange neon tongues lapping around them. I looked to see the Bike Rider, arm extended post throw, in her other hand, the largest handgun I had ever seen. The remaining monsters bolted to her, and with a practiced aggressive stance, she brought her hands together and raised her weapon. The Desert Eagle barked like a cannon, every shot well placed and decimating. She leaned into it as she shot, putting down each of them without hesitation. As the last one screamed inches away, she stuffed the bulky barrel in its mouth, the blast splashing the black goo all over the helmet's visor. They were gone.

She moved toward me, ejecting a wide magazine that thudded in the sand. She pulled another from a holster on her thigh and slammed it home, racking the slide as she watched the smoldering fire that was Rodger's grave. She reached her hands up and removed the helmet, releasing the cascade of curls it contained. She looked at me, her eyes alert and mesmerizing. Her skin a smooth, deep tone. She walked with grace, each step bouncing her wide, styled hair. She holstered the gun and offered a hand to help me. With my arm weak and shaking, I reached for it.

***

I blink to see a dirty molding ceiling, and I am hit by the clear, gut-wrenching stillness of sobriety. My eyelids are heavy and drag across my retinas like gravel. I cough dryly, my breath a fog in the chilly room. The coughing leads to hacking, and as I shiver and convulse on the dirty couch, I am painfully reminded of where I am. I look around the dim derelict house, its cobwebbed walls feel like they're closing in on me. My head throbs, and I wrap my frail arms around myself, trying to keep warm in my stained sweatshirt. I want to curl up in a ball and sleep on the couch, but it's the sight next to me that stops me. Rodger sits next to me in a recliner, his mouth held still and open.

"Rodge? Rodge, you awake?" I say between coughs, my raspy voice a whisper in the damp room. His mouth agape, I see the black fluid, thick and caked in his scraggly beard and unkempt mustache. The stain is splashed all over his neck and chest and has long since dried, like it happened hours ago. His eyes are closed and his face is pale, almost white. I nudged him, even though I know in the back of my mind he's already dead.

I want to cry, but my eyes are too dry. I look at him perfectly still, frozen in the chair. His hands were stuffed in the front pocket of his hoodie, the same thing he always did when he used. His hair is tangled and greasy. His lips are scarred and his teeth, the ones he has left, are decayed and misshapen. We had only been squatting together for a few weeks, but I feel his loss like the death of a brother. He looks peaceful, but I get a glimpse of pink and black, and for a second, I hear his screams. I rub my eyes and they fade away.

In front of me is a coffee table, covered in dust and garbage. There's a battery powered boombox, weakly trying to play a tape that ran out of film hours ago. It was Rodger's. Next to it is the score, the little plastic bag that brings back memories of days prior. I'm painfully reminded of the struggle it was to get it; two days panhandling, a shady back-door deal behind a bar called The Sixth Shot, with a new subordinate we'd never heard of before. We squatted in the first hole in the wall we could find; a safe place to use away from the eyes of cops. We bought four, I took one, Rodger took two.

I see the little black pill hiding in the plastic bag like the devil himself. I grab the little baggy and feel the pill between my fingers. As I touch it, I hear the music, see the palm trees, and the bright neon sun. I tuck it in my pocket. I shut off Rodger's boombox and eject the tape. I pocket that too; it will be the only thing to remember him by once my own mind has rotted away. I set his boombox in his lap, and with a solemn pat on the shoulder I left him there, just as we had done time and time again to the ones we've met along the way. I have no phone, and even if I did, I've burned every bridge long ago of the ones I would call and even if I did tell someone, they wouldn't care. With a shiver I duck out of the abandoned house and return to the dark messy streets of the city. There's an anxiety welling in my gut, and as the cars pass I feel into my pocket for the little plastic bag. The feeling is sickening, the same feeling every time. Through the screams that echo in my head, I find some peace in the little black pill as I roll it between my fingers.

Deep down, I already know I have to go back. Just to have one more taste.

MY LAST HOUSE BLESSING

I've been blessing houses for three years. Three years of distressed parents, shaken kids, and superstitious elderly. From bumps in the night to shapes in the woods, I've answered calls far and wide to clear the terrified of their fear of the supernatural. I started small, in my hometown, and slowly worked my way to taking jobs out of state. I did it for free at first, but after the donations started rolling in and my name got around, I was able to earn a decent living from saving the innocent from otherworldly threats. My growth in popularity led to my persona, the young and prestigious Father Cain. I maintained a dedicated online presence, building groups and pages on social media to stay engaged with the community. Answering every question, responding to every text.

Each successful blessing brought more follows and shares. Before I knew it, Father Cain was a household name, and I was booked daily for months to come. My hair was gelled right, my pencil thin beard immaculate, professional. I dressed clean and drove even cleaner, rolling up to houses in my waxed Cadillac Deville and knocking on doors in black, lambskin gloves. Every time an old man or frightened woman would call, I would deliver. Every ghost banished and aura lifted soothing the minds around me. Each time they ask me how I perform such miracles, and each time with over-exaggerated theatrics and heavy mysticism I keep them from learning my hidden secret: I'm a fraud.

That's right, I'm a total fake. It started as a prank, just to see if I could do it, really. But after I actually got away with it, I realized I could help people by the power of placebo alone. Built upon my own arrogant skepticism, I cloaked myself as a "warrior of light", and boy, was I welcomed with open arms. With just a bit of innovation, I put on a front that sold anyone at the end of their rope. Some well-versed scripture, sprinkled with buzz words. A cheap rosary off Amazon, scuffed with sandpaper for authenticity. A vial of holy water, courtesy of the tap. I plan each "blessing" accordingly, using the information gathered beforehand. I go in and put on a good show, leaving the family feeling rejuvenated with their newly cleansed house. I've had nothing but success over the years, and my social media is filled with nothing but praise and delightful reviews. Over a hundred successful cleanses, with nothing but thanks to follow. That was until yesterday. Yesterday I blessed a house, and I will never do it again.

Yesterday started like any other routine job. After some messaging back and forth with the client on Facebook, I knew the gist of what was going on. The client's name was Lacy Stephens, and she was concerned about some strange occurrences going on in her house. The same stuff I had heard a hundred times before; unexplained noises, a chilly draft in the house, doors opening and closing on their own. The more significant detail was an apparent leak in the basement, some kind of ooze seeping from the foundation (my guess was septic). I decided before I went out that the "issue" would be solved in the basement, the discovered "origin" from which the problem stemmed. In and out, no big deal.

I pulled my car into the driveway, taking in their gorgeous property as I parked in the front. It was an old Victorian style house, a few acres of forest serving as a backdrop. A field neighbored the property on either side, and less than a block away was construction for what looked like a new subdivision. I stepped out of the car and walked up the drive, smoothing my peacoat with my shiny black gloves. In my right pocket was the rosary, and on the left was a bundle of sage with the vial of "holy" water. I went over my lines in my head, a smug grin already starting to form.

Lovely evening, Ms. Stephens. Blessed day, Ms. Stephens. How are we faring today, Ms. Stephens?

I stood at the front door, re-teased my hair, and raised my hand to knock. Before my knuckles could rap, the door shot open.

"Good afternoon, Ms.—"

"*Jeeeeeeesus.* You look more ridiculous than I thought." A man stood in the door, tall and broad, his face twisted in a scowl. Wife beater, basketball shorts. On his head was a large gaming headset, a thin cord trailing down from it to a controller gripped in his hand.

"I'm sorry?" I asked, confused. The man eyed me up and down and scowled again.

"Look here, pal. I don't know what kind of shit you're trying to sell to my wife, but do me a favor. Make this quick, let her down easy, and get the f——" he was cut off by a much shorter woman, who shoved past him.

"Father Cain! Thank you for coming out today!" said Lacy Stephens, who beamed under the man's shadow. She was very pretty with long brown hair, her curvy body accented by a spaghetti string top and leggings.

"Pleasure's mine," I said, shaking her hand with both of mine, much like a priest would in a church. I flashed a smile at her, and then to the husband, who proceeded to groan.

"Come in, come in. Don't mind my husband. He's in the middle of a game." She motioned inside, and the husband shambled away, his slides dragging on the floor. He sat on the couch, giving me another warning look before unmuting his headset. On the wall opposing the couch was a large flatscreen displaying a Call of Duty queue.

"Sorry guys, I'm back. Lacy actually invited that *Criss Angel* guy."

"Would you like some tea?" she asked, heading to the kitchen.

"That sounds wonderful," I said, watching her go. I looked around the living room at the furnishings and wall decorations. It gave the old house a much more modern look, your standard *Live Laugh Love* giving a taste of Instagram home happiness. I looked at the pictures on the walls, taking in additional information in my head.

Young couple. Bubbly Wife, Stubborn Husband. No kids, no pets. Should be easy, as long as the Husband doesn't heckle too much.

It wasn't my first time dealing with a skeptic and it wouldn't be the last. We exchanged looks for a moment, him taking the time to remind me he didn't approve while his character sprinted through smoke. Luckily, Lacy returned quickly.

"I put the kettle on. So, how do we start?" she asked.

"Tell me about what's happening here, and we'll go from there," I said, putting my hands together.

"It started a couple months ago. Nothing really crazy, just weird. I've had a couple doors close on their own while he's at work. Sometimes in the middle of the night, the house creaks, and I can hear scratching in the walls. It didn't happen often, at first. But lately it's been every night. My husband thinks I'm overreacting. Not that he would hear it anyway, the way he snores," she said, her eyes traveling like she was searching for something invisible.

"I see. Sometimes darkness works in mysterious ways, Mrs. Stephens. The devil always looks to bend the ear of those willing to listen," I said, pulling the rosary from my pocket. Behind us, the husband scoffed.

Lacy gave an annoyed look past me and motioned toward the kitchen.

"Most of the activity is in the kitchen and the basement. The entrance to the basement is next to the pantry."

"Let's have a look, shall we? I want to reach the epicenter; it'll be there where we'll cast our blessing. If that is what you want," I said, letting the beads unravel until the cross dangled in the air. She went to turn, and I put up a hand to stop her.

"What? Is something wrong?" she asked, eyes wide and worried.

"Ah, yes. There is definitely a presence in your house. I can feel it now, and it beckons from the basement. The devil's dark touch reaches out, and I believe—"

"Alright, alright, cut the theatrics," The husband cut in, his headset and controller left on the couch, "Just let her show you the damn basement, so we can get this over with." He brushed past me and stood next to his wife protectively. She gave an apologetic look.

"Of course. Let us see the basement," I said with a smile.

Bumps in the night were a common occurrence. Every chilling noise mistaken for a haunting could easily be debunked by rational thought and a little bit of research. Creaks in the night was always an old house settling on the earth it was built upon. Scratching in the walls was most likely squirrels, flying squirrels with the sheer amount of wooded land in this town. Doors that closed on their own were usually all chalked up to overall gravity and pressure changes in the rooms themselves. In conclusion, old country houses, doing old country house things. Not that I would tell them that.

"What sort of noises have you been hearing, Mrs. Stephens?" I asked, following them in slow, steady steps. I felt it helped in the act. Lacy turned to acknowledge while her husband rolled his eyes and waited with impatience.

"The scratching has only happened a couple times. There's been a few knocks, too. Sometimes I think I hear whispers, too," she said, rubbing her arm as if suddenly chilled.

Varmints, old plumbing, perhaps a forgotten television?

"The most unnerving one is the clicking though. I can't explain it. It almost sounds like gunfire," she said, looking at her husband.

"I told you Lacy, nobody's firing off machine guns in the neighborhood. We live in a nice part of town. Here's the basement, come on," said the husband, rushing the tour along.

Machine guns?

I entered the kitchen and actually felt a chill waft over me. I could see the culprit immediately, a pair of single pane windows by the sink. I kept my smile to myself and followed the husband, the wife following close behind. The husband opened the door next to the pantry to reveal the dark entrance to the basement. With a sigh he reached into the dark and flicked the light switch, and the stairway filled with soft yellow light.

"It's down here. Watch your step, Copperfield," he taunted.

"Of course. This is where the energy is manifesting. Would we like to say a prayer before we head down?" I asked, and Lacy considered.

"No. I don't want to deal with this all day. Let's get it done," he said.

"Brian, don't be a dick," Lacy said.

"It's quite alright. The Lord is with me now, every step of the way," I said, looking down the old wooden steps.

"Sure, sure. Don't hit your head," Brian led.

We went down the stairs, each step creaking as we descended. The basement was unfinished, the crude cement walls damp and dimly lit. Lacy passed us and walked to the old washer and dryer, her bare feet slapping the concrete floor. There were two green rugs on the floor, one in front of the machines, and another in the far corner.

"This is where I hear it. Every time I do laundry. He thinks I'm crazy." She put her arms out in the empty space.

"Hear what, exactly?" I asked.

"The clicking," she said.

"Probably just a jackhammer or something. They're putting in that new neighborhood, I'm sure you saw the construction," Brian said.

"It's only when I'm down here. Alone," she said, hugging herself.

I hadn't heard of any clicking in the past. An old clock, sure. But a sound as fast as a jackhammer? That was a new one for me. I walked to the closest wall, running a gloved hand over the bricks.

"You said there was a leak? May I see it?" I asked.

Lacy walked over to the second rug and peeled it up. It separated from the ground with a wet sucking sound, and I moved closer to inspect it. Septic leak would be anywhere from clear to brown, not to mention the smell. This "leak" was black, like the color of tar. Underneath the rug was a wooden padlocked door, and the black ooze had been seeping from underneath it.

"I had a guy check out the septic. We should be good now," Brian said.

"That was two days ago. It's leaking again," said Lacy.

"Then I'll call him again."

I looked at the trapdoor, and the rusted lock that looked like it hadn't been touched in a decade. I could feel a breeze coming from it, like a damp breath pushing out. There was something about the door. It didn't feel right. I looked at it, feeling my ears get hot. The longer I looked, the more I thought I heard something. Slowly rising beneath it. I clutched the rosary nervously, the noise getting louder.

"The Kettle!" Lacy said and made her way upstairs.

I chuckled. Always an explanation.

We watched her go, and when she was out of sight, Brian narrowed his eyes on me.

"We finished here? Come on, man. Don't drag this out," he said.

"What's with the door?" I asked, pointing to it on the floor.

"It's a crawl space. Never seen one before?"

"Why's it locked?" I asked, crouching down to get a closer look at it. Trying to look more concerned than necessary.

"I dunno, man. Realtor said it floods. The lock was there when we bought it. We just left it there. Covered it with the rug, it's pretty gross," he explained.

Excellent. The Realtor already explained it, so the only one concerned here was the wife. The husband already didn't want me here. He could give his "blessing", feign some sense of clarity, and be on his way.

"Evil enjoys dark, damp seclusion, Mr. Stephens. It gives it an adequate place to hide, *fester.* It burrows into the property and grows. The longer it's there, the more mischievous, more unrelenting it gets." I played it up, gently grabbing the lock. The surface of the rusted metal deteriorated on my gloves. I rubbed my fingers together, and it smeared into a disgusting paste. "Do you believe in God, Mr. Stephens?"

I waited for an answer, but none came. No attitude, no jab, no sigh. Above me, the door slammed hard, and I jumped. I looked for Mr. Stephens, but he was gone. Standing alone in the basement, the lights went out.

I sighed. I felt a chill on the back of my neck and chuckled to myself. So, this is how it was going to be. I felt through the dark, heading to the stairs. I cleared my throat and spoke aloud.

"I understand my presence here aggravates you, Mr. Stephens. But pranking me isn't the way to solve this matter," I said, my footsteps echoing on the old steps. I reached for the basement door and opened it, expecting them to be waiting, possibly laughing. Maybe they were playing me. But there was no laughter, no pointed fingers. There was nobody at all, just an empty, cold kitchen. Even the appliances were gone.

"Hello?" I called, watching my words come out as fog.

The house was bare, and unbelievably *gray.* I walked into the kitchen, my footsteps kicking up dust. My first thought was to just leave, the irrational fear of the unknown gripping my spine like ice. I headed for the front door and shoved it open. My car was gone. The driveway was gone. Nothing but open fields, no construction, nothing. The sky above was the color of ash, overcast for as far as you can see.

"Mrs. Stephens? Mr. Stephens? Helloooooon," I called, but my voice barely reached. The sound wouldn't carry, it was being suppressed by something else. It was an odd noise, and my mind conjured the only thing to make sense of it.

Clicking.

There was movement in the monochrome landscape, about as far away as my car had been. Long, twig legs attached to white, elegant feathers. A pair of storks in the grass, their legs robotic under a seemingly fluid body. They looked at me, eyes beady and wide, as if they were alarmed. Their bodies contorted, long necks bending backwards in unison, like they were dancing. Together they pointed their beaks to the sky, a loud chattering erupting from their bills. It sounded like gunfire over the valley.

I slammed the door to block out the noise and hide from their beady eyes.

"No, no, no-no-no-no," I stammered. Feeling helpless, out of control. The rosary in my hand was steaming, the beads radiating warmth. I looked around the living room, the flatscreen, the couch, video games, all gone. Bare walls, fogged windows. There was a loud crash, and I squeezed my eyes shut, the rosary held close. Whatever it was, it came from the basement.

"H-hello? Anybody there?" I cried weakly. Over a hundred houses. Never anything unordinary. This didn't make sense. It just wasn't possible.

I stood there in denial for a time. I knew what I had to do, or rather, the only thing I could do. My feet moved on their own when they were ready. Slow, creaking steps, one by one. Back to the kitchen, the air getting colder as I moved. I shivered, the chill stiffening my peacoat. No hot burner, no piping kettle. My attention felt drawn to the basement doorway, to the dark passage that seemed to push wind from it. Like it was breathing.

I went in, holding the beads close. Pushing forward, down the steps. I waited for something, like a hand to grab me, but the sensation was different. I felt eyes on me, but there was no one in sight. At the landing I turned hesitantly, knowing what I would find but afraid to see it. No washer and dryer, no rugs. Only the cellar door, thrown wide open. The padlock and latch littered the floor in pieces.

The dark hole beckoned, its mysterious black luring me in. I didn't want to go. It was something that just happened on its own. I could hear sounds coming from it, like someone was plucking a tight guitar string. It was metallic and *wiry.*

I stood before the hole and looked in. There was nothing, only a void. Black so thick it looked like you could grasp it. The noises came from the hole, the metallic *ting,* with a whisper on the cold breeze. Whatever it said, it didn't make sense.

"Our Father, who art in Heaven, hallowed be thy—" A loud pop interrupted my mumbling, and I clutched my stomach in pain. It felt like someone had punched me. I felt the sensation of trickling water and assumed I pissed myself. To my dismay I did not, the leak was coming from my coat.

I reached in to feel my glove soaking, and pulled it out to find a handful of glass. The vial of holy water had burst. My mind raced. With a shaky hand I tried to get all the glass out, wet shards hitting the concrete like pebbles. I kept trying to mumble, to say something in comfort, but the words felt scrambled in my head. The now wet bundle of sage tumbled out with the glass and I watched it fall. As soon as it hit the floor it shriveled, igniting in embers and a puff of smoke.

God help me, I thought, the smoke stinging my eyes. I stepped in front of the hole, peering in like it was an open casket. I felt the wind, and there it was again, the metallic twine. I didn't have a choice. I had to go in.

"B-blessed is the man, who remains s-steadfast under trial, for when he has stood the test…" I stammered; the irony was not lost on me. I was a joke. I deserved this.

Holding the rosary, I closed my eyes and jumped in.

Falling, endless black. I hugged myself, the wind flapping my cheeks as I yelled, plummeting into nothing. There was nothing but gusting wind, my stomach twisting as the blind momentum continued. I thought of prayers, something for comfort, but it didn't matter. Even if I could find the words, I didn't deserve to use them. Eventually my shoes felt surface, softly at that. I landed gracefully at my destination, and once I had the courage, I opened my eyes. I was in what looked like a cavern, but a manmade one. Carved out ten foot ceilings in the stone, like a larger, cruder basement. Torches lined the walls, fire that burned white. I wanted to call out, but my breath was ripped from my lungs. Whatever I was meant to see I had found, and it was right in front of me. I watched in horror, unable to speak, unable to breathe. The sounds of metallic plucking clear as day.

Hanging from the ceiling on a long braid of barbed wire was a woman. Blind folded and gagged, she hung like an art piece, a complicated Shibari tie forcing her pose upside down. Her naked skin was scuffed with a slick black rub, an oily substance that reflected the torchlight. She swayed slightly, the barbs *tinking* off other strands. It looked terrifying and painful, the way the wire bound her. Arms tied tight behind her back, each leg positioned individually with the grace of a ballerina, like she was twirling in the air. Through the horror of the bondage was a beauty, her figure displayed like a twisted sculpture.

The rosary was hot in my hands, steaming against the lambskin glove. My fingers wouldn't let it go, like it was the only thing I had left. I could hear the sound again. The maddening clicking of the storks, bouncing off the walls from some unknown location. I took a step toward the woman to try and help her, but froze. A shape emerged from the shadows of the cavern, a broad figure garbed in what looked like layers and layers of leather. I could hear the fabric of their clothing as it moved, whatever resided beneath was being restrained. I guessed it to be a muscular man from the build, but its face was shielded by a porcelain mask, arced slits for eyes, and a long shoebill beak. It looked like a plague doctor, but *tainted.* Behind the eyes of the mask, two globes glared, bloodshot and depraved. I could hear his breathing now, heavy and labored.

The dominator came to the woman's side, their hulking presence casting a shadow over the helpless pose. A leather hand moved across her body, sliding over the slick rub, caressing the breast. The woman writhed in her restraints, her whimpers indiscernible from pleasure or fear. The hand rested on her stomach, fingers tapping the skin like this was a carnival show. With a heavy step, their boot pressed into the floor, an indent in the stonework causing a groaning shift. The floor split apart, opening a pit beneath them. They floated in the center, a small platform serving as a stage. It was now the noises got louder, reverberating so intensely it shook the walls and rattled my teeth. Dozens, no, *hundreds.* The chorus of clicking blasting from the pit.

Below the stage, an army of wild-eyed storks clacked their beaks. They jumped excitedly, wings smacking each other as they reached for the bound woman. They didn't notice me there, every beady eye locked hungrily above. The masked man reached behind him slowly, and the birds clicked in anticipation. Theatrically he withdrew his hand, a long sickle shining in the white torchlight. The commotion grew as he placed the cold steel against her abdomen, and she twitched under its touch. After a pat of admiration, he pulled the blade fast, and her lean stomach separated. A geyser of black and red rained into the pit and the dominator let her go, her sculpture body spinning, her legs curled. Like a Stork.

Below the birds went wild, clacking wet beaks at the splashing blood. They shoved and fought for it, stark white feathers stained a vibrant red in the light. It covered everything until all you could see was a writhing mess of beaks and claws. Their pupils dilated, and the clicking got erratic, unsynchronized. As she ran dry, the woman gave her final convulsion before going limp.

In my hand, the rosary exploded. The sound was deafening, beads bouncing off the cavern walls like a shotgun blast. The squawking and clicking stopped, and all fell silent. Ahead of me, the hulking dominator looked my way, a long finger unraveling from his fist as he pointed. Those bloodshot eyes looked angry, offended even.

Like a sonic boom the birds cried together, bursting from the pit like an erupting volcano. Red feathers, sharp beaks, eyes dotted like pin pricks. They were on me instantly, pecking and slashing with their extremities. They squawked in my ears before pecking at them. Their talons tore my clothes, ripped my coat. I felt the beaks puncture my scalp and knock my skull, a volley of spear-tipped stabs picking me apart. My flesh peeled away; their solid beaks rattled against my bones.

"Get off me! Get off, get—"

"What the fuck is your problem, man? It was just a fuse!" said a familiar voice.

I thrashed wildly and opened my eyes, Lacy and Brian looking at me bewildered. We were back in the kitchen. I huffed for breath, sweat trickling down my back and beading on my forehead. At my feet was a shattered teacup, China glass crunching under my feet.

"Wha—what? What happened?" I asked, taking off my gloves and wiping my face. I unbuttoned my peacoat, I was burning up. The beaks tearing my flesh. The holy water, sage, and rosary. I patted my pockets; they were empty.

"What do you *mean* what happened? The breaker blew, I went to fix it, you said you would burn some sage and sprinkle some water or whatever. Said you'd be right up," Brian said, his brow furrowed, "then you come up here, mumbling and shit, and she handed you some tea. You squeezed the cup until it broke. Reached out for her, all crazy. Now look at this mess. What's wrong with you, man?"

My mind raced. I looked at Lacy, who put her hands up and backed away, moving behind Brian. I thought of it all; it replayed in my head on fast forward. The barb wire, the girl, the storks. I looked at Lacy's face, the hair, her skin. It was her, the bound woman. I blinked and rubbed my eyes. My face was flushed, and I felt a hot trickle from my nose. I touched it to see the red drip of a nosebleed.

"You need to get out of this house! It's not safe!" I pleaded, and they flinched when I stepped forward.

"You guys gotta go, I don't know what it is, I can't expl—"

Brian cut me off.

"No, it's *you* who needs to go. Get the fuck out of here. C'mon, let's go. Now," he said, grabbing me by the arm, hard.

"No! You don't understand! Your wife, she's not safe! You gotta' get her out of here!" I begged as he shoved me through the living room.

"Yeah. Not safe from you, no doubt." He opened the door and tossed me out, jabbing a finger in my face.

"Don't come back here, understand? Don't message my wife, don't show your face here again. I'll call the cops. Psycho!"

He slammed the door in my face.

I walked to my car, my head foggy, my nerves shot. My hands were shaking, and when I got into my car, I sat there for a moment. I looked at the house, with all of its color returned. I looked to the front window. Lacy was there, mouthing the words *I'm sorry* briefly before her husband was there, phone in hand. They started shouting at each other, and I started my car, tires spinning gravel as I turned around. I drove home, not really sure of what to think. Not sure what to do, I drove home in silence. I couldn't get it out of my head. I pulled into my driveway. The tears started to fall when the adrenaline wore off, and I bawled at my steering wheel.

It was wrong. Everything was wrong. My whole world came crashing down. No more blessings, no more cleanses. I took it all down. I'm done. The charade is over. I shut down the website. Canceled all meet and greets and future appointments. I ghosted everyone like the fuckin' fraud I am, and now I'm done. I see their eyes when I sleep. In the back of my mind, I see the hanging pose. The geyser from the gaping wound. The clacking beaks.

Days have passed now. The phone calls are getting less frequent, and the messages have died down. I made a post on social media, announcing my resignation. My fans deserve better, but in the end I'll only hurt them more. I'm moving soon, far enough away to escape the stain that is my own existence. I check in on the site from time to time, seeing the love from those I have helped in the past. I hope I really did help them somehow. Maybe it wasn't all a waste. I'm sorry everyone. Really.

Lacy sent me an email. It's two in the morning. I've read it a dozen times, and I don't know what to do. Every time I read her name, I'm reminded of the clicking, the beaks echoing in my mind. Nothing makes it go away. I can only turn down the volume, but it never leaves. Why? Why won't it stop?

Father Cain. It took me a while to track you down. I'll understand if you don't respond, but I don't know who else to talk to. The door is open. My husband doesn't see it, it's always closed for him. But I can. It opens at night. It calls to me. I know you warned me. But I don't know how long I can resist. I just heard it open. I can hear it. The clicking. It's getting louder.

THE OLD MAN THAT FOLLOWED ME

I'll never forget his face. I can see it now, the way he stared, cloudy but focused eyes locked on me like I was the only thing in existence. We were on our honeymoon drive when it happened, gassing up at the only available stop before our three-hour homestretch. We were heading to a cabin far from home, a wedding present gifted by her family. I don't know if it was the lonely roads or the dark endless tree line, but I was on edge.

I had just started pumping when I noticed him hovering next to a beat-up Ford pickup. It was an older one, with square headlights and boxy frame. He was minding his business initially, but once his eyes saw me, they never lifted. At first I gave a friendly nod, but when he did nothing but stare, I found the awkward crawl of discomfort setting in. He looked uncomfortable, confused. He reminded me of an extra in a horror film, the figure that was standing off to the side and out of focus. That's how he lingered, even after his nozzle 'clicked' as it was topped off. I stared at the digits on my pump impatiently, keeping him in my peripheral vision as I watched the numbers climb. He was just standing there. Staring.

Once mine was done, I hung the nozzle up and got my receipt. I gave the old man a parting wave, and he gave me the slightest of nods. He almost looked offended. Yanking the door and ducking in, I could even feel him watching after I got in the car.

"You see that?" I asked my wife, who was sitting in the passenger seat. Her face was buried in her phone, scrolling through videos of people doing embarrassing dances.

"Hmm?" she said tiredly, not quite looking away. Her eyes were haggard, the screen time keeping her awake until we were on the road again.

"That old man. He was staring at me," I said, turning the key in the ignition. Our little Honda started up, and I buckled my seat belt.

"What? Where?" she asked, looking up away from her phone. She looked around until she saw him; he was still there, standing next to his truck.

"Creepy," she said, turning back around.

"Maybe he's looking at you," I joked, putting it in drive and pulling away. I watched in the mirror, the old man's head swiveling slowly as we left. It gave me the chills.

"What? At my boney ass?" she snorted, and I grabbed her hand, interlocking our fingers.

"Maybe. You get the GPS back up?" I asked, pulling back onto the road. The load stretch of lines reflected off the headlights.

"Oh, right. Sorry," she said, bringing it up again. The bright GPS screen lit up the cab, and when the blue line on the grid collected itself, the voice spoke over Bluetooth.

In two miles, take a right.

"We almost there?" she yawned, nestling back in her seat.

"Not really," I said, adjusting the rear-view mirror.

Off in the distance, a set of square headlights was turning out of the gas station.

"Can you wake me up when we're close?" she asked, already falling asleep. I watched the headlights for a moment, heading in the same direction as us. I pressed the accelerator further.

"Sure thing, honey."

Surely it was just a coincidence. I kept my eyes forward, watching for deer in the passing trees. I messed with the radio, trying to find something to listen to. Behind me, the headlights were getting closer. I tuned the dial, and found a station, only for it to be cut off by the automated voice.

In 500 feet, take the next right.

I slowed down, watching both the headlights and the upcoming turn. I thought of the old man's stare, and how he stood perfectly still, never looking away. Just picturing it made me shudder.

Turn right.

I slowed and cut the wheel, turning onto another long backroad, one that looked shadier than the last. My wife opened her eyes for a second before snuggling back against the door.

In three miles, take a left.

I kept driving, both hands on the wheel. I was tired as hell, every yawn watering my eyes and making me drowsier. I rubbed my face, massaging my cheeks to remove the stiffness. I watched the mirror subconsciously, waiting for the truck to fly past. I watched silently, seeing the glow come closer and closer. I watched them slow and pan over, the headlights bouncing on the old suspension. The truck was still following.

"Honey. Honey, wake up." I nudged her, and she groaned.

"Hmm, what?" she stretched.

"That old man. He's following us," I said, my hands gripping the wheel.

"*What?*" she said, looking behind us.

The truck was gaining, chugging behind us through the night. I tried to go faster, but it kept speeding up, the headlights getting closer and closer.

"Maybe it's just a coincidence. Maybe he lives around here. You didn't say something to him, did you?" she asked.

"No, nothing. I tried to wave. That's about it," I said.

"Huh. Maybe he'll turn off."

Ahead was a traffic light, the soothing green glow like a beacon. I sped up to try and catch it, but almost as if in spite, it started changing.

"Damn," I said, slowing down again.

My eyes darted between the traffic light and the truck. It practically flew up on us, headlights blinding in the mirrors as we stopped for the red. The truck was loud, a big engine and old exhaust echoing right behind us. My wife looked behind us and shielded her eyes. I stared at the red light, as if my will would make it change faster.

"He's getting out," my wife said, and my blood ran cold.

"*What?*" I asked, checking the side mirror.

"Fuck, babe, he's got a knife." She squeezed my shoulder, looking frantic.

In the mirror I saw him close the truck door and start walking up to us. I saw the light hit the blade in his hand, and he started shuffling faster, his image growing as I watched.

"What the fuck, what the—" I said, clamming up.

"Go, babe, go-go-go-gooo!" she yelled, and I looked both ways. The light was still red.

The old man was at my window. I stomped on the gas and the tires squealed, the car lurching as it caught traction. We blew the intersection, and I watched the dark silhouette shuffle back to his truck and throw open the door. In the light of his cab, I could see him hitting his steering wheel.

In one mile, take a left.

We sped away, trying to put as much distance between us as possible. The truck was moving again, but my head start had bought us time. My wife turned in her seat, watching the truck struggle to keep up. Ahead, I saw the green rectangular sign for a backroad.

In 500 feet, take a left.

"Hang on!" I shouted, slamming on the brakes.

"For what?" she shouted, but grabbed the overhead handle anyway.

Spinning the wheel quickly, I turned right instead, and gunned it down an unfamiliar, unkempt stretch of road. The pavement was poor and cracked, the lines barely legible in the center. I swerved to hit potholes and broken sticks.

"What are you doing?" she shouted, holding on for dear life.

"We gotta lose him!" I said, nervously watching the mirror.

Make a U-turn.

The road was dark and winding, taking us up hills and under old railway bridges. I squealed on every curve, our little car struggling to miss the many obstacles in the road. Garbage bags. Old mattresses leaned against brush. The trees were dead, towering above like withered giants in the dark.

Make a U-turn.

The road grew thinner and more desolate, the shoulders turning into deep, treacherous ditches. I checked the mirror again. Nothing but darkness. It was getting harder to see. I turned the brights on, and it only added to the discomfort, lighting up hundreds more wicked branches and scattered trash.

"What do we do?" My wife asked. My mind raced. I didn't really know.

"I don't know, call the police!" I shouted, and she unlocked her phone. The bright light hampered my view, the glare reflecting in every window.

Ahead the road straightened out, getting even more narrow. The tires bounced as the pavement transitioned to gravel, the static of it droning and *plinking* against the wheel wells deafening us. Ahead, a large orange sign reflected our light, but the high beams were too bright to make out the old lettering.

"Babe?"

Make a U-turn.

I squinted at it, having no choice but to slow down to the lack of road. I read the sign, big black capital letters echoing in my mind.

"Babe? I don't have enough signal."

Ahead the road was gone, the sparse gravel blending to dirt, then grass, then… nothing.

-DEAD END-

The ground ahead ceased to exist, the sheer drop of a cliff waiting on the other side of the old sign. Behind us, the headlights were coming. I parked the car, witnessing the impending doom of the light catch up. Not enough room to turn around. Nowhere to go. Frantically I searched the inside of the car, looking for some kind of weapon. Tossing aside old documents in the center console, I found a flashlight.

The truck pulled behind us slowly, blocking us in.

I tested the flashlight; the batteries were dead. Still better than nothing.

"Stay in the car!" I yelled and threw open the door.

"What do you want me to do?" she cried, looking from me to the truck.

"Lock the doors."

I gripped the flashlight in my hand, hoping the weight of it would give me courage. It didn't.

The old man emerged from his truck, hinges creaking loudly as he pushed his door shut. The knife was in his hand, like a spike protruding from his arm. He was breathing hard, his shoulders hunching as his chest heaved.

"What the hell do you want!?" I shouted.

He took another step forward and stopped, his shadow in the headlights frozen. He craned his head for a moment and stepped back. He moved stiffly; his moments slow.

"Why are you following me?" I shouted again, stepping forward with the flashlight. I could hear my wife sobbing in the car.

I was tired of running. I raised the flashlight and marched toward him. He raised the knife, ready to stab. I grit my teeth and reared back, ready to swing. I saw his face in the dark, his piercing eyes staring just as they had at the gas station. I brought the flashlight down, hoping to knock the weapon from his hand, and stopped.

The old man was crying.

"I'm sorry… I'm so sorry," he said, his voice choking. I lowered the flashlight slowly, and he lowered the knife.

"Why were you following us?" I asked, lowering my voice. He looked so thin and frail, even in the dark.

He put his arms down, both hands squeezed into fists. He looked like he wanted to walk away, his steps hesitant, shaking.

"I'm sorry. I thought you were my son. I was wrong. I'm sorry." He looked away, trying to shield his face.

"Wait, what?" I asked. I looked to my car, where my wife sat on edge, her mouth hanging open.

"When I saw you at the gas station, I thought you were my son. You, you look just like him. But it couldn't be. My son passed away a long time ago now. In a car accident. But you look just like him. I wanted to be sure. I had to be sure. But your voice… you're not him. You're not Peter. I'm sorry for scaring you. You must be terrified," the old man said.

"But the knife! At the light, you were coming at me with a knife!" I said. It didn't make any sense.

"I know, I know. I didn't think that through. I let my emotions get the better of me. I'm just an old fool. I got this for my son all those years ago. I thought you were him. I thought maybe, if I could get it to you, you could move on. And I can move on. But I made a mistake. I saw what I wanted to see. I'm sorry," he choked and started backing up.

I looked to my wife, who threw up her hands in confusion. I held up a finger and mouthed "wait a minute"

"If you want to press charges, I understand. I'll wait here. For the police." He turned and started walking back to his truck. I went after him.

"Wait, hang on a second!" I called after him, and he stopped. He was so much smaller and thinner up close. I guess at the gas station, I saw what I wanted to see too.

I gave him a hug. He resisted at first, but when I didn't let go, he gave in and returned it. We stood there for a while. I let him cry for as long as he needed, standing in the square headlights in the middle of nowhere. No pressed charges, no stabbing or clubbing. I motioned for my wife to get out, and when she joined us, I explained what happened.

"My name is Tom. This is my wife, Gina. I'm sorry for almost hitting you. And I'm sorry about your son," I said.

"It's alright. My name is Wallace. I'm sorry I scared you good people tonight. But thank you for giving me your time. You didn't have to do that, I appreciate it. Before I go, I think I'd like you to have this. I can't hang on to it anymore." He held out his hand, the hunting knife in his palm. Inscribed across the blade were the words "For my son."

I took it, and promised to take care of it, under the stipulation that he take my number so we could talk again. He seemed to enjoy that, and after a hug farewell, and even a few laughs, we parted ways. I watched him walk back to his truck; his head held higher than before. He opened the door and looked at me for a moment, giving a final wave before ducking in. I found myself freezing briefly, before nodding and waving back. Behind him, barely visible, was a man, his hand resting lightly on Wallace's shoulder. He nodded to me with a smile, and after the old man climbed in and shut the door, he was gone.

COOPER

"Nine-One-One, what's your emergency?"

"H-hello? I'm being stalked. I need help."

"Being stalked? By whom?"

"My neighbor."

"You're being stalked by your neighbor?"

"Y-yes. I'm not safe. He's going to get me."

"Okay, sir, where are you now? I'll send a unit right away."

"No, you don't understand. I'm on my way to the police station right now. He killed Cooper!"

"He killed who, sir?"

"He killed Cooper. The cat, he killed the cat."

"He killed your cat?"

"No! He's not my cat, he's just a cat. He's a stray. I'm bringing him with. You have to help me!"

"Sir, how far away from the station are you? Where are you now?"

Brief pause.

"*Oh, no.*"

"Sir?"

"Oh god. Oh no."

"Sir, what's the——-"

"*He's in my car.*"

"Sir, pull over, you need to——-"

There was a panicked scream, followed by an electric crackling over the phone. Muffled thumps and interference are all that can be heard from the caller's end, with a faint sound of squealing tires.

"Sir! Sir?"

The line goes dead.

That was a transcript of a dispatch call to the sheriff's department. This was a couple weeks ago, and the man who called never made it to the station. I was not dispatched to this call, nor did I have any knowledge of it at the time. This is the only place I can tell this story, *you* guys being my only possible audience. I have to tell somebody. There will be specifics I will have to leave out, but I will tell you everything that I can. Maybe those who are looking can get some closure. It's the best I can do.

I'm a police officer. I've only been on the force for two years. My dad was a cop in the big city, just like his father before him. He always said he wanted his daughter to follow in his footsteps, but was ultimately shocked when I joined the department in the next town over. The city was too congested and noisy for me, and I wanted to try and make my own way without working under his shadow.

There's something wrong in our town. It started two months ago, like a dark cloud had just hovered over our town and never left. The start of my career has been quiet if I'm being honest. The extent of my police work consisted of traffic violations and petty theft. A wellness check every once in a while, or a call for a domestic disturbance. It almost seemed a little easy, like maybe I should've joined the academy in the big city instead of this sleeping town. It all seemed to start when they found that girl under the bridge—the first murder in our town in a long time. I drive over that bridge every night to go home, and it serves as an odd reminder of how peaceful things used to be. Ever since then, things have been chaotic. There's always tension at the station. There's always calls to be answered. Some people go missing, others call in to report strange sightings. It's like a madness is looming in the distance.

I was on the way home the night it happened. I had just finished late on a night shift. I changed at the station and drove home, long stretches of back roads through the farmland. I live in the country in my grandparents' old house. It's got some land, but it's really marshy. I had to start getting in my uniform at the station because my driveway was a muddy wreck. Most of my gear is at the station as well, in my locker. All I had was my phone and a compact Ruger 9mm I carry when I'm off duty. It had been a long day, and I was ready to be home.

I was on a particularly long stretch of road, my headlights the only light in the vast fields of beans on either side. They were alternating from corn this year, and it was only a few weeks away from the fall harvest. I had the radio playing lightly—some kind of seasonal ad for a local haunted house. An announcer was trying really hard to be edgy, talking of ghouls and frights for the low-low price of twenty dollars a ticket. I turned it up out of boredom and was surprised when it cut to loud static. I usually had good reception all the way home, so the interference was unusual. I sighed and changed the station, only to find more static. I tried them all, and they yielded the same result. That's when I saw it out of the corner of my eye.

A strobing light, blinking quickly across the field.

Instinctually, I slammed on the brakes. Sitting in the darkness of the road, I stared into the darkness of the trees, waiting for it to happen again. The static continued cutting through the advertisement, the voice warping against the interference as I white-knuckled the wheel. Just as I started to wonder if I had imagined it, it happened again.

The blinking was slower this time, but definitely there.

The clock on the dash read 1:39am. I shut the radio off and sat there in silence. Something was wrong, I could feel it. Nobody lived in the area, nothing but weeds and trees once the beans ended. Hunting was out of season, and even if it wasn't, it was nearly two in the morning.

A few feet off the road there was a beaten gravel path, one of the lanes the farmers use to pull harvesting equipment in when they till the fields. I grabbed my phone from the passenger seat and tried to ring the station.

Holding the phone to my ear gave me nothing but a long silence. I looked at the screen to see I had no bars, and I started to feel sick. It was ten minutes back to the station. *Five* to get home. But if someone was in danger, they wouldn't have time for me to be dicking around to find a landline. I wasn't in uniform and there would be no calling for backup. If something bigger was going on out there, I would be just as shit out of luck as the person calling for help. I tried the station again. Nothing.

With my eyes on the dark gravel lane, I felt in my purse for the 9mm and my badge. I always kept it loaded, but I checked out of habit, half-cocking the slide to make sure it was chambered. I didn't have a choice, really. I would get my ass chewed for going without backup, and I wouldn't be able to forgive myself if someone couldn't escape danger because of my negligence. I let off the brake and turned into the path, my Suburban bouncing over the uneven ground of the farmer's lane. The headlights shined down the stretch of gravel, barely hitting the trees in the distance. I saw the eerie strobe light again—it was coming from the forest, near the base of a tree. I periodically checked my cell for reception, but was rewarded with the same results. Driving down the path made my palms sweat. I kept scanning the trees for movement, for a sign of life or a struggle, anything. I decided I would start where I saw the strobe and I would go from there. Hopefully by then I could get some kind of signal.

The gravel lane ended with a tree line. There was a gap between the trees with waist-high weeds that looked like someone drove through them. I couldn't really see what was behind the weeds and there was no visible path from here, so I took it as my cue to get out. I put the phone and badge in the pockets of my high-waist jeans and grabbed the handgun. I decided to leave the car running and use the headlights for visibility, along with the hazards, to draw attention from the road.

Stepping out into the chilly midnight air, I felt the immediate squish of mud. I always wore my hiking boots because of my shitty driveway, and I was thankful to have them on now. I closed the door and tucked the handgun into my coat.

A toxic smell wafted on the night air, like something burning. I checked my phone a final time in desperation before swallowing hard and committing. Leaving my truck behind, I headed toward the tracks in the weeds. Someone had definitely been through here. The mud sucked at my boots as I approached, feeling clumsy and vulnerable the further I got away from my car. Ahead, the weeds started to rustle, and I froze, pulling the gun and readying it tightly with both hands. I trained my gun on the weeds, clicking the safety off and lining up the sights. A white and brown mass of fur slinked out, a collar jingling on its neck.

It was a cat.

With a sigh of relief, I lowered my weapon, and the cat *meowed* at the sight of me. It was a calico cat, his marbled fur untouched by the surrounding mud. It pranced up to me and purred loudly before rubbing up against my leg. I knelt down and scratched its chin.

"What are you doing all the way out here, little guy?" I asked as I pet him.

The cat looked at me with intense eyes, its whole body radiating an odd warmth in the chilly air. After seconds of scratching and purring, I heard a loud popping in the distance, like a firecracker going off. I stood and looked into the forest, down the tracks of flattened weeds. There was a faint orange glow in the trees, but from *what* I couldn't make out. I decided to take the cat back to the truck, but when I looked down, it was gone. Confused, I looked around for it, almost slipping in the mud when I whirled around. It was nowhere to be found. No meow, no jingle, nothing. The sudden reminder of being alone again gave me goosebumps, and I gripped the gun tighter as I scoped out my surroundings. Having no choice but to leave the mysterious cat behind, I headed into the forest to find the source of the noise.

Once I started down the trail, the mud lessened with the foliage of the forest floor. The further I walked, the stronger the stench became. A few more steps, and my eyes started to burn. Smoke. I couldn't really see it in the dark, and the headlights weren't helping as much as I had hoped. I was embarrassed by my lack of preparation, but it was better than shrugging my shoulders and driving home. I followed the smoke, scanning the woods for any signs of movement. As the glow ahead was slowly getting brighter, I started walking faster. My adrenaline was rising, the gun held tight in front of me. Something was definitely burning. The smell was strong, and the smoke was getting thicker. It was like smog with the hints of charred meat, like a cookout in the middle of a refinery. I chanced a look at my phone. No bars. I don't know why I expected anything different.

I started running. The glow got brighter and brighter until I could see it radiating. There were trees and brambles blocking the view, but I pushed on. I needed to get there. Too much time had been wasted already. I ran through the weeds, blinking at the sting of smoke. My boots snapped twigs and kicked up leaves as I went. I could hear the fire now, the crackling and sizzling of something burning hot. Thick smoke hazed through the light of the fire, and as the trees broke into a clearing, I could finally see the source.

In the center of the clearing, a mini-SUV sat like a ball of fire. Wicked tongues of flame licked from all sides, billowing black smoke trying to reach the sky through the crowded treetops. The twisted figure of what was once a person sat in the driver's seat, their contorted hands frozen in perpetual scorched agony. I felt sick to my stomach, and my hands started to shake. I suddenly felt… out of my depth. Something brushed my leg and tore my gaze from the wreckage.

The cat was sitting next to me. It was looking ahead, the reflection of the roaring blaze burning in its eyes. It looked up at me for a moment before focusing on something off to the side of the fire. I followed his gaze and suddenly felt my knees weaken.

Sitting near the fire was a man. He stared intently into the flames, his hands messing with something in front of him. His face was emotionless, but he sat like he was enjoying a campfire on a cool summer night. I felt the panic rise within me, and I forced it away and sprang into action. I ran into the clearing, badge held up with my gun trained on him.

"Police! Hands where I can see them!" I shouted. For a moment he ignored me. He just kept looking at the fire.

"What are you doing here? I just wanted to watch," he said quietly, his hands gripping the object in front of him. It looked like a taser.

"I said get your hands in the air! Now!" I yelled again, and this time he looked at me. His blank face slowly twisted into anger. He started getting up, the taser held at his side.

"Did you come to watch too?" he said, taking a step closer.

"Take another step and I will shoot! I'm warning you!" I shouted, pulling the hammer back.

There was a sizzling in the wreckage, one that was starting to slowly get louder. We both seemed to look at it at once, and right before our eyes, the hood of the SUV exploded. The sound rattled my ears, and I shielded myself from the debris as the wave of hot air threw bits of glass and metal. I looked up just in time to see the man rushing toward me. As I tried to raise my weapon he slammed into me, and the gun fired into the trees. We hit the ground in a grunting mess, my hip and elbow jarring into the ground. I lost my grip on the gun, and it tumbled away. With an electric crackle the man thrust the taser down, and I put up my hands to fend him off. I grabbed his wrists desperately, the arcing tip inches from my face.

"I just have to play with you next, that's all," he said, and kneed me in the stomach. I faltered, and he shoved the taser into my neck. The pain coursed through my body like lightning as I involuntarily spasmed. It was like all my veins had caught fire at once. He laughed as I struggled, and I could only shut my eyes and suffer through it. He hit me again, and through my agony I searched the grass for something to fend him off. My teeth rattled as they were forced together, and I screamed as the tremors rolled me onto my side. My fingers flexed and twitched, and as my vision blurred, I felt something in the grass. Something solid and pointed on one side.

The badge.

As my fingers wrapped around it, I squirmed for an opening. He grabbed the collar of my coat like he wanted to slam me on the ground. I slammed my palm inside his elbow to buckle his arm, but I was too weak. He laughed at my futile attempt and ignited the taser again. As he arrogantly laughed, I thrust the badge upward, shoving the point of the shield in his eye. He screamed and covered his face, trying to climb off and pull the shield out. I kicked him away and looked for the gun; I could barely make out its shape sticking up in the firelight. He stopped and pulled the badge from his eye, tossing it into the weeds as I crawled for the gun. At the sound of him rapidly gaining on me, I mustered all the energy I had and leapt for it. The man grabbed my ankles and pulled. I whipped around and squeezed the trigger.

Three shots, center mass

He clutched his stomach and fell to his knees, blood seeping through his fingers as his face twisted from a look of anger to sadness. With an exasperated groan, he doubled over, his eyes resting on the fire, the lights of them fading slowly as the profound sadness melted into a softened look of what I could only describe as… relief.

I sat up, gasping for air. Through the sounds of the inferno, I could hear the faint wail of sirens in the distance. My skin burned and my tongue itched. The world spun as I coughed. The fire was getting bigger and consuming the grass surrounding it. I looked around for the cat, but it was nowhere to be found.

***

When the cavalry showed, I was put in an ambulance and treated. Minor scrapes and bruises, along with the burns from the taser. Nothing major, I would recover in no time. I was thankful for the arrival but confused about how they found me. Before the fire department drove back to put out the fire, one of the officers on the scene told me the station had received several calls from drivers, all talking about a strobing light in the distance.

"The funniest thing," the officer said, "we didn't think we'd find anything. The only reason we were able to find you, well, there was a cat. It was standing in the middle of the road—I almost hit the damn thing. When I stopped, it took off down the farmer's path, and I could see your car with its lights on. Could smell the smoke from the street. Radioed it in, the cat practically led us to you. Like a little guardian angel. It must have ran off, though. Some of these feral cats live off the mice in the fields. We see 'em all the time. Probably the most excitement it's had in a while." He chuckled, scratching his head. All I could think of was the fiery eyes of that cat as they closed up the ambulance and sent me on my way.

The next day, I filed the incident report. I told them about everything, the strobing light, the car fire, the guy with the taser. There was a lot of information to go over, and I struggled to retain all of the details. They pressed me on why I didn't call for backup, and when I said I had no signal they treated me like I was lying. After some evaluations they deemed me fit to leave. I was allowed to go, and I was given a couple of days off to recuperate.

While I was off, I eagerly awaited the news reports revolving around the incident. I left the television on in hopes of catching it, and even browsed the web to find an article about it. It was strange. No network had coverage, there wasn't any mention of it. Social media was quiet, and there was no official statement made by the police department. I called one of my fellow officers and they said something was going on at the station, that the perp's family had *money*, and they sent a representative to sweep everything under the rug. When I asked him to elaborate, he said there was some "shady shit" going on, and they were paying off everyone involved to keep their mouths shut.

When I returned to work, it was like the whole thing never happened. Everyone kept their heads down, and when I asked them about it, they made up some kind of excuse or redirected me to the chief. When I spoke to the chief, he said the investigation was no longer our jurisdiction, and I needed to "let it go". He said an agent from the FBI turned up while I was on leave and collected all the evidence that was for the investigation. When I tried to pry further, the tone seemed to change, and there were threats of suspension and possible relocation to a different department. I was given *thorough* instructions on what to say if the issue ever came up again, and I was reassured that the media had been handled. The chief said both men were deceased, and as far as they were concerned, it was an "open and shut" case. Further attempts to get information only angered him, and I left his office baffled with my head hung low.

The rest of my day was an uncomfortable crawl. Eventually I got to meet up with the officer I called while I was off, and he slipped me an envelope discreetly, when we were away from everyone. He told me it was "all that was left", that everything else had been pulled and labeled confidential.

I didn't feel comfortable opening the envelope until I got home. *All that was left* consisted of the positive IDs for the perp and victim, and the forensics they had been able to pull off the wreckage before they were locked out.

As far as I know, this is the only physical evidence remaining of the incident altogether. I can't give you names, but they both lived in the same complex, their apartments directly across from each other. The driver who burned up in the car had lived in his condo for a couple of years and kept to himself the whole time he lived there. The perp, however, had just moved in a couple days prior. Neighbors said he had an expensive moving crew with lots of nice stuff. The department had gone door to door asking questions to the other tenants in the beginning, and the only thing they could tell us was the perp was acting strangely. There was no way of telling what really happened between them, but I later found the dispatch call above that came from the driver in the car.

After several online searches I was able to learn more about the perp's family—they were extremely wealthy—like *Gates* and *Bezos* wealthy. There wasn't much on the perp himself, but I can only assume they moved him here because he was a problem child, or something like that. The landlord said the guy didn't personally apply for his apartment, that a representative did. The landlord made a statement saying something about generous donations to the district, and it was an offer he couldn't refuse.

The forensics weren't as complete as I had hoped. They were leaning toward electrical being the cause of fire, but were unable to draw any accurate conclusions before the investigation was pulled. The man behind the wheel had been so badly burned, but there was a residue of adhesive left behind, like he had been duct taped to the seat when the car caught fire. They didn't get a chance to do an airway examination, whether he was alive when the fire broke out is unknown. The only other thing they were able to find was the remains of an animal on the passenger side floor. It was hard to tell with the fire damage, but it seemed to be dead beforehand, this being concluded due to the "large flashlight forced down the animal's throat". The temperature in the car fire had gotten so hot, the flashlight had fused to the remains.

Forensics were unable to remove it for further testing.

If it wasn't for the file and my own eyewitness account, it's almost like this whole thing never happened. Nobody had spoken since the evidence was collected, and as the days go by, I find some of my fellow officers avoiding me altogether. Everything was business as usual at the department, and I was back to making my rounds and answering calls. Nobody ever reached out to follow up, and after a few weeks, I almost wondered if this whole thing was just my imagination. That was until I found a post online. It was a story from the point of view of a man in a condo; a man who loved to watch, and the cruel demise of a stray cat named Cooper. I'm going to link these stories together and save it, because I think it's the closest thing I will get to closure.

I still take the same route home after work, just as I did the night it happened. Sometimes when I pass that farmer's lane I'll catch static on the radio, and sometimes I feel like I'll catch something out of the corner of my eye. If I look fast enough, I swear I can see the strobe in the trees.

TV GUIDE

I shambled from the steamy bathroom, jet-lagged and tired as I dried my hair. Another flight, another cheap hotel, only to rise early and do it again tomorrow. The room was clean but bare, not the worst I'd had in the past. White walls with edgy art pieces, glass end tables next to a fainting chair, complete with comically large ashtrays, and what I assumed would be a stiff queen-sized bed. The Sunset Hotel, a bargain grab from the plethora of the cheapest inns. It looked like it had *zest* once, but seemed to have lost its spark a couple years ago. The only real issue with the room was the TV across the bed. It was on when I got here, the same infomercial TV-guide type program running in a loop.

There was no remote, not that I had seen, anyway. The screen itself was bolted into the wall, the manual buttons on the back out of reach. I only spent five minutes searching for it when I got here, and it was about as much as I felt like dedicating. It was a self-check-in hotel, and there was no one on sight to actually phone for room service. I was only here to sleep after all. The TV would just provide white noise while I slept anyway. The only annoyance was it was just a *hair* too loud. You could always hear it, like it refused to be ignored.

After draining a few of those little courtesy liquor bottles and setting my alarms, I killed the lights and hoped for a decent recharge. I just needed a few hours. The infomercial cast a white glow in the room, playing randomly scripted programs as I closed my eyes. Under the cool sheets, I felt my muscles relax, and sleep seemed not far off.

"Thanks for tuning in, folks. Here at Intelleguide, we seek to find you the right program, whenever you need it. You don't even have to call," the voice chuckled, scripted and fake enthusiasm for an invisible crowd.

I ignored it, trying to channel my exhaustion into a slumber. Thoughts of meetings and TSA danced through my head. I would be back home soon, just had to get through tonight.

"Want a quick laugh? Check channel 6 to see PrankFail Emporium, and their ever-expanding collection of pranks, and you guessed it, fails." The same voice talked, just loud enough to hear the words clearly.

I lifted my head from the pillow and squinted at the screen, just to match a face with the voice. A Chris Hansen type was standing there, hands motioning to a green screen thumbnail on his right. Gelled hair and a plastic grin wearing a brown suit. The thumbnail blinked away, leaving the white backdrop. The man in the suit looked at me, a little bar of channel suggestions scrolling past. I rolled over and closed my eyes again.

"Looking for love? We got you covered. Drama.Net can pull at your heartstrings, you'll be reaching for that tissue box in no time!"

He went on and on, one bit to the next.

"Intelleguide. Here to serve you whenever you need us. We're always here."

"Still here? May I suggest an action flick? Who doesn't love Stallone? Channel 10, KevlarMetal. All action, all the time."

I started drifting in and out, the voice of the host continuing on as I felt my limbs get weightless and my mind quiet. I was almost out, the program fading away. Under the bright glow, I found my eyes opening when the monotony changed in my white noise. At some point, the guy had stopped talking.

I lifted my head and looked at the screen. He was just standing there, watching me. Like it was paused.

I sat up and rubbed my eyes, thinking it was a dream. The program continued, the suit guy moving like nothing had happened.

"We're a big ol' happy family here at Intelleguide. And we seek to serve you like one of our own," he said, an arm reaching to his side. A family faded in, an attractive wife holding a pie, teenage daughter with her phone in her hand, and a young son holding a football. They all laughed together, like someone had just told a hilarious joke. It looked fake like it always did, but something about it bothered me. It felt off. Like it was forced.

They all smiled together. A big, happy family. When the laughter subsided, they all looked at me with a picture-perfect pose. I checked my phone; it was almost 1am. I rubbed my eyes and laid back down, wishing I could find a remote and shut the damn thing off. Just a couple hours of sleep, that's all I needed. I sandwiched my head between the pillows, trying to block the light and sound.

The voices muffled through the pillows, and in my restless annoyance, I found sleep returning to me. It was a slow, soothing embrace. But even as my mind wandered, that voice still seemed to poke through.

"Hey there, partner! Still here I see."

"Haven't found something to watch yet? Watch all the best sitcoms on Channel 2. Lots of love and laughs, there. Family living, at its finest. Like *ours*."

Under the shield of the pillows, it persisted. Every time I felt myself drifting away, that voice would catch me. I couldn't ignore it.

"Still here, huh? Let's see if we can find something for you here."

"Whatever you say, that's the Intelleguide way."

"So many channels to choose from. How *do* you choose?"

"Channel 5, nature and exploration! From the Arctic to the Jungle."

"We appreciate your audience. Thank you for choosing Intelleguide."

"We're here when you need us, *always*."

"People usually don't hang around that long. For that, we thank you."

"We'll be back, after a word from our sponsors."

The eerie quiet set in again. I tossed and turned, keeping my eyes shut. I just wanted to sleep. It was there, just barely out of reach. I could feel it. I was lying on my side, head still stuck between pillows. Slowly I opened my eyes and saw the window of the hotel. The infomercial was still on, I could see the reflection in the window. Same guy in the suit, and the wife holding the pie. The teenager daughter with the phone stood next to the younger son with the football.

They were watching me through the television.

I could feel their eyes on me, like they had been paused again. I felt frozen, unsure of what to do. There was something in the ambient ringing of the program, something soft I could barely make out. As I watched their stare through the reflection, it finally dawned on me, and the restless knot in my stomach was replaced by a welling pit of anxiety.

They were whispering to each other.

"Is he still awake?"

"I think so."

"How much longer do we have to do this?"

"As long as I say."

"Can't we just go? *Please?*"

"Can I put the pie down? I'm so tired."

"You drop that pie, *and I will break your fucking fingers.*"

In the reflection, their mouths didn't move. They just looked ahead; the same smile stuck to their faces. I could barely see through the reflection, but it almost… almost looked like they were crying. I didn't want to look, but I had to.

I threw the pillows down and sat up. The frozen family looked at me, all of them paused in the same white backdrop.

Everything except for their eyes.

Their eyes were shaking, begging for help. The camera zoomed in on their eyes, moving from one to the next. The son, the daughter, the wife. A single pixelated tear ran down her cheek. The screen flickered and was replaced by static. Total silence, the glow consuming the room. I felt alone and afraid under its glow. Afraid to move, afraid to look away.

The screen flickered again, and the static was replaced by a new scene. The same white backdrop, but this time, splattered with red. Separated body parts and gore strewn everywhere. The phone and football laying there, the pie destroyed. In the center of the screen, the guy in the suit was working an axe, a wet chop echoing with every overhead swing. In the silence, I could hear their screams.

At the bottom of the screen was an infinite scroll of the same short message:

HELP US HELP US HELP US HELP US HELP US HELP US

I woke up, my pillow soaked in sweat. The same infomercial playing, the same guy in the suit. I checked my phone. It was 3am now. It was all a dream.

My heart was racing. I wiped my brow, trying to make sense of the fog in my brain. On the screen, the host was combing his hair. He looked at me, stopped mid stroke, and tucked the comb back into his pocket. He stared for a moment, his face blank. After a moment, he smiled.

"Hey there, friend. Glad to see you're still around. Guess you'll be joining us after all."

He lurched toward the screen, his hands breaking through with a rip of static. With the sound of a static scream, his head came through, his face cold and withered, like a corpse. His eyes melting, oozing streams down ghoulish, toothy jaws. Piercing through the noise was a single grumbling voice.

JOIN US

I screamed and jumped from the bed, reaching for something, anything. My fingers felt one of the large ashtrays. I hefted it up and chucked it as hard as I could. The object broke through, and with a flash of light, the screaming was gone. The host blinked from existence, fading away until there was nothing but a jagged, discolored screen. I stared at the gaping hole in denial, a faint whisper still breathing through. I couldn't make it out, and I didn't take the time to listen.

I packed my things and ignored the TV, shoving everything into my suitcase as fast as I could. I grabbed my phone, left the key, and slammed the door behind me.

Out on the street, I called a cab. They arrived quickly and gave me a ride to the airport. When we drove away, I didn't look back in fear of whatever could be seen from the hotel windows. I rescheduled my flight and paid every premium and fee I had to just to get the hell out of there. Even got a window seat.

As we took off, I sighed with relief, finally hoping to catch some rest.

Beside me, an elderly woman indulged in her in-flight movie.

"Anything good?" I asked, closing my eyes.

"Not really. Can't seem to get it to change off the TV guide."

CAUGHT PEEKING AT THE GYM

.53 miles. I remember the number clearly, the orange digits that tracked the distance on the treadmill interface. I was going for three miles, just a standard run for me. It was a run I had completed many times, just a warmup for me before I would finish the session with moderate weightlifting. I don't remember anything significant other than the fact I was feeling particularly sluggish that day.

The gym was pretty busy, like usual. The three o'clock crowd was in, relieving the day's stress through cardio and powerlifting. It was the most crowded time of the day. Every time I walked in, I felt a twinge of jealousy for those working third shift. I had music playing through my earbuds to black out the repetitive drone of the belt as my shoes skipped across it. Gyms are noisy places.

Ahead, a gym monster finished his set and returned the dumbbells to the rack. A sound that would've been loud if it wasn't for my own tunes. I watched him pop his pecs one at a time, briefly marveling at the symmetrically sculpted rocks before looking at something else. Like any other run, my eyes wandered, going back and forth between the other people working out and the line of TVs hanging ahead. Half the battle of going to the gym is rationing your people watching and making sure they're not looking at you when you're looking at them. You see everyone do it, eyes moving non-stop to appear super focused on your workout. Even when you were checking yourself out in the mirror, everyone was watching everyone and trying to appear not to. Looking more than a split second was just… weird. It was easier to just focus on the many

TVs, but that day I found my eyes wanting to wander more than usual.

Ahead of me, a younger woman was cooling off from a treadmill sprint. Her ponytail bobbed as she checked her watch, power walking unbeknownst to the beat of my music. I gave her a glance, a brief scan of the yoga pants stretched over lean legs. Just a quick peek. After getting my look I returned to the TV line, each screen playing something different. The news, *Dr. Phil,* a program about the stock market, a rerun of the show *Friends.* I kept my practiced pace, feeling a little more tired today than past days. I watched Ross and Monica go back and forth in the apartment. I looked at the subtitles, and realized they were several seconds behind, and gave up trying to fill myself in on the plot.

Back to people watching. Dozens of people sitting at machines, half of them on their phones. Those monopolizing the free moving benches were shamelessly flexing in the mirror, making triceps bulge with legs like toothpicks. Groups of girls in spandex, doing every body weight exercise to exclusively grow their lower half. Another man in a sweltering tracksuit sat with extended legs, punishing his calves to no end.

Sweat collected on my brow, feeling chilly from the current of the large overhead fans. I wiped at it, wondering if I had eaten too little earlier. Maybe I was crashing? Ahead, the gym monster grabbed a heavier set of dumbbells and was heading to an inclined bench for presses. I tried to guess the number, somewhere between fifty-five and seventy. It was something he did often. I felt the urge to look at the woman ahead again and brought my gaze back over, but not immediately, just one sweaty person at a time.

The woman in front of me had lessened her pace and was walking it out slow. I couldn't help but look again, pulled into the tantalizing rhythm of her walk. Lean, muscular legs. The mesmerizing *swish* of her butt with every step forward. I knew I was looking too long, but it's not every day you get to just stop and *really* look—

The old woman on the treadmill next to her was staring at me. I looked away immediately in shame, mentally kicking myself for being so careless. I had never been caught before, and now that I had, it felt pretty shitty. I looked ahead and kept running, unsure of what else to do. After several strides I checked to see if she was still watching, hoping it would just all go away. She was.

I looked at the old woman guiltily and tried to give her a polite nod. She didn't return it, only keeping the same expression awkwardly. Her treadmill wasn't even on, the belt at a halt under her bright little sneakers. The stare painfully persisted, and I felt the sudden heat of embarrassment in my cheeks and ears.

The old woman's face. She wasn't scowling or smiling. She was just *there*. Her face was blank, almost like she was lost.

I kept running. I hoped her judgmental look would pass, and I could forget about it. I felt an itch on my right calf, and I resisted the urge to scratch it. You know how sometimes your scalp itches when you get frustrated or stressed? That kind of itch. Instead, I turned the speed up higher, the *beepbeepbeep* faintly coming through my music. It was suddenly hard to focus on it. I ignored the old lady and pushed myself harder. She would walk away eventually, and I wouldn't look that long again. Lesson learned.

I scanned the line of TVs again, trying to busy my eyes with something, anything. The same programs played on with their delayed subtitles and cringey commercials. I tried to focus on them, sweating harder as I chugged away. The programs all seemed confusing, like I couldn't make sense of them. I shook my head and wiped my face. The itching on my leg got worse, almost burning.

The old woman just kept looking, face pale, eyes unfocused.

Come on man, I get it, I thought as I looked away. If it kept up, I would just have to call it for the day.

I tried to just stay focused ahead, finish the run so I could just go. Ahead, the gym monster had stopped at the beginning of a rep, holding the massive dumbbells still above his shoulders. I waited for the lift, but he just held them there, like he was just stuck anticipating it. It wasn't until I looked into the wall mirror in front of him that I realized he was watching me too.

Wait, what the fuck?

The gym monster's deadpan look didn't match the rest of his body, like he was frozen from the neck down. It gave me the chills; he was looking at me the same way the old lady was. It gave me a sense of discomfort I couldn't explain. While I looked back, I could hear something coming through my music, some kind of interference in the lyrics and beats. Jumbled words I couldn't understand. I felt a hot flash, and I wiped my brow again. My leg burned like someone was holding a lighter to it.

The old woman had stepped off the treadmill at some point. She was moving closer.

I felt out of breath. Sweating bullets. My legs felt like they were draining away. I hadn't even been running that long.

The girls in spandex were next, frozen mid squat with medicine balls in their hands. All of them stared with the same blank look. The old woman crept closer.

In my earbuds, the mumbling continued, remixing my music to the point it was unrecognizable. I could almost make out the words, but I just didn't have the energy to tune in.

The track-suit man on the calf machine was looking now, toes pointing out in his own paused rep. Others followed. Everyone I made eye contact with was eyeing me somehow, either directly or through the walls of mirrors. Nobody moved, everyone held still like human mannequins.

The old woman was close now, only two steps away. Her face didn't change, and I couldn't bring myself to look at it. The woman ahead with the sculpted legs was watching. I could only see half of her face in the reflection, but she was looking right at me. My chest was getting heavy. Two needle-like stabs pinched my chest, one on each side. My leg burn had shifted into a slow rend, like someone was peeling my flesh slowly. I couldn't think, couldn't bear their staring. I looked at the TVs for salvation.

I couldn't breathe.

Every program was paused. They were all looking at me.

Each music video, news program, and sitcom had halted. Everyone completely still. *Dr. Phil* watched from his chair; the cast of *Friends* had all turned to face me. News anchors stopped at their desk; pop stars paused mid-shuffle. Hundreds of eyes, all watching me.

I wasn't running anymore. I couldn't remember when I stopped, I just... did. I looked at the treadmill interface, at the bright orange letters: .53 miles.

The old woman was reaching out with a finger, her long digit inches away. She was saying something quietly, but I couldn't make it out. The ear buds were blocking the sound. I took them out, a calming silence replacing the noise that had been in my head. Exhausted, I tried to hear what she said.

"What? I can't... I can't hear you," I said, my voice unusually loud. I craned my head toward her, and the mumbles started to come together. I started to recognize it. She was saying letters and numbers, over and over.

"C... P... R... 9... 1... 1... A... E... D..."

The walls of mirrors shattered, reflective glass exploding to reveal a void behind it. A wind blew through the void, voices carrying in the air. It sounded like calls from hell. I flinched and covered my face, and the old woman lowered her finger and started to frown.

"Help! This man needs help!"

"I think... I think he's having a heart attack!"

"MOVE! I KNOW CPR!"

"Somebody call 911!"

"Oh god-oh god, what do we do?"

"Don't crowd around! Get back!"

"I know CPR too, I'm here to help."

"Somebody shut that thing OFF!"

"Get the AED!"

I opened my eyes, feeling like an anvil had been dropped on my chest. Through the crushing weight I sucked in a breath, the best tasting air I had ever tasted. Someone was patting my shoulder, asking me if I was okay. Another assured me help was on the way.

It was the woman in yoga pants and the gym monster.

Shouting orders with their arms outstretched were the girls in spandex, keeping back the crowd.

Pacing around us was the guy in the tracksuit, a cell phone held to his ear.

They all stopped when I opened my eyes, each looking incredibly relieved. I tried to move, but they stopped me. Wires and little pads were stuck to my chest, a horrible stinging echoing from them. My right leg burned so badly and was sticky with blood. It had been laying limply against the treadmill. The belt had been shaving into it after I collapsed.

I had experienced a heart attack.

It took me months to recover, and several hospital visits before I got back to any kind of normalcy. I couldn't go back to working out for a long time, and even after I was up and about, I knew it would take me even longer to run like I used to. I saw the people that helped me when I returned, still going through the same routine. They all stared at me when I walked in, and I felt that familiar chill of the day I almost died. They smiled and asked how

I was doing. Everyone was happy to see me come back after so much time. Turns out the girl in yoga pants was a nurse, and the gym monster was a physical therapist. The tracksuit guy was the first to dial on his phone, and the spandex girls were the only ones that listened to their instructions and kept everyone back. I still see them now and again, and each time we take a moment to catch up before moving on with our routines. The strange thing is, every time we go over the story of what happened, no one remembers an old lady. None of them do.

I started running again. On a different treadmill this time, though, and I keep my eyes to myself. It'll take me a while to get back where I was, but I'll keep steadily building until I get back there. I still get a little short on breath as I pass the .53 mark, but it's a victory every time.

I've had to go through a bit of therapy since the incident, to help me move on from the trauma. It's mostly a mental wall I have to hurdle, and I'm doing the best I can not to live in fear and keep moving forward. I recently started using earbuds again, and things are starting to feel normal again. Despite my achievement, I'll need to keep going to therapy to totally get over it. Sometimes when I'm on my runs, I look at the hanging TVs at the same news channels and sitcoms. I know it's the trauma, and I'll get over it soon. But sometimes, when I look too quickly, I swear I can see them side-eyeing me.

PUBLIC RESTROOM

I had to go, like bad.

The sensation hit me as I pulled into the Wal-Mart parking lot, a terrible gurgling that bubbled in my stomach. I gingerly put my car in park, and placed a hand on my gut, as if it would help me thwart the uncomfortable churning. Suddenly I realized the error I had made and was now cursing myself for eating the pizza my company had bought for lunch. It was a band-aid for the erratic change in hours we had been working, and we ate it like we've never eaten before. I should've known better. The pizza they ordered was the same as they always did, and it fucked up my stomach every time.

I opened the car door and started stepping out of the vehicle, looking across the dark lot. There were only a handful of cars in their giant lot. Shopping after midnight was both a blessing and a curse; for the most part you had the store to yourself, on the other hand the ones who happened to show had a habit of being sketchy as hell. I had gotten so sick of fast food in recent weeks, and I was dying to have some home-cooked leftovers in my lunch for a change. I was willing to roll the dice on tonight's midnight shopping crowd.

One foot out of the car, and my stomach started bubbling again. I stopped moving, hoping it would soothe my stomach. I didn't have much time. Whatever was upset in there was ready to get out. I chanced disrupting my stomach and got out of the car. I made my way to the store, clamping my ass together as hard as I could while blindly aiming the keyless remote to lock the doors. I marched like I was on a mission, each step bringing me closer to losing it. I knew I looked ridiculous, but there was nobody in sight, so I shamelessly shuffled in.

Through the automatic doors and past the carts. I immediately beelined left, my shoes squeaking as I hurried along. I didn't see any employees, and hoped to God there wasn't one cleaning the restrooms. Past the shutters of the closed Subway restaurant and the darkened corner for customer service. I looked around embarrassed, clearly walking like I was trying not to lose my bowels. Relief washed over me as I saw the sign for the restrooms, and I quickened my pace. I swerved left again down the tiled corridor for the "Men's" section, and promptly died on the inside.

The path was blocked, a large yellow cart keeping me from entering.

"Fuuuuuuck," I seethed, and looked past it to see if there was anyone in there.

An old man in an apron and gloves was spraying a urinal, one slow squeeze at a time. I considered going to the other restrooms, but they were on the other side of the store. Another rumble in my gut told me I wouldn't make it.

"Hey, excuse me!" I tried to say politely, my knees shaking.

The old man looked at slowly, panning over like an owl.

"Just finishing up. I'll be a minute," he said, pausing his leisure spray of disinfectant.

"I'm gonna be honest man, I'm about to die. I'm not gonna make it," I said, dancing in misery next to his cart of cleaning supplies.

He stared at me for a moment, taking his time, probably on purpose. Finally, he let out a labored sigh and started walking slowly to his cart.

"Fine. If you're in such a hurry." He grabbed his cart and started pushing it out of my way.

The wheels squeaked as he slowly created a gap, and I squeezed by as soon as there was enough.

"Thank-you-thank-you!" I said, and power walked in.

There were five stalls in a row, with the larger handicap-accessible one at the end. My stall of choice was obvious. Picking one in the middle of the row would've just been weird. I slammed the door, locked it, and silently praised the old man for cleaning the stall before I could ruin it. Sitting on the cold seat, I listened for the squeaking cart to go away. I heard it finally leave the bathroom entrance and immediately unleashed the hell in my stomach. It wouldn't surprise me if the sound echoed through the entire store. I would never eat that pizza again, probably.

Aside from the shame, I felt much better. I yanked on the bouncing toilet paper roll, finished my business, and flushed. Chaos successfully averted. As the ambience of the toilet filling faded away, I prepared to stand and get out of there. I grabbed the waistband of my jeans, and a loud noise made me jump out of my skin. It sounded like someone had kicked open one of the stalls further down as hard as they could. My heart jolted in my chest. I thought of the employee that had been cleaning it and assumed it was his attempt to get back at me for interrupting his job in the shittiest way possible. I sighed and tried to laugh it off.

"Man, you got me," I said with a chuckle, my voice ringing in the silent bathroom, "good one old m—"

WAM.

The same sound echoed again, louder and closer this time. Whoever was doing it had moved down a stall in my direction. I found myself holding my breath in disbelief. I heard nothing, aside from the creaking of the stall door as it bounced on its hinges. As quietly as I could, I leaned forward and tried to sneak a peek at whoever was responsible. I expected to see the old man's shoes walking to the next one, but was shocked to see none.

"Hello?" I called, feeling very vulnerable with my pants at my ankles. I wanted to pull them up, but I didn't want to advertise my presence with the jingling of my belt and keys. I received no answer, only complete silence.

Goosebumps crawled over my skin. I listened for movement, footsteps, anything. It was just so quiet; I couldn't even hear anything by the checkout line. I heard a single drop from the sink, then what sounded like a wheezing exhale.

WAM.

Two stalls away, the door flew open and bounced loudly.

"Hey man, c'mon, it's not funny!" I pleaded and fumbled through the pocket of my jeans for my phone. I didn't know what else to do.

WAM.

The door next to my stall was next, and it bounced so hard it rattled the toilet paper dispenser next to me. I cringed and waited for mine to fly open, and whoever it was to burst in. I cowered on the toilet and raised my hands to protect myself.

The stall doors creaked in a frightful chorus. Ahead, I watched the turn lock jiggle, like someone was trying the flat portion on the other side.

"Occupied! Be out in a minute!" I blurted, my words stuttering.

They tried the lock several times and seemed to give up. I could hear heavy breathing outside the door.

I looked through the cracks in the stall, but there wasn't anyone there. All I could see was the mirror's reflection above the sink outside, my own awkward pose with my phone in my hand. I aimed my phone at the door, thinking if I could record it, I would be able to file a harassment charge or something. I opened the camera app, hit record, and froze.

Through the video feed was a large figure, tall and lanky. I couldn't see it directly, only its back in the mirror's reflection. It wore no clothes, and its skin was pale. Blue veins scrawled across its body. I held my breath, unable to look at the sight my phone revealed. Whatever it was, it was watching me through the stall.

I sat there for a time recording, and the figure refused to move. Its heavy breathing echoed in the bathroom, and I wished for the first time in my life that someone else would come in and also use the restroom.

With a low groan, it turned and walked away. I heard it push past the door in the stall next to me and get in, the sound of bare feet plopping on the tile. I heard it sit on the toilet next to me. I sat there for a moment, the recording still going. Trying to breathe as quietly as possible, I leaned painfully slowly and angled the phone under the stall.

Oversized, shoeless feet lay flat on the floor. Its toes were too long, its ankles where they shouldn't be. I could also see its knees, like its limbs were too large to fit in the stall. Next to me there was a painful groan, followed by the sound of a horrid mess hitting the toilet water. The stench that followed was just as disgusting as the sound.

With it occupied, I took it as my cue to leave. I sat straight and pulled my phone to my lap, and switched the camera to forward facing so I wouldn't get my junk in the recording. My empty stomach twisted as my mind tried to make sense of what I saw. Behind my face in the camera's view was another, along with two sets of long fingers over the top of the stall. Its head was bald save for some wispy strands, and its eyes were hollow, different sized pits.

It had been peeking over the whole time, and its neck was getting longer.

I screamed and fell off the toilet. The tile was hard and cold, and I writhed like a worm on the floor. I struggled to simultaneously pull up my pants and flee, the stall door knocking my head as I ran into it. Without my phone I couldn't see it, but I felt its breath on my face. Still screaming, I squirmed underneath the stall, scooting my way out and kicking my feet until I was out. I could hear the stalls creaking under its weight as I thrashed to my feet. I bolted out of the bathroom, pulling my pants up as I went.

I immediately crashed into something heavy and screamed again as I stumbled to the floor.

"Hey! Watch it!"

The old man looked bewildered, his janitor cart knocked over, cleaning supplies rolling everywhere. I was on my feet in a second, and running as fast as I could, one hand holding my unbuttoned pants up, the other still clutching my phone. I ran and ran until I was out of the store, nearly hitting the automatic doors as I fled to the parking lot. Chest heaving, I sprinted across the dark lot, barely buttoning my pants and getting my keys. Hands shaking, I got my keys and unlocked it as I approached.

I swung open the door, barreled in, and slammed it behind me. I locked the doors and started the car.

I shifted to drive and took one last look at the store before driving away. My throat was hoarse, my heart beating hard against my chest. There was nothing there, the automatic doors closing on their own. No one had followed, no one bothered to chase me. I looked at the doors for a time, wondering if it had even happened in the first place. It had all happened so fast; I was still trying to make sense of it.

I wiped my forehead with my shirt. When I looked again, the automatic doors opened on their own. There was nobody there.

I peeled out of my parking spot, blowing every stop sign out of the lot. I left the store behind me, not even wanting to look back. Maybe if I got far enough away, I think I would be able to handle fast food one more night.

THE PAPER MACHE MAN

Emily wanted to be scared. At first, I shared her enthusiasm, setting up movie nights twice a week and chewing through an ever-growing list of the scariest films we could find. I was a pretty big movie buff myself, so I contributed my own favorites to the list. It started innocently enough. Emily had just gone through a bad breakup and was trying to take her mind off the hurt. As her roommate, I was happy to lend a helping hand. It had nothing to do with the fact I was infatuated with her. I knew she didn't see me that way; it was something I had to stomach and forget about. Sometimes someone just needs a friend.

We started with the classics. Michael, Jason, Freddy, Pinhead, Leatherface. Bowls of popcorn, cans of light beer. Some nights we ordered Chinese takeout, laughing and pointing with chopsticks as unfortunate individuals screamed and met their demise. It was really fun and experiencing the thrills once more built up a sense of camaraderie. It felt like it was more than a trip down memory lane. I thought the excitement wouldn't last for long, but it became a ritual of ours.

On the days we didn't work, we would go sit on a little bench by the lake and burn, excitedly scribbling more titles in a little red notebook to the list as we passed a joint back and forth. She would always wear this oversized *Coheed and Cambria* hoodie she bought online; two sizes too big from a shipping error. It was adorable, watching her jot things down, hood pulled up like she was hiding.

I hooked up an old PC rig I wasn't using to the living room TV, and we would use it to either stream or play DVDs we picked up from the bargain bins at the store. We would plot out the week's movies, twice a week, sometimes a third. We would always watch two movies back-to-back, often staying up too late discussing cheesy on-screen kills or chilling scenes.

As we crossed names off the list, we had the pleasure of revisiting old favorites. I always thought it would fizzle out when she found another boyfriend, but would always come back with more for next time. As the weeks passed, we relished one iconic scene after another. Leslie Nielsen's stone-cold killer in *Creepshow*. The terrible Achilles tendon cut in *Pet Sematary*. Angela's unforgettable face in *Sleepaway Camp*. As the films slowly haunted my dreams with childlike nightmares, I noticed a strange theme with our movie binges; none of it seemed to scare Emily.

Soon, she started to dig deeper. She started checking forums, going through list after list of top chilling horror movies, the ones that stuck with you for days. Soon, the movie nights felt less like a fun hangout and more like a trial. I know it was lingering grief from the breakup, or a crisis of some sort. Everyone goes through the phase of "gritty soulless movies", but it was starting to feel like punishment. I wanted to be there for her, but I started having to brace myself for each session. The uncomfortable silence in *Calvaire*, the way-too-long scene in *Irreversible*. I was rapidly approaching my limit, but Emily didn't even wince. Her eyes were glued to the screen, the awful imagery reflected in her gaze. As I fought the urge to look away, she was looking for something. Looking for more.

That night she opted for a third movie, and with that, a bottle of liquor. We usually didn't party like that, aside from the tokes on the lake and the light beer. Despite my reluctance, I agreed. We poured some roughly measured shots and sat in for the latest showing we had done yet. It was a movie I hadn't seen but had heard rumors about. *A Serbian Film*.

I… Couldn't finish it. I was completely repulsed; it was nothing like the other movies we had watched. It was disturbing for the sake of disturbing. This wasn't what our movie night was supposed to be about. I was a little drunk, and the night ended in an argument. The movie nights were over, whatever magic it held evaporated as I walked to my room to go to bed. She finished the movie on her own, her eyes devouring the screen alone in the Tv's glow. She just sat on the couch, her hood pulled up. I felt guilty for leaving her, but her search for terror had driven a wedge between us.

We didn't speak for a couple of days after that. We went our separate ways, avoiding unnecessary contact before and after work. I wished we could go back to the fun stage instead of walking on eggshells in our own home. Emily spent a lot of time in her room on her computer. I could see the light still on under the door, the faint sound of music playing into the late hours of the night. I just let her have her space.

"Have you heard of the Paper Mache Man?" she asked one morning. I was about to leave for work, and she caught me as I was about to walk out the door. It was like the sour end to our movie night had never happened.

I told her I didn't, but I was curious.

She elaborated that she had spent the last couple of days surfing the web in search of something actually scary. This had taken her down a rabbit hole in the shadiest parts of the internet, where she had seen a bunch of clips and photos that surpassed the horror of the last film I had bailed on. Straight up snuff films, live decapitations, worksite accidents. This went way beyond "Ten harrowing images taken before disaster". Just the thought of the videos she mentioned made me uncomfortable.

I asked if she was alright, and she shrugged me off. She looked tired, and I could tell she had been drinking. Whether she started early or was still going from the night before, I didn't know. She wasn't wearing her hoodie anymore, just a tank top and pajama pants. She looked flustered, like she was burning up. Deep down I was really concerned, but I didn't want to drive the wedge forming between us further.

"Alright, who is he?" I asked. She went through the reel of pictures on her phone and held it out to me.

It was a picture of a dining room, with a table and chairs in the middle. The table was set and filled with food, almost as if people had been there, and just vanished. Behind the table was a dark doorway, like it was leading to a kitchen, but you couldn't quite see. I tried to make sense of the picture, but I felt like it was going over my head. Like I wasn't let in on the joke.

"I… don't get it," I said, scratching my head.

"You're kidding, right? *Look* at it," she said, pointing to the screen. The phone was shaking in her hand.

"Yeah, I see it. But I don't get it. You went to the dark web and found *this* scary? Anyone could've staged this photo," I said.

She looked at the screen again and looked at me like I was crazy. With her thumb and finger, she zoomed in on the photo, to one of the chairs at the table. She made me look again. It was just an empty chair.

"I don't get it. It's just a chair," I said, and there was a flicker in her eyes like I had insulted her.

"*Oh,* I see. So you're just gonna fuckin' gaslight me? I thought I deserved better than that," she said, eyes tearing up.

"What are you talking about? Where is all this coming from?" I said. I didn't know why she was getting so defensive.

"The chairs. The paper mache. Look at them. They're all there. It's horrible. You see their faces? And he's right there. *There.*" She pointed to every empty chair, then to the dark doorway.

There was nothing new, just the same scene.

"Who?" I asked.

"The Paper Mache Man. I found a thread about him on one of those sites. But it's barely a whisper online. They say he's behind a bunch of disappearances around the world. Like, eventually he finds you and sends a warning. That means he's coming for you. Then he turns you into paper mache."

"Sounds creepy, but it also sounds ridiculous."

"Then he adds you to his collection or something like that. I've been trying to get information on it all night. Every time he gets mentioned, whatever thread it's on gets removed quickly. Pictures, too. Not long after you see a comment, or see a picture with him in it, the content just ceases to exist. I managed to download this one and made some backups so I could show you."

Except I didn't see whatever she was pointing out. What she described was something you could find online but simply in a different representation. Internet legends, carefully crafted online spooks, with people going through the trouble to keep the bit alive. Anybody could meticulously monitor and toy with posts if they had enough time on their hands and alt accounts.

Between her tired, distraught eyes and the undeniable smell of alcohol, one would say she was just sleep deprived and reaching. I made the mistake of being that one. I looked at the picture again and rubbed my eyes. Emily was nervously biting her nails, eyes wide and impatient as she waited for my response. It was still just a dark, empty dining room.

"Look, Emily," I sighed, wishing I could just go along with it, "someone is probably just baiting you, and you're eating it up. There's no such thing as a cyberspace ghost. Cursed images are made in Photoshop. Behind every scary creepypasta, is someone hoping people will believe it is real, if only for a second. You need to get some sleep. Take a break from the scary shit. And maybe take it easy on the drinking a little bit," I said and braced myself for the backlash. It came immediately.

"Oh, *fuck you.* If I wanted to talk to my mother, I could've just called her. You're just going to *pretend* you don't see it? This shit is real. It's fuckin' scary, and I'm gonna show you. And when you see it, who's gonna be the asshole here? You!" she yelled, her lip trembling. She stormed off, leaving me there alone, feeling quite like the asshole.

"Emily, c'mon," I said, but she was already gone. Seconds later I heard her bedroom door slam, and the volume of cranked music echoing from the hall, leaving me to go to work in frustration.

I didn't understand the sudden, consuming obsession. I thought of the Paper Mache Man, and the things she said about him. I thought of the dining room photo, and the general lack of fright it provided. The scene itself was creepy, with the set dinner table and the empty chairs. But it was something *I* could've made in ten minutes.

I thought of looking into it on my phone, but I was still pretty salty over the whole thing. In the end, I just decided to let it go, and hope maybe it would pass and she would get over the whole thing.

The next couple of days passed in awkward silence. I only saw Emily a couple of times by chance on the ins and outs for work. She still looked as haggard as before; she no longer styled her hair and her make-up was the bare minimum, her outfits thrown together and wrinkled. Our conversations were minimal, if we talked at all. I would only know if she was home if lights were on under her door, the soft tune of music emanating from within. After a couple of days of radio silence, I texted her a few times, most of which she barely replied to, or simply left on read.

Looking at the gloomy apartment, I found myself thinking of the fun we used to have. The back and forth with the films, bullshitting about life, and the chill vibe we shared at the lake. I thought of the dwindling friendship and wondered if there was any way to try and salvage it. I ordered Chinese food and sent Emily a text, one I hoped to use as a life raft.

"Have you learned anything else about the Paper Mache Man?"

Shortly after the food arrived, I heard the music in her room stop, and she appeared at the end of the hall. I held up the takeout as a peace offering, and a hint of a smile shined through her mask of increased exhaustion.

We sat on the floor and ate at the coffee table, silently slurping noodles and picking odds and ends from several containers. Emily ate more than I thought she would, and I wondered if she had been eating at all in the past few days. Her face looked a little thinner and her eyes were shadowed like a raccoon's. Whatever rabbit hole she had found herself tumbling down, it was obviously taking a toll on her.

"How are you holding up? Work going alright?" I asked awkwardly, slumping against the couch.

I winced at my own words, thinking I could've done a better job breaking the ice. Emily paused and gave me a startled look, much like a deer in headlights. When she processed what I said, she slowly put the takeout carton down like she was embarrassed. She wiped her mouth, took a long drink of Sprite, and cleared her throat.

"Look, I'm sorry—" she started.

"It's cool. Really."

She nodded and looked away. She looked guilty, lost. Bothered. I could tell she had a lot on her mind, and she was sifting through it to find something to say. After a moment she took a deep breath, then let out a defeated sigh.

"I shouldn't have pushed so hard with the movies. And I shouldn't have blown up over the picture. I was just a little… frazzled, I guess. And drunk. It's not your fault you didn't see it anyway. I was just so caught up in it, you know?" Emily said, resting her chin on her knees.

"What do you mean?" I asked.

She looked confused for a moment before elaborating.

"Oh. Sorry. I looked into it some more. The leads are almost non-existent. Like I said, every time someone spills something, it's gone pretty quick. But showing you wouldn't have amounted to anything anyway. You only see what's there when you're *supposed* to. When *He* wants you to."

"The Paper Mache Man," I said. It felt weird to say it aloud, like I was talking about the Boogeyman or Bloody Mary.

"Yeah," she mumbled and chewed on her lip.

"Would you like me to look at it again? Just to be sure. I was in a rush when you showed me. I might've missed something. I won't make fun of it or anything, I promise."

"No. It's alright. It's gone anyway," she said, yawning.

"What? You didn't have to delete it," I said, leaning in. I was starting to feel bad.

"I didn't. *He* did. Like I said, everything that has to do with him doesn't stick around for long. It just… vanishes. Not sure how it happens, but it *does* happen. I had that picture on my phone, backed up on my desktop, and on a flash drive. And the flash drive was unplugged and sitting in my dresser. Still, gone," she said, and I felt a surge of anxiety.

"What the fuck? Do you think somebody broke in?" I said, standing up. Emily just shook her head and looked out the window.

"No, nobody broke in. It's more like a virus, I think. Or something like it."

"How can you be sure? If you were on the 'dark web' and all that. How do you know that shit's safe? Who knows what lengths they'll go to." I looked out the window at the parking lot outside the building. The sun was starting to set, the bright orange globe in the sky descending like a slowly closing eye.

"I have a camera set up in my room. To catch him," she said, nudging a piece of General Tso's chicken with a chopstick. She shivered under her hoodie and seemed to sink further into it.

"And did you…" I trailed off.

"No."

I looked outside again as if to reassure myself. There was nothing there, only our cars and the cars of other tenants. I collapsed on the couch, feeling suddenly exhausted. The whole thing felt off, like something had changed in the air. The apartment felt dusty and cramped, despite our furnishings being pretty bare. I couldn't help but look down the hall at the shadow that led to our bedrooms. There was nothing there, but you know that feeling you get when you're looking into the dark? Like maybe, just *maybe*, something could be?

"Wait, you said the other day, something about a warning. '*He sends a warning*'. Did you get one?" I asked.

She shook her head and set the chopstick down.

"No. The lack of evidence is about all there is. Convenient, right?" she chuckled nervously.

I rubbed my eyes and let out a bit of a chuckle from the sudden paranoia. It was just some sort of messed up prank. It had to be.

"Look," I said, scratching my head, "You wanna get out of here? Go do something? Get out of the house. Maybe ice cream? Bowling, or something?"

"Nah," Emily started, then yawned again, "Too tired. But hey, we can do something else, if you wouldn't mind keeping me company? Would you mind watching another movie together? Like old times," she said, perking up.

"Oh?"

"No-no-no, nothing scary! Just something normal. I promise. Please?" she said, putting her hands up.

I looked at her for a moment and started to laugh. Soon, she did too. I got off the couch and agreed.

"I'll make some popcorn. And... I think there's still a few beers in the fridge. Want one?"

"Please."

Twenty minutes into *The Princess Bride,* Emily was asleep, snoring softly on the couch. Once the popcorn was made, we got some pillows and blankets from our rooms and settled in the living room. We cracked open some cans, had a brief 'cheers', and settled in. I found myself downing mine in no time. Emily left hers mostly full. I settled in the old recliner we had and kicked back, listening to her faintly recite old lines we had both heard a hundred times.

It was nice to see her smile, but as her eyes grew heavy, I noticed her looking down the hall, as well as glancing outside. After she passed out, I made sure the door was locked, dead bolted and chained, and checked the window as well. I decided to let the movie play and sleep in the chair, hoping the bright lights would keep the mood light and make it easier to fall asleep.

I watched the movie for a while, and as I started to get drowsy, I double checked the alarms on my phone to make sure they were set for work. As I went to set it on the coffee table, I found myself hesitating.

With the phone still clutched in my hand, I looked at Emily, who was fast asleep on the couch, her hood pulled up and the drawstrings tight.

I sat back in the recliner, unlocked my phone, and opened the web browser.

I entered the words, my thumbs moving reluctantly. Paper Mache Man. Search.

I held my breath as it loaded, casting glances at Emily, down the hall, and to the window.

The search results gave me instant relief. Nothing but Etsy purchases, pictures of ugly art projects, and paper mache tutorials.

No forums. No haunted pictures. No madness.

I locked my phone, set it down, and kicked my feet up. Before I knew it, the lures of relaxation and ease grabbed me, and I drifted off to sleep.

***

I awoke to Emily nudging me. I opened my eyes and jumped at first, not expecting to see her hunched over me. With one arm she had shaken me awake, the other hugging herself tightly. She was shivering.

"Hmm? What's up?" I mumbled, wiping the drool from my mouth. She backed up so I could lower the footrest. When I sat up, I looked out the window, my drowsy eyes and brain still trying to boot up. It was dark out, save for the spotlight in the parking lot.

I checked my phone. It was just after midnight.

"There's something at the door," she whispered, motioning quietly.

"*What?*" I said incredulously. Through my confused grogginess, the icy crawl of goosebumps spread across my limbs. I looked at the door to see the deadbolt still turned, the chain latch still hanging.

"I was asleep. And I kind of just found myself awake. I tossed and turned, but before I could fall back asleep, there was a really loud knock at the door. I'm surprised you didn't hear it," she said, pacing slightly.

"Are you sure?" I asked, cautiously moving toward the door. I turned on the living room lights, and the room lit up.

"Of course I'm sure. I'm not fucking making it up!" She hushed, wincing against the light.

"Ok, ok," I whispered, approaching the door silently. I waited to hear another knock, or someone making noise outside. There was nothing. We looked at each other and shrugged. Emily chewed her lip. I could tell she was terrified.

Holding my breath, I pressed my cheek to the door and looked through the peephole.

There was nobody there. The apartment hallway was empty, nothing but the bare white walls and the doors of adjacent apartments. I half expected something to lurch up and scare the shit out of me. Luckily, the jump scare never came.

"I don't see anyone," I said, pulling away from the door.

"I heard it. I fuckin' heard it. Swear to god," Emily was saying, shaking her head in frustration.

I unlatched the chain and retracted the deadbolt. With Emily hiding behind me, I opened the door.

We cowered behind the crack at first, both of us trying not to make a sound. Nobody jumped out, no footsteps running away, no distant slamming door. I threw the door open and stepped out, whipping my head down both ends of the hall. Nothing out of the ordinary, until I looked at my feet.

There was a small rectangular package on the welcome mat, wrapped tightly in newspaper and tied with raffia yarn.

"What the hell..." Emily said words I found myself repeating.

She picked it up, and against my better judgment, brought it inside. She set it on the coffee table, scooting aside half-eaten egg rolls and cartons of fried rice. It was thin, like a small paperback book.

"It's really light," she said, tugging on the straw-like yarn.

"You think we should open it?" I said, and Emily shrugged.

"What else are we supposed to do?"

"I don't know, call the police?" I said, but as she started unraveling the newspaper, my curiosity kept me in place.

Underneath several layers was a white, unmarked DVD-style case, much the one you'd see at a video game store. She picked it up, and after we exchanged bewildered looks, she cracked it open. Inside was a CD, simply labeled: your turn.

"What the hell is that supposed to be?" I said, looking at the message written in marker. It was scrawled so neatly, almost like it had been printed on there. Emily said nothing for a time, just staring at it like she couldn't believe what she was seeing.

"It's for me," she said plainly, her words hanging in the air.

"How do you know it's —"

I thought of something she had said a few days ago, ringing in my head over and over.

Eventually, he finds you and sends a warning.

Emily popped it out of the case and was already on her way to the old desktop.

"What are you doing? You can't be serious," I said, moving to intercept her.

"I'm watching it. I'm sorry. But I have to," she said, pushing the tiny button at the top of the tower. The disc tray squeaked out, and she swapped *The Princess Bride* with the new mysterious disc. After watching the tray recede, she looked at me, her eyes sad and guilty.

"You don't have to watch it with me. I can watch it by myself. I got myself into this, anyway," she said, and the computer started to *hum* as it recognized the disc.

But even as the media player auto booted, I found myself moving closer so I could clearly see. We stood together in front of the coffee table and waited; the disc reader loudly got itself together. I hoped it was just a meme. I prayed for a Rickroll. Despite my wishful thinking, I just *knew* it was something worse. There was an unmistakable animosity to the disc and the program itself. Dread welled in my stomach, and I felt myself sweating.

As the video buffered, the title of the video file showed at the top of the window as an illegible string of text. We waited, visibly wincing, for the snuff film, live torture, or some other unthinkable horror to begin. However, what we got was the furthest thing from that.

The video started as a feed from an old camcorder, a heavy distortion that was slowly coming into focus. There was no sound to the video, and no time stamp, just little black bars where the time and date would be. The whirling static started to fade, and in the clarity, we could see a girl. It was hard to make out at first, but she seemed to be in a store of some kind, looking at a display shelf full of what I assumed were DVDs.

She was hunched down, taking her time looking at each title, chewing at her thumbnail. She was wearing a hooded sweatshirt, a black frilly skirt with leggings underneath. The knot in my stomach worsened, twisting uncomfortably as the hair on the back of my neck rose. It was an outfit I had seen many times because it was something Emily wore. The girl in the video was her.

"What the hell is this?" I asked, and looked to see Emily was shaking. Her eyes were locked on the screen, her pupils shaking as she took in the video.

On the screen, Emily was browsing alone, kneeling down to inspect a copy of *Friday the 13th.* Her hood was pulled up as it usually was, little wisps of brown hair hanging out the front. She bounced on her heels, something she did when she was lost in thought. Totally unaware of the camera's presence, she returned the movie to its spot on the shelf. The camera followed her motions, tracking her hand as she reached for another DVD. It focused on her hand, lingering to show her painted nails before zooming back out.

"They're fucking stalking you. Did you know about this? Did you see them?" I asked, and she was shaking her head, her eyes glued to the screen.

"I know when this was," she said, shivering, "this was the day before we started doing the movie nights. I had seen these when I was out... I texted you that night. Because I wanted to be scared. I remember. I didn't... I didn't see them. I didn't know."

She trailed off, her eyes dilating as she watched herself peruse the horror movies. I recalled her text from that day. That was the night we set up our first hangout.

"That was weeks ago. Before you were looking that shit up, right? That doesn't make any sense. How would they have known where to find you? How..." I couldn't think straight.

Emily started pacing the room as on-screen Emily browsed, taking her time reading the back material of *Hellraiser.* The camera caught a glimpse of her face, zooming in as she smirked at something she read. The video paused, not from us, but of its own accord. The TV was nothing but Emily's face, her little smirk immortalized in the grainy footage from the stalker's camera.

"I'm calling the police," I said, looking for my phone. I dug through the graveyard of Chinese takeout, moving aside containers and soy sauce packets. As I found it, Emily mumbled something inaudibly.

"What?" I asked, unlocking my phone and glancing at her.

She was frozen in place, staring deeply at the video. On the screen was the same paused frame. She looked confused, like she didn't know what she was supposed to be looking at. I touched her shoulder, but she didn't move, her eyes frantically looking around the screen. *Searching.*

"I don't want to watch this anymore. I don't want to… oh god… oh god… OH GOD, NO-OH-GOD!!!!" Emily's screams ripped through the silence, her face twisted in a look I can only describe as pure terror. She swatted at my hand as she bawled, tears flooding as she recoiled from the screen, all the while unable to look away.

"Emily, what is it? What's wrong?" I asked, trying to calm her down. I looked at the TV. Nothing had changed.

"OH-MY-GOD-NO, PLEASE NO, OH GOD, OH MY GOD!" Emily wailed hysterically, so loud it rattled my ears. She pointed frantically at the video, her words breaking into irrational screams of fear. I panicked. I didn't understand. I tried to grab her to calm her down, but she was inconsolable.

"What is it, Emily? What—"

"MAKE IT STOP, MAKE IT STOP—" she cried, pulling at her hair so hard I heard the strands rip. Her eyes were wild and bloodshot, streaked make-up running as the invisible horror tormented her.

As Emily's cry melted into an agonizing scream, I stumbled to the TV. Out of desperation, I reached behind the stand and yanked the cord from the wall. The TV shut off, and the video was reduced to our reflection on the black screen. Emily collapsed on the couch, her face buried as she sobbed into the pillow. As she settled down, I opened the dial pad and called the police.

By the time I could see the blue and red strobe through the window, Emily's sobs had started to subside. She had curled up into a ball on the couch and receded inside her hoodie. I tried at first to communicate, but every attempt only made her shift further away. The invisible horror that lurked inside the video had reduced Emily to a shell. When no words could provide comfort, I took to watching out the window until help arrived.

I heard the police in the hall, the jingling of keys, and the chirp of radios echoing along with their footsteps. The sounds brought a hint of relief to the air, but with that a nervousness I wasn't prepared for. I had been so focused on them getting here that I hadn't even thought of what to say.

"The police are here," I said to Emily, which seemed to pull her out of reclusion. As the authoritative knock rattled the door, Emily sat up and wiped her eyes.

I opened the door to see two officers: one male and one female. The man was tall and broad, with tanned skin and bleach-blonde hair. The woman was considerably shorter, her hair pulled into a tight ponytail, a shade of pink lipstick offering a polite smile.

"Hi there. I'm Officer Regan, and this is Officer Henry. Are you the one who reported harassment?" The female cop said.

"Y-yeah. But it's not me, it's my friend. Here, come in," I said, holding the door open and stepping off to the side.

The officers walked in. Regan looked around the apartment for a moment and moved towards Emily when she saw her. Henry came in close behind, but stayed by the door. He hooked his thumbs in his Kevlar vest and took his time looking around the apartment, eyes darting as his jaw worked at a piece of gum. They both looked tired but alert, taking in everything in the living room surprisingly fast.

"Hey, I'm Officer Regan. Do you mind telling me what's going on here?" Regan knelt next to Emily, who was looking at the officer weakly.

"She's being stalked. They sent her a—" I started, but Henry cut me off.

"Let her talk, kid," he said sternly, pausing his chewing long enough to make sure I understood. I nodded compliantly.

Regan readied a notepad, ignoring us both. She cleared her throat and clicked a pen.

"Start from the beginning. When did this start? Do you have any idea who it is?" Regan said, posed and ready to write.

Emily said nothing for a moment, hugging her knees to her chest.

"He's watching me," she said, looking out the window. We all followed her gaze. Regan looked at Henry, who left without a word.

"Who's watching you? Ex-boyfriend? Girlfriend?" she asked, scribbling briefly.

"I went looking for him and I found him. It was my fault. I shouldn't have. I should've listened," she said, the tears threatening to return.

"Who, honey? Who did you go looking for?" Regan said, speaking a little softer.

Through the window, we could see Henry pass, flashlight panning into the night.

"He sent me a warning. It's too late now. He's going to get me, and I can't stop him. *You* can't stop him," Emily said, hugging herself tighter.

"Uh-huh, this guy got a name, sweetie?"

More scribbling.

"The Paper Mache Man," I blurted impatiently. Regan looked at me in a way a mother would look at their child for touching something they shouldn't be.

"Is this true? Is that our guy?" she asked Emily, who nodded weakly.

"You said he sent a warning. What do you mean by that?"

Emily lifted a finger to the computer tower, which was still humming by the entertainment stand. I cleared my throat and spoke up.

"He sent her a CD. There was a video on it. Of him watching her. I... unplugged the TV when she got upset. You want me to hook it back up?" I asked.

"Could you please?" she said, before addressing Emily again. "Did you happen to get a good look at him? This 'Paper Mache Man'? Either of you see him out the window? Or dropping the CD off?" she asked.

"You *can't* see him. Not until he's ready," Emily said.

"Ready for what, honey?"

"For you to join him," Emily said. Regan paused her scribbling, but only for a moment. The words gave me the chills.

While I plugged the TV back in, Officer Regan continued her soft prodding. She asked her many questions, each time jotting down notes and flashing the same sweet smile.

Where did you find him?

Have you met in person?

Do they have another name they go by?

Have you seen them around here before?

Do they have any reason to hurt you?

The last question hung in the air, only to be cut off by the chirp of Regan's radio. The stern voice of Henry crackled over.

"Perimeter clear."

"10-4."

I turned the TV on and grabbed the dusty mouse on the TV stand, giving it a wiggle to preemptively pull it out of the screen-saver.

"Now I'm gonna need to see this video, honey. You want to wait in the other room? Would that be easier for you?" Regan asked, pocketing her notebook and putting a hand on her shoulder. Emily shook her head.

When the desktop screen appeared on the TV, I saw the video had closed itself out. I moved the cursor across the screen to the 'My computer' tab, and double clicked. I looked at Officer Regan, who nodded for me to continue. I double clicked on the DVD tray reader icon and waited for the video to play. We waited in silence, the spiral buffer icon taking its time.

Behind us, the door opened, and Officer Henry stepped back in. He joined Regan as we waited.

"This the video?" he asked, and his partner nodded. I waited for the window to launch, and the static to follow. The feed with Emily, looking at the old horror movies. When a window did finally pop, I felt like I had been kicked in the stomach.

Error: File not compatible. Unable to launch.

I hovered over the options to cancel or troubleshoot, feeling myself starting to sweat.

"It's not working. I'm going to try again," I said, and the officers nodded. I looked at Emily, who was now solemnly looking at the floor.

I canceled it out and clicked the icon again. Same error, except faster this time. I tried again, and again, but each time it yielded the same result. After the tenth try, officer Henry cleared his throat.

"You two do some drinking tonight?" he said.

My cheeks grew hot. I already knew where this was going.

"What?" I asked, my tone flaring up.

"Did you two do a little bit of drinking tonight?" he said a little slower and batted an eye at the cans on the coffee table.

"You don't believe us," I said.

"I didn't say that."

"Look, I'll prove it to you!" I opened the disc tray and reached for the DVD. My fingers stopped just short of the tray, my hand shaking in the air.

The disc was gone.

"What the hell? Bullshit." I looked at the screen for the icon for the DVD reader. The icon was gone as well.

Emily buried her face and started to cry softly. I checked the screen again, closed it out, opened it again. I closed the disc tray and opened it a second time. Nothing.

"That's wrong, it was here. She opened it. It was wrapped in…" I looked underneath the coffee table for the newspaper and raffia yarn. There was nothing. I looked around the takeout containers. Nothing. Henry cleared his throat.

"Alright. So, you two did a little drinking. Watched some scary movies. Some of those movies, they can be a little scary, can't they?" he said, chewing his gum.

"We're not making this up! It was here. *He* was here," I said, standing up.

"*Who* was here?"

"The Paper Mache Man," I said, feeling suddenly foolish with my hands balled into fists.

Henry exchanged a look with Regan, then sighed.

"Look, kid—"

"No, we're telling the truth! She found him on the dark web. Now he's stalking her. He sent the disc, and I saw it."

"*The deep web?*" he said incredulously.

"C'mon Emily, tell him!"

Emily did nothing, only sank more.

The silent tension built in the living room like a hot breath, and I wiped at the sweat forming on my forehead. Henry looked about out of patience. I looked at Officer Regan, who just raised her eyebrows.

"*Look.* If you find the CD, the wrapping, *anything,* give us a call. We can't stay here all night catchin' ghosts. I looked, alright? Whatever it is, it ain't out there. No footprints in the dirt, no nothin'," he said.

"We'll send a unit out here to make some patrols throughout the night, ok?" Regan offered, "And if you see anything else, call. We'll come back out. In the meantime… maybe you should get some rest."

Henry left first, talking into his radio in the hall. Regan gave an apologetic look before following. I closed the door behind them and locked it again, both deadbolt and chain.

I walked to the window to watch them leave. Emily sniffled and got up from the couch, wiping at her puffy eyes. Outside, the officers killed the strobe, and after sitting there for a moment, the cruiser pulled away.

"They're leaving. They're really just gonna…" I looked for Emily and was shocked to find her no longer there.

I looked down the hall, just in time to see her door shut.

***

I remember lying in bed for a while, tossing and turning through the night. I would open my eyes at every noise outside, sitting up and checking my phone before uneasily rolling back over. I felt an odd paranoia I couldn't shake. Each time I would start to drift off I felt like someone was watching me, and it would pull me from the lull of sleep.

At one point I couldn't help but get up to check the apartment, creeping out into the hall and turning all the lights on. I checked every closet and corner, even going as far as checking the peephole to make sure no one was lurking behind the door.

I decided to look for the wrapping again, picking through the takeout trash to find some validation for the past events. I checked under the couch and inside the cushions, then in and around the recliner. I gathered up the containers to throw them away and even picked through the trash can to be sure before dumping it in.

I found no evidence of the Paper Mache Man.

Before trying to go to bed again, I peeked out the window to the parking lot, my last ditch effort to find *something* before returning to my room. To my surprise, the only thing out of the ordinary was a police cruiser, parked and idling next to the dumpster. They had actually sent a patrol as they promised.

Seeing the car made me feel emotional. The stark vehicle creeping in the night made me question myself, my thoughts, and everything I had seen. Had I *actually* seen this shit? Or was I just fooling myself to be there for Emily?

I killed the lights and walked back to my room. I could see Emily's light under her door, the faint tune of music whispering from within. I wanted to knock and try to talk to her... but in the end I was just too *tired*. Too tired to be awake any longer, and too tired of this internet ghost conspiracy. I returned to my room; my last shred of evidence spent wincing at how late it was.

***

The next day I awoke, cursing my alarms for doing what I asked of them. I dressed like a shambling corpse, pulling on a wrinkled uniform through the fogged lens of drowsiness. My body ached from the lack of rest, each routine motion labored and irritated.

I brushed and combed, trying to make myself presentable aside from feeling dead on the inside. Putting on my shoes, the soft playing music could still be heard. Emily was still holed up in her room, and I wondered if she had been missing work. After pocketing my keys and wallet, I fished out my phone and sent her a text:

Off to work. How you holdin' up?

I promptly left. Getting out of the apartment felt liberating, and it seemed to ease the paranoia lingering in the backseat. Maybe I just needed to get out more. Maybe *she* did.

I felt a little better as the morning went on. I found the distraction of work to be welcoming, and focusing on the day's tasks seemed to put me at ease. Time moved consistently, and I didn't even realize it was time to take my lunch until my boss mentioned it. I hadn't even realized I was hungry. On my break I grabbed some lunch from down the street, deciding when I got back I would just chill and eat it in my car. I looked at my phone for the first time since I left the house and found my text message had been left on 'read'.

The incessant nagging that had been lying dormant sprouted at the sight of Emily's name, and the text I had sent the day prior.

Have you learned anything else about the Paper Mache Man?

Seeing the words provoked a discomfort deep inside my soul. I felt a pressure in my head, a painless migraine pushing on the insides of my skull. Like a vibrating cell phone worming its way out from the compacted folds of my brain.

I read the text again and again as if I had sent it to myself.

I thought of last night, standing at the TV next to Emily as we watched her browse the horror movies on camera. The look on her face when it zoomed in on her skin and how she couldn't look away. The way her eyes *buzzed.*

My thumbs moved of their own accord, opening the web browser and typing the name into Google. I hit 'search' and waited.

The same results as the night before. DIY projects with glue and paper. Recipes for the perfect adhesive. Newspaper sculptures in all shapes and sizes. I looked at dozens of links, each leading to something crafty and innocent. I took to Reddit, and when I exhausted all points of interest there, I went to 4chan. I found nothing conspicuous, no inclination of The Paper Mache Man's existence in any way, shape, or form.

No-name websites were next, pages and pages of third-party forums. Each of them was ages old and chock full of ads. I kept scrolling, patiently waiting as my phone struggled to load the poorly optimized content. Threads that had burned out years ago, inconclusive conversations that had been buried by a decade of old domains and forgotten email activations. The longer I looked, the more time it took for the pages to load.

I spent so much time staring at my phone I hadn't noticed my break was over. My food sat in the passenger seat, cold and uneaten. I sighed and rubbed my eyes. I needed to head back in, I would have to continue this later.

I gathered my things, threw open the car door, and stopped. Part of an old thread I was reading had finally buffered, now showing several comments posted that lacked an actual message. Each comment showed up as <removed>, but one attachment had lingered, something that looked strikingly familiar.

It was a picture of a dining room, with a set table and a darkened doorway in the background.

A family sat there, each recoiled in their chairs. White hands brought to their chests, the fingers fat and contorted. Their faces were pulpy and gray, no features save for the smeared and matted text of newspaper.

Standing in the doorway was a figure so tall it had to hunch over to fit. With one lanky arm, it grasped the doorway, the other outstretched and pointed forward.

Pointing at me.

***

I drove away from work to the sound of a dial tone drumming in my ear. My call to Emily timed-out to voicemail. A cheerier, past version of her told me to leave a message. I found myself rambling into the phone with an urgent stuttering that could've been simplified to:

Emily, we need to talk, it's important. I can see him.

My second call was to my boss, apologizing for running off without saying anything. I told him I really wasn't feeling well, and on my lunch break I had thrown up all over myself. He was understanding and told me to take some time off until I felt better.

Driving home, I couldn't shake the feeling of being watched. I kept checking the rearview mirror, expecting the malformed shape of a man to be there. Each time I would see nothing but the fleeting stretch of the road behind me.

I called Emily again. Straight to voicemail. I drove faster, a cold sweat chilling my neck. I caught every red light in town, subconsciously looking behind me at every stop. The image of the dining room photo was burned into my mind, and everywhere I looked I anticipated the long pointing hand.

When I arrived home, I practically jogged into the building. I fumbled with my keys, glancing down the hallway sporadically until the door was unlocked. I yanked it open and shut it behind me.

The apartment was dark, except for the light trying to fight its way in through the blinds. The house was still clean from the night before, but everything felt dusty, *dingy.*

"Emily?" I called out, my voice sounding unnaturally loud in the complete lack of white noise. Silence was my only response.

I made my way to the hall, turning on every light as I went. Before I even made it down, I noticed something missing, something I hadn't realized I was relying on until it was absent.

Emily's door was closed, and the light was off.

"Hello?"

There was no murmur of music from within, no comforting tune to assure me of her company.

Nothing but a ringing that had started in my ears.

I knocked on Emily's door and called her name again. I stood close to the door and listened for movement, keeping my eye on the front door. The apartment felt so *empty,* and I expected something to peek around the corner every time my eyes drifted away.

My phone chimed and scared the living shit out of me. I dug it out of my pocket and was simultaneously overcome with a rush of relief and worry. The text had come from Emily.

Ran into town. Had to get out of the house. Be back later.

I felt myself sinking. In the past few days of me coming and going, Emily had locked herself in her room and spent her time trying to make sense of the anomaly. And after days of not listening, I was now alone.

When you see it, who's going to be the asshole here? You.

I locked my phone without responding to her text. Even if I knew what I wanted to say, hounding her over it now... didn't feel fair. I would just have to wait until she got back in.

I went to the living room and opened the blinds. I was in such a hurry when I got here, I hadn't even noticed that her car was gone.

The ringing in my ears made the silence unbearable. A tight knot was forming in my stomach, the anxious twist of stress hampering my breathing as I looked outside. There was nothing out of the ordinary, but I still felt the eyes on me.

I splashed some cold water on my face and tried to relax. Looking at my own distraught reflection, I realized there was only one thing I could do. The exact same thing Emily had done: try and find out what the fuck was happening.

I closed myself in my room and booted up my desktop. I opened the web browser; I decided to try to retrace my steps. If I could just find something she might have missed, maybe I could help us both. The ringing continued, and I put on some music of my own to alleviate the crushing silence.

Hours passed in front of the screen. I combed dozens of threads, scrolling through every comment until each domain was useless. When I reached a dead end, I would backpedal until I found another fork in the road. My browser became littered with tabs, reference points saved in case I snagged on whichever forum I was currently on. The longer I dug, the older the threads got. But everywhere I went, everything was <removed>.

I imagined Emily doing the same, typing and clicking at her computer in the safety of her bedroom. Thinking back, it astounded me how well she had handled it alone. All the time she spent searching, trying to find some concrete assurance that she wasn't crazy. I thought of all the times I dismissed her, and how I could've *helped her look* instead of just letting her sink. I could've asked more questions; I could've *tried* to understand.

After searching the whole day, I turned up nothing. I was exhausted, my eyes aching from staring at the screen, and the swell of the migraine lingering behind it. It was mentally jarring, looking for something that didn't want to be found. Every time I thought I was close, the trail would stop completely. The information just wasn't there.

Almost like it didn't exist.

I rubbed my eyes and stood from my desk, feeling too tired and frustrated to continue. Maybe if I could rest my brain, I could try again tomorrow with a clearer start. I collapsed on my bed, thoughts of the photo slipping away as sleep found me.

***

I was standing at the bathroom mirror.

I don't know how long I had been there, hands gripping the sink, staring at my own reflection. My palms were slick with sweat, and I felt clammy. I stared at myself, eyes struggling to focus on a mirror image that didn't look right.

The tap was running, ice cold. I felt the stream with my fingers, and hunched down to splash some water on my face. The water was freezing, and my skin tingled as I massaged the water in. I felt nauseous and dehydrated. I cupped my hands and brought them to my mouth, slurping greedily as my body shivered.

When I looked back at the mirror, I could see it.

The difference.

My eyelids were slack. I got closer to the mirror, using my fingers to stretch the lids open. I looked at my own eyeball, then at the flesh around it. It wasn't the normal shade of pink and red. It was pale, white even. With my other hand I picked and prodded, surprised to feel nothing as my fingers explored the open cavity of my eye. There was something *beneath* it. I could feel it.

The first scratch was the hardest, a hot trickle of blood chilling as it streamed down my face. There was no sensation of pain, and my need to see what lay beneath surpassed my concern for the damage I inflicted.

I burrowed into my own skin, digging until I could get under it with my fingertip. I worked the digit in, paying no mind to the sprinkle of red that was peppering the sink. I pinched the flap and pulled, ripping a strip under my eye until it came free. I could see it now, the hiding layer of blurred lettering that continued underneath. But it wasn't enough, I couldn't quite see.

I needed more.

With both hands I clawed and raked at my face, each swipe peeling a little more than the last. My nails dripping as they worked through my face, my eyes fierce and focused on my deteriorating doppelganger. Blood splattered the sink, collecting in a thick pool as bits of my skin clogged the drain. The running water of the tap churned the mixture as it rose to the edge.

It started to come free. My fingers dug deep, hooking into the flesh over my cheekbones. I took a deep breath and started to pull, removing the mask that disguised my true face. Each revealing tug spurted the mirror in dark streaks. I watched through the stained glass as I ripped, my nose and lips coming free in one long strip of bloody skin.

My trembling hands let the mask fall, and it fell with a splash. The dark pool gushed over the sides of the sink as I stared at what had been hiding all along.

A face made purely of paper mache.

I awoke gasping, clammy hands touching my face in a panic. I felt my skin, hot and sweating from the terrible nightmare. It took me a while to come down, gasping for breath as my eyes struggled to discern the dream from reality. A sense of familiarity slowly returned, and I realized I was in my bed.

My bedroom was dark, the soft lullaby of music still playing after hours of shuffling. The daylight that had previously shone in before had retired to the veil of night, leaving me to squint at the features of my room. Just as I started to relax under the covers, an unmistakable detail filled me with discomfort.

My bedroom door had been opened while I was asleep.

The door was slightly cracked, a narrow beam shining from the light in the hallway. I pulled the covers off and swung out of bed, keeping my eyes on it as I stood. I left it shut when I laid down, I was sure of it.

I grabbed my phone from the nightstand and checked the time. It was just after 10p.m.

Creeping toward the door, I began to hear a noise from the other side. It was a familiar sound, a *skrit-skrit-skrit* that I swore I had heard before. I froze next to the crack, trying to place it as I looked down the hall.

Skrit-skrit-skrit. Click.

Skrit-skrit-skrit. Click.

Skrit-skrit-skriiiiiit.

It was coming from the living room. I opened the door quietly and looked down the hall. All the lights I had turned on early still remained, but it didn't make me feel any better.

Skrit-skrit-skrit... click.

Emily's door was shut, still dark and quiet as she had left it. I walked down the corridor, hugging the wall as the sound continued. It was moving around, each time just a little further from the last.

Skrit-skrit-skrit...

At the end of the hall, I could hear the scuffs of socks on carpet. I peeked around the corner to see someone standing next to the sliding door.

Click.

Emily was looking outside, standing perfectly still. In her hands was a tiny camera.

Skrit-skrit-skrit.

"What are you doing?" I asked, and she jumped.

"Jesus, you fuckin' scared me!" she said, flashing me a look of startled anger.

"Sorry."

Emily walked over to the coffee table and reached for a bottle that sat in the center. My guess was vodka. She unscrewed the cap and took a swig, one that looked like it hurt.

"I'm taking pictures, obviously," she said, wiping her mouth. She offered it to me, and I shook my head. She shrugged, her little shoulders bobbing in her tank top. Her lower half was covered by the massive *Coheed and Cambria* hoodie tied around her waist, the legs of plaid pajama pants poking out from under it. Her socks were covered in little cats.

"I didn't know they made disposables anymore," I said, sitting on the couch.

"Me neither, until today," she said, aiming the camera into the kitchen.

Click.

"I wasn't having any luck with the phone," Emily began, her thumb working the plastic wheel on the corner of the camera, "so I'm trying physical copies. See if he shows up. Maybe if I hold on to the pictures, they won't go away. This is my third one." She held the camera up.

"You think he's *here?*" I asked, trying not to sound worried, and failing. I looked around the apartment, feeling the uncomfortable ringing returning.

"Maybe." She aimed the disposable down the hall and clicked the button.

"I uh, saw him this morning," I said, shifting my weight on the couch.

"Did you?" she said, working the wheel again. It wasn't a question, more like an acknowledgement.

"Yeah. He was…" I went to the gallery on my phone, to bring up the screenshot I had taken before leaving work this morning. It wasn't there.

Emily walked to the kitchen and stood in front of the refrigerator. Facing the front door, she raised the camera and clicked the button.

"Did you get a warning?" she said. Her words hung dead in the air as she readied another picture.

I saw the recording of Emily in my head, and the sounds of her frightened shouting cut in like interference as I remembered her paused face.

"No."

"Hmm." She inspected the camera closely, and without a word, came and sat on the couch.

We said nothing for a while. Emily sat the camera on the table and grabbed the vodka bottle. I watched her take a drink, wincing harder this time. I felt like I should say something, something important, but every conjured thought ended with a pale hand pointing from a photograph.

"What are you gonna do now?" Ended up being the best I had.

"Gonna get these developed. Then maybe go see my mom. I don't know. I feel like I should," she said, resting her head on the arm of the couch, cradling the bottle upright.

"They still have 24-hour photos?"

"Yeah."

"Wow… hey," I swiveled on the couch to face her, "you want me to take you?" I asked.

She perked up for a moment, but it didn't last.

"Nah. Probably call an Uber or something. You got work, don't you?" she said.

"I don't think I'll be making it in tomorrow." I chuckled, scratching my head.

"It's cool. Besides, I don't want anyone waiting on me. Rather make my own way, you know? But if you're not going in…" she held the bottle out with a smirk. I took it.

The mouthful was warm but comforting, an instant burn accompanied by something… fruity? I coughed afterwards.

"It's supposed to be pineapple." Emily laughed.

"It's not." I choked and took another swig. Emily sat up and grabbed the camera.

"Hey, I got one left. You wanna…" she held it out, mimicking a selfie.

"Yeah, sure," I said, and she scooted over. I put an arm around her shoulder and she snuggled against me, provoking a smile I hadn't thought possible until then. Emily held it up and pushed the button.

Not long after, Emily called a ride, like she said she would. While we waited, we continued to pass the bottle, and as we got tipsy, we talked about horror movies. The more we drank, the more we laughed, until we wiped at tears from cracking up so hard. We reminisced about the movie nights, and in that moment, there was nothing else that mattered. There was no Paper Mache Man.

When her ride honked outside, we both frowned, and Emily pulled on her hoodie. I asked if she would rather stay and we could sort it out tomorrow, but she was adamant about leaving. I wanted to convince her to stay, but I knew once she had made up her mind there was no changing it. She took a drink for the road and left me the bottle, a sad look in her eyes as she put on her shoes. She hugged me goodbye, both of us swaying from the lull of alcohol. I let her go, wishing it would have lasted just a little longer. She left, and I found myself wandering back to the couch, unsure of what to do next. Without any better ideas, I reached for the bottle again.

To my surprise, Emily poked her head back in.

"Thirteen Ghosts," she said, without elaborating further.

"What?" I asked, confused.

"It was one of the movies I meant to watch. Always forgot to put it on the list," she said with a frown.

"Next time. We'll watch that first," I said, pointing at her with the neck of the bottle.

"Yeah. Next time." And she was gone.

This time I got up from the couch and watched her go, leaning against the slider as she shuffled to the little hatchback car that came to pick her up. She opened the door to the back seat and saw me, giving me a wave and a smile before ducking in. I waved back, and as I watched her go, I finished the last inch of the bottle.

I tossed the bottle in the trash, my steps sloppy and exaggerated. I locked the door and headed to my room, wondering if I should've done something different. Maybe *said* something different. Looking back, I would have.

I stopped at the bathroom and looked in the mirror. My reflection was tired and drunk, breathing too hard as I leaned forward to inspect myself. I looked into my glazed eyes and saw nothing out of the ordinary. The corners of my eyes were soft and pink, with nothing lurking underneath. The ringing had ceased as well, and before I left the bathroom, I was even smiling a little.

When I got to my room, I left the door open and shut off the music. I sprawled out on my bed, the cool pillow and comforter soft on my skin. In the drunk serenity of peace and quiet, I fell back to sleep.

The next morning, I woke up late. My head was pounding, and the daylight from the window was suffocating. I grabbed at my head, regretting the drinks I had the night before. I shambled out of bed with a groan, feeling for my phone as I shielded my eyes. I hadn't called work to tell them I was staying home. As far as they were concerned, I was a no-call-no-show.

I found my phone on the floor and squinted at the screen. It was 11a.m. I had overslept three hours. I went to swipe, but something stopped me. I had received a single text while I was asleep, a simple message from the only name I hoped to see. Emily.

Want to meet me at the lake at noon? The usual spot. For old times' sake?

I pulled up to the lake forty-five minutes later. It was a small portion of an otherwise long stretch of beach, with a pavilion stuck between two fenced off private property signs. I could hear the waves as soon as I got out of the car, accompanied by a cool breeze that rolled off the water. It was a beautiful place aside from its eternal gloom, a shore cursed with overcast skies the majority of the year.

After a quick shower, change of clothes, and some Tylenol, I was starting to feel less like a walking corpse. The dull ache in my head was starting to pass, but the ringing had returned full force. I called work before I left and informed them I would still be out sick, and they were sympathetic. I guess I could thank my hangover for that.

I locked my car and walked into the pavilion, old pines dancing above the masses of beach grass. It was mostly empty, something you would expect on an early weekday. I looked around for Emily but didn't see her; she wasn't one to typically linger for friends to show before going. I assumed she would already be at the shore.

Through the pavilion was a set of concrete stairs that had been built into the dunes, a kind of winding path that changed structure several times before hitting the sand. I went down the steps quickly, and passed the spouts for rinsing off sandy feet. There was nobody around, except for a couple walking their dog. The breeze got chillier the closer I got to the water. The boardwalk was the last stretch before sand, a wooden structure built over massive rocks used to thwart erosion.

I crossed it briskly, the old boards creaking with every step. My hands glided over the rails, beach grass tussling on both sides as I made my way. At the end of the boardwalk was a staircase that led to the shore below; knotted and faded lumber that was eventually swallowed by sand.

I stood at the landing and admired the view. The dreary water stretched for miles, a seemingly infinite blue-gray with a pleasant sight on either side. On the left was the neon silhouette of Chicago, and on the right was the Lighthouse pier. Between the two landmarks was Emily, sitting on a bench on the shore below.

The sight of her made me quicken my pace. I descended the steps quickly, skipping every other step as the excitement welled within me. Even as I hit the dead resistance of the sand, I kept my eyes on Emily. She was sitting with her back to me with her hood up, watching the waves quietly. Beside her was the little red notebook, the wind flipping the pages as her gaze held on the water. I had a stupid smile on my face, my legs burning as my shoes slogged through the sand with every stride.

"Hey, Emily! I made it!" I called, trying to catch my breath. She didn't move.

The wind whipped at my face, and I raised a hand to combat it.

"Hey! Sorry I didn't text. I was pretty hungover. Got here as soon as I..." I stuttered as I got closer, a sense of foreboding weakening my legs as I was within arm's reach.

She wasn't moving at all, like she was frozen in place. Her head was hung low, her hands stuffed in the front pocket of her hoodie. Like she had fallen asleep.

The wind tore at the notebook, pages turning sentiently at her side.

"Emily, it's me," I said, and grabbed her shoulder. Her shoulder felt *wrong,* impossibly thin and bony, even for her. Her head lolled to the side, and her hands slipped out of her pockets. They were contorted and white, knocking against the bench like rocks.

I screamed.

Emily's face was gone.

In its place, a crude husk of paper mache.

I fell back into the sand. The body remained still, tossed to the side like a discarded puppet.

No hair, no nose, no mouth. Only black holes where the eyes should be.

The newspaper husk stared at me, the drawstrings of the hood swaying weakly in the wind. I tried to speak, but the words were caught in my throat. I couldn't breathe. My hands shook in the sand. Despite the boiling urge to run, I approached the replica, thinking it had to be a joke. I looked up at the boardwalk, hoping to see Emily laughing or waving her arms. Nothing but an empty pavilion and dancing grass.

I tried to laugh, tried to convince myself it wasn't what I thought it was. It had to be a joke. I looked at the clothes it wore, shaking my head in denial. The newspaper husk looked at me, the wind whistling through the cutouts in its face.

Coheed hoodie. Plaid pajama pants. Socks with little cats.

She didn't take any clothes with her.

I could see something poking out from the front pocket, a white corner contrasting the black of the hoodie. I delicately pulled it out.

It was a photograph from last night, the last photo selfie Emily and I took together.

It showed me on the couch, my arm curled around nothing, and empty space where Emily should've been.

I touched the replica's face, tears falling as my fingers brushed the dry, pulpy skin. The surface withered away at my touch, bits of paper breaking and blowing away. I started to cry, sobbing as the replica started to break down and blow away. I averted my eyes as it wasted away, my eyes falling to the notebook next to it.

Every page was filled with words, the same phrase penned over and over.

MAKEITSTOPMAKEITSTOPMAKEITSTOPMAKEIT-STOP

In the distance, a blood-curdling scream echoed across the water and over the shore. The paper mache replica collapsed, and an uproar of dust scattered on the wind. As the last of the dust blew away, I ran, leaving the pair of deflated clothes swaying behind me.

***

I don't recall the drive home. I remember pulling up to the apartment and crying at the wheel, not wanting to go inside. I didn't know what else to do. I thought if I could make it back home, Emily would be there, holed up in her room just like she had been before she left. Her light would be on. Her music would be playing. I would knock and she'd answer, and we would order takeout again. Or maybe we would just go somewhere and get away from all this.

The thought urged me forward. Out of the car and into the building, I readied my keys and unlocked the door as soon as I got to it. I could see Emily's face, her smile. I could hear her laugh; the combination of shy and obnoxious rolled together. She would be there. She had to be.

I turned the key and opened the door.

The apartment was dark and empty, the ringing of the noiseless void deafening as I closed the door behind me. All the lights were off, the blinds closed to shut out the brightness of the outside world. I didn't remember shutting them off, but it didn't matter. I marched down the hall, determined to get to Emily's room even as the darkness grew. I looked for the light, for the sign of her presence. But there was no light to be found.

Her door was open, nothing but black peeking from the open crack.

I wanted to turn around, but I couldn't. I had to make sure she wasn't here.

I pushed the door open, the soundless void beckoning me.

I swallowed the knot in my throat and flicked on the light.

The entire room was covered in photographs. 35mm prints littered every surface, from her computer desk to her bed. The floor was a sea of film, white bordered polaroids fanned out in all directions. I took a step in and heard the rubbery squeak under my heel. I looked at my feet to see I was already stepping on them.

I crouched and picked them up, the feeling of churning bile rising in my throat. The ringing rattled my brain, but I kept my gaze on the photos, taking in the similarity they all seemed to share.

In every picture stood The Paper Mache Man.

His hulking mass was caught one way or another, but in some you could see his entire frame. He was unnaturally tall, hulking in every room Emily had snapped a photo in. His legs were long, but his arms were longer, often bracing himself on the ceiling or the walls as he struggled to fit in the apartment. Sometimes he just looked toward the camera, other times he reached for it, his fingers elongated and uneven across his hand.

In some pictures they looked like hooks, others like tentacles. Whenever he pointed, they were long and rounded, a dozen digits with a protuberant tip. His head looked heavy and bulbous, with two unopened slits for eyes and a blank canvas for a mouth. His skin was layered and pulpy, with a pinkish tinge that blurred at the edges of his body in the photo. His skin was shiny and glistened like glass in the light.

I looked through dozens of photos, each showing the lurking horror in different spots in our home. The kitchen, the bathroom, the corners of the ceiling. Taking up the hallway, standing in her closet, kneeling by her desk. He had been right there the entire time, even waiting as we sat on the couch.

And when Emily left, he followed her.

I fanned out the pictures, looking at each one. There were several that were similar, where Emily had gotten the same angle several times, just in case. I looked at all of them, each one serving as the evidence she strived to find since the beginning.

On her desk was a large orange envelope, with the photo center's logo stamped onto the side. Holding it open, I gathered them all up, stacking them together and tucking them in as I worked my way across the room. Once the floor was clear, I moved on to the desk, removing the photos that blanketed Emily's keyboard and mouse pad. I picked up so many I stopped looking at them, wanting to close them in the envelope and never peek again. Just when I thought I got them all, one photo remained, one that was much different from the others. When I picked it up, the ringing blared in my ears, and I felt a hot trickle seeping from the inside of them.

The photo was of me sleeping in bed. The Paper Mache Man was standing next to me, his large head craned as he watched me sleep.

One knock, thunderous and absolute. The ringing was gone.

I stood in pure silence, every nerve lighting like a switchboard. I tucked the photo into the envelope and closed it. I left

Emily's room and closed the door, looking down the hallway to the source of the noise. In the living room, I set the envelope on the coffee table and booted up the old computer, listening to the hum as I powered up the TV as well.

I took a deep breath and opened the door, knowing what I'd find.

Wrapped in newspaper and tied with raffia yarn, was my warning.

I picked it up off the welcome mat and closed the door behind me. I pulled the string loose and let it fall to the floor, then unwrapped the layers of old Sunday papers. The case was plain white with no decoration, just like Emily's. I cracked it open and looked at the disc, with a label so clean it had to be printed. I ejected the tray and placed it in, and watched it retract in silence. As the computer hummed and the video loaded, I sat on the couch and waited, gritting my teeth so hard it hurt.

When the video loaded, it lit up the living room like a home theater.

My video started with soundless distortion, just as Emily's had. I waited for it to clear, anxious and unable to look at anything but the screen. I even tried to close my eyes, but they wouldn't obey me. I *had* to watch. As the deformation cleared, I could slowly make out the scene around me. Little things at first, until the shapes bled together into a sudden clarity. When I recognized what I saw, I felt the air flee from my lungs.

In my video, Emily and I were on a bench at the beach.

The view captured us from the side, from a spot that would've been impossible without us seeing. Old pines swayed in the distance, with a chorus of beach grass at their feet. Overhead, a seagull passed by.

The video zooms in on Emily, rearing back in laughter in her oversized hoodie. She's writing in her little red notebook, a beaming smile on her face as I light a joint behind her. I take a big drag and hold it in, smiling stupidly before exhaling a plume of smoke. Emily takes it and does the same, except she coughs several times afterward. We pass it back and forth, both of us laughing as we kick our feet in the sand.

Emily looks happy. *I* look happy.

The video zooms in gradually, until our legs are removed from the picture. It's focusing on our faces now, and the more I look at it, the more it starts to make sense.

This was our first time at the beach, the first time we planned a movie night.

The feed continues to zoom, but it's moving differently now. It's cutting Emily out of the frame until the screen is mostly my face. I'm saying something to Emily, something I can't make out. When I'm done talking, I smile at Emily, a half-stoned smile that she probably doesn't see.

The video pauses.

I look at my face frozen on the screen, and I'm squeezing the cushions in my hands. I don't know what's coming, but the image is getting larger, my eyes forced forward as I watch it grow.

I thought the video was zooming in, but it's the *screen* that's getting bigger now. I'm moving towards it, or it's moving towards me. I don't exactly know. Everything around me is getting tunneled out, and I'm forced to sit and look as the screen gets closer, until it's all I see.

I hear something through the screen, the sound of ripping paper, followed by a low-pitched bellowing that vibrates the screen itself.

Then there is no screen.

The room is dark, with a single overhead lamp shining above. It looks like a basement or a cave, something dark and damp and unnatural. The walls… are bleeding.

There's someone in a chair, they're tied up or stuck, with something wet like glue. Their eyes are bloodshot, their lips trembling as they try to free themselves. They can't get free, whatever is binding them is too strong.

At their feet are dozens of bodies. They're trembling on the ground and moaning, a choir of agony and suffering. Their hands are contorted and white, their faces wrapped in the pulpy shell of paper mache. There are footsteps, loud and heavy. Some of the bodies twitch, some of them start to wail. One of the bodies starts to sob, its oversized hoodie stained, the logo unreadable.

The video doesn't zoom; it doesn't pan. I am there, watching firsthand.

The footsteps continue. The naked, genderless monstrosity stepped into the light, its skin polished and shiny like glass. Its head is massive, its slit eyes looking in the direction of the person in the chair. The individual kicks their feet in fear, but there is no hope. Even if they could escape, there is nowhere to go.

The person is me.

I watch as The Paper Mache Man gets close, a low-pitched growling vibrating deep within his chest. The low echoing sounds of a lion's purr, but it's something abnormal, not of this world. Its face is in mine now, its pinkish head five times the size of mine. I'm whimpering, tears leaking from distraught eyes. The rumbling purr gets louder, and I watch as I piss myself. Inches away from my face, the entity's eyes open, revealing two black globes the size of bowling balls. The abyssal globes of black and deep purple, swirling like wormholes in space. In its eyes I see what it wants, and I see there is no escape. It raises its hand to touch me, and I look away and start to bawl.

The Entity's hand is large and grotesque, its fingers twisting and reforming constantly before my eyes. They are drenched with a crystalline slime, a clear mucus that steams as it trickles onto the ground. Slowly, benevolently, it smears it on my face, the rumble in its throat growing louder until it's almost screaming. Its eyes widen, and the globes in its faces glow like burning stars.

The misshapen hand closes around my face, squeezing the skin until it bruises and bleeds under its touch. It pulls the skin away effortlessly, peeling it from my body in a sanguinary spray as I scream helplessly. When the skin is removed, it holds it to the light, the dripping gore coagulated with the rest on the floor. The electric clicking from its throat settles as it's satisfied.

In the chair my screams are jumbled and hysterical, the skin gone from half of my face to my chest. A singular exposed eye darts around the room, looking for help, looking for death. But there is no hope, only the groans of the ones littering the ground.

The Entity stretches the skin tight, and wraps it around its torso. It smooths it out over its own hide, the mucus from its hands glazing it as it smooths it out across its body. It continues this for a while until it is time for the next piece. Each freshly peeled strip is applied to its body. First its torso, then one of its thighs, then the back of its head. Its wicked fingers flatten every applied piece until it is perfect.

I watch until the end. And even when I run out of skin, it isn't finished. My skinless body convulses in the chair, beady eyes scrambled like a faceless animatronic. The entity returns, and once again applies its secretion to the bare tissue on my face. My wailing has subsided to groans like the others, and as it unravels the newspaper, I nod obediently so it can apply it. The malformed hands work gently, delicately, until I am wrapped like the others around me. I groan under the shell of my new skin, and as it leaves, the light above me goes out. My groans mix with the others, until I'm unable to discern my voice from theirs.

***

When I open my eyes, I'm in my living room. I don't know how long I was there, but my eyes are swollen, and my throat is hoarse from screaming. I lay there for a time, processing it all. Every time I close my eyes, I see the horror unfold, and as I finally get up from the couch, I find myself trying not to blink.

I climb to my feet, find my keys, and grab the envelope on the way to the door.

I get in my car and drive away, leaving the apartment behind me with no intention of going back. I keep the envelope close to me,

I drive for a while, taking roads without any real direction or course in mind. I don't look in the rearview mirror, and I don't check the streets around me. The ringing is gone, and I roll the windows down to hear the outside and feel the wind on my face. I keep driving, looking at things in town I never paid attention to. Shops I never noticed, people walking down the street. I look at everyone's cars, what they're driving, and who they're with. Everything looks so peaceful.

As night falls, I keep driving until I'm at the edge of town. I find a bar, with a neon sign of a smoking gun, and I pull in to have a drink. I keep the photos on me, tucked under my jacket so I don't lose them.

The place is pretty busy, but as I walk to the bar, it seems like two gentlemen are ending their night. One is bald with a mustache and full of muscle, the other is particularly average but smiling wide. I let them pass and take their spot, enjoying the music as I settle into one of the stools. The barkeep comes over, and I order a drink. Two inches of vodka with a pineapple slice. I tilt it to my lips and drink slowly, savoringly. It tastes terrible.

I enjoy my terrible tasting drink and ignore the growing feeling of being watched. It won't be long now, I'm sure.

Emily wanted to be scared. At first, I shared her enthusiasm, but after setting up a few movie nights, she set out to look for something *more*.

In the ruins of the internet, buried under old forums and long forgotten pages, she found what she was looking for. I still don't know what it is. But what I do know, is it was waiting for her, lurking in the graveyard of left behind IPs and dormant threads until someone dug too deep. I don't know where she is, but I have a feeling that soon I'm going to find out. And I'm scared. But she's alone. She left behind a blank spot in a photograph in the crook of my arm and I remember what is missing. I remember her. That memory makes the waiting almost bearable. Sometimes someone just needs a friend.

EMPTY AISLES

It didn't make sense, the way he was standing there. Just on the other side of the automatic doors, like some kind of cardboard cutout. Standing there waiting, that fuckin' smile, toothy and wide and unexplainably unrealistic. Eyes an extreme contrast of black and white, looking at me through the glass—

"Uh, helloooo?" The guy at the register snapped, startling me.

"Gosh, I'm sorry. What did you want again? The menthol?" I said, embarrassed. I had been on my way to grab his vape pods when I noticed the guy (thing?) outside. The man sighed exasperatedly, leaning against the counter like I had ruined his night. He was tall and lanky, wearing a tuxedo that seemed to shrink whenever he moved. Dressed like some sort of gentleman, but moved like Jack Skellington.

"No. Virginia tobacco," he said impatiently.

"So sorry." I grabbed the pods from the shelf and scanned them, unable to help myself from side-eyeing the automatic doors. He was still there.

"Nineteen, twenty-six. Would you like a bag?" I asked, and he shook his head while reaching for his wallet.

"H-hey, do you see that out there? That guy?" I whispered, nodding at the automatic doors.

He inserted his card and raised his eyebrows.

"What?" he said, annoyed.

"Outside. The guy, standing there." I motioned to the entrance, at the guy who was very much still there, very much looking like a photoshopped disaster. His eyes were just as menacing as his broad smile, and he was still staring—

"Look, lady, I'm in a hurry. Places to be. Receipt?" he asked, holding his hand out. He looked at the automatic doors briefly, then back at me.

"Right. Sorry, it's my first night." I printed the receipt and handed it to him, and he stuffed it into the pocket of his slacks.

"There's nothing out there," was all he said, and walked away.

I leaned over the counter, watching the tall gentleman leave. The automatic doors opened with a *hiss,* giving a plain view of the man lurking outside. I could see him clearer now, a paper copy stuck in time and space. The gentleman paid him no mind, walking past him like there was nothing there. He didn't see his intense eyes, didn't notice his exaggerated grin. The teeth were long and rectangular; the corners pointed impossibly like a PowerPuff Girl's smile. He didn't move, didn't blink. Kept lurking even as the headlights on the gentleman's car passed over him as he drove off into the night. Just standing there. Watching me at the register.

I looked away, pretending he wasn't there. I scanned the aisles, looking for someone else, someone who could assure me I wasn't crazy. I could see two, and I found comfort in the fact I wasn't alone. In the liquor aisle, a bearded man with a ponytail and sunglasses was browsing the whiskey. Two aisles down was my manager, Katherine, who was straightening things up before she left for the night. I tried to motion for her to come over, but she wasn't paying attention.

Outside, the cartoon man watched, unmoving.

I looked at the monitor on the counter that displayed the live camera feeds. One view pointed at me, standing behind the counter. Another was at the pharmacy, which was currently closed. The view showed the counter and the dark delivery window. The third view was the liquor aisle, where the bearded man had made his selection. Lastly was the front entrance, where the cartoon man stood. Although on the screen, his toothy face was turned toward the camera.

I looked outside to see he hadn't moved at all; he was somehow watching both at once.

"What's the word?" said the bearded man, putting a bottle of Woodford Reserve on the counter. He ran a hand over his ponytail and pointed at my nametag, "Cool name, like the Disney movie. With the lions."

"Heh, thanks," I said, but I wasn't looking at him anymore. My gaze unintentionally pulled to the entrance of the store, "Hey, do you see him out there? The guy. Outside."

I scanned the whiskey and put it in a bag, while the bearded man lowered his sunglasses, his slightly glazed eyes looking outside.

"I see him," he said, and I felt a rush of relief.

"Oh, great, it's not just me—"

"He's coming in. Oh god, he's got a knife!" He said, and I leaned over to look, gripping the counter.

The cartoon man hadn't moved, his blown-up eyes still glued to me.

"Sorry, couldn't resist," he chuckled, putting his shades back on, "seriously though, there's nothing out there. Sorry, kid. Are you alright?" he asked.

I rubbed my eyes, a desperate attempt to make him disappear. But the strange cartoon man remained, still watching me through the glass.

"I'm fine. Must be my imagination, I guess." I sighed.

The man paid for his booze and left, approaching the cartoon stalker as he left. I watched him go, and he made a point to look around outside before shrugging and leaving.

I tried not to look. As the seconds crawled, I could *feel* him outside, lingering there like an antagonist from a 1930s cartoon. Silently watching, begging for my attention. Every customer that came in walked right past him, some of them even *through* him. In the end I couldn't help it, and my eyes would wander discreetly to the monitor where he would be waiting.

"Alright kid, I'm finished up. You cool with holding the fort?" Katherine said, startling me for the second time.

"Y-yeah. Hey, you ever have any issues here at night?" I asked awkwardly. To my surprise, she looked nervous.

"Whatever do you mean?" she said, and I could tell she was sweating.

"Do you see him? Out there?" I asked, pointing discreetly.

Katherine didn't look. Or blink.

"I don't see anything out there, dear." She kept her eyes on me and readjusted her purse on her shoulder.

I looked outside and at the monitor. He *was* still there.

"Look, if this is some kind of joke—" I started, but Katherine interjected.

"The first night's always rough. It's weird, working the night shift. But you'll be fine. It gets easier. Just make sure you're IDing for alcohol and tobacco sales. And try to keep the area clean." Katherine leaned over the counter and inspected my area, her eyes browsing over everything. Everything but the monitor. Once done, she started walking away.

"Everything *should* be just fine, dear. As long as you're not the only one in the store. Have a goodnight," she said, making her way to the door. When they automatically opened, she immediately turned right onto the sidewalk, scrunched up like she was warding off a winter wind. The cartoon man's eyes followed her briefly, before snapping back to me.

I started to sweat. The feeling of being stared at made me uncomfortable. I looked for the other customers, each doing a late-night run for something specific. Even though it was after ten, it was still pretty busy. I tried to pay him no mind and focus on work, restocking cigarettes and straightening candy bars in between transactions. I spent more time looking at the people walking in, so I knew I wasn't alone at least. Each time I started ignoring him, I thought of the smile and those eyes. When I looked back, he would be there. Just when I thought I'd get used to it, I couldn't help but ask the next customer if they saw him.

A tired Mother with the stroller thought I was joking.

A muscular man buying protein powder just shrugged.

The teenager buying condoms didn't even look.

The man in the Hawaiian shirt asked if I was high.

The man buying manga books *was* high.

Not a single person could see the cartoon man. I started to think I was crazy, but after a while I started to get used to it. Eventually I stopped looking all together.

By the time a mustached man came in to buy Guinness, I had stopped asking people if they could see it. I handed him back his change and told him to have a good night. Once I turned to see the next customer, I realized he was the last. From the counter I looked down the aisles and saw nothing but empty tile and shelves. With nothing else to look at, I found myself looking outside.

The cartoon man was gone.

A moment later, I heard a crash from the back of the store.

I checked the monitor, to see the delivery window busted, the distorted cartoon man rapidly moving out of frame. I could hear his footsteps, running down the aisles fast and growing louder as they approached. I whipped around to look, just in time to see him duck behind a row out of sight.

He had gotten inside. I could hear him back there, pacing back and forth.

The automatic doors opened, and a couple walked in holding hands.

The footsteps stopped.

I don't know what they're looking for, but I hope it takes them a while to find it.

PRISONER TRANSPORT

He had an air of blatant arrogance about him. Even as the transport van bucked us with every pothole in the backroad, his eyes never left mine. As he stared at me, his face would transition from emotionless to amused, sometimes offering a smile or furrowing his brow like he was some kind of AI trying to troubleshoot a human reaction. I looked away often, not wanting to feed him the attention he seemed starved for.

My eyes wandered to the floor, at the shackles around his ankles. A jingling chain swaying between his legs that seemed almost overkill for the scrawny individual it was fastened to. I found myself trailing up from the shackles, over the red jumpsuit, to the straightjacket that had been used in place of handcuffs. A thick leather strap was fastened tightly across his chest, holding him firmly in place as the van bounced down the road. The man before looked so small and helpless, like a little kid that had been cast to play a prisoner in a movie.

Stuart Cavanaugh was a high-profile prisoner transport on his way to death. Seeing him in person was almost disappointing, his lack of muscle or tattoos making him look like a pitiful vanilla suburban househusband. He was supposed to be some kind of mass murderer, a 2020 Charles Manson wannabe that had a few dozen deaths under his belt. Some kind of "master-manipulator", leaving a harrowing trail behind him wherever he seemed to shuffle. People would die gruesomely, but never by his hand. One way or another, he would always get someone to do his bidding.

No one could figure out *how* he did it.

It had become enough of a problem that the State, out of desperation, was ferrying him to the closest prison that still practiced the death penalty.

Death by lethal injection, or "whatever deems successful", effective as soon as possible.

Transport Stuart William Cavanaugh immediately, only the highest of clearances.

Extremely low profile. No news, no announcement.

This had been my first taboo transport of sorts, one that wasn't funded by the rich family of a known kidnapping or a political power move from behind the curtain. They wanted this guy gone, bad. Our route consisted mostly of erratic backroads, with a cut through the town of Dyer Falls. All in an attempt to dodge the press, and whatever theoretical peons Cavanaugh had working under him.

As he stared at me, it boggled me what was so *dangerous* about a shrimp like him. Thin, geeky glasses. Arms like toothpicks and beady little eyes. I could probably beat this man to death in four seconds. I was twice his size, and I could bench three-times his body weight. He knew it, too.

And still he stared at me, like some kind of fuckin' animal.

Another pothole shook our cabin, one that stifled a muffled groan from my colleague next to me. He readjusted on the bench and returned to browsing his phone, the popping of his gum almost inaudible under the suppression of the earplugs. The only thing of interest in the bare transport van was a first aid kit and a fire extinguisher.

The earplugs were the only known foolproof defense against Cavanaugh's bullshit. It was a rule we had to follow during the transport, one I kept hearing on repeat from the tired voice of the Commissioner.

Do not, under any circumstances, remove your earplugs.

I thought of the plugs lodged uncomfortably in my ears and couldn't help but look at Cavanaugh's face. He raised one eyebrow, much like Tim Curry in *Rocky Horror Picture Show*. The taunt was met with silence, as I had done many times before, with many people much bigger than him. His jest made me think of the gun holstered at my side, and the weight of it hanging. An incredibly expensive but equally deadly sidearm, loaded to the brim with .50 Action Express hollow-points, but that special kind that would bloom into a star-shape through the trajectory. It was grossly overpowered and by all means unnecessary, but when you contact "private" security firms to cab-ride your problem child, they "privately" outfit.

Next to me, my colleague known only as "Webber" was busy burying his nose in his phone. A major infraction by the company's standard, but this was the norm for him, even though he looked like a teenager out of his element, this was my third ride with Webber, the second of which I had witnessed him killing the transport in self defense. Brutally.

Cavanaugh watched Webber, and when he saw him looking at him, he simply winked at him and went back to perusing his phone. Tinder, from the looks of it. Cavanaugh looked to scowl at Webber, but whatever noise he made I couldn't hear. After failing to get a rise out of him, he turned back to me and settled in like he was watching a movie.

It was annoying, sure. But this was nothing.

We once had a guy who bit off his own tongue and would collect the blood in his mouth until he had enough to jet-stream our visors like that dinosaur from Jurassic Park. The worst part was, we had no idea when he actually *did* bite his tongue off. He did it silently, without emotion.

For a while, we all wobbled in silence. The ride was only supposed to be two hours, and this one felt like three already. Not a good sign, but it was how it always went. Eventually we would jump out of this shuttle, and the money would spend the same.

Cavanaugh continued to stare at me, cycling through facial expressions as we maintained eye contact. It looked very unlike him, like the actions that didn't match his face. He looked like the type to grill on a Saturday get-together, flipping burgers in khaki shorts with his socks rolled up to his knees. To see him do stupid shit like cross his eyes intentionally or make silent fart noises with his tongue was just… strange. Despite my lack of engagement, he still continued long after I stopped paying attention.

Another pothole shook the vehicle, and Webber almost dropped his phone. He proceeded to pound on the wall of the van with a gloved fist and yell something I assumed was "Settle down, you goofy bitch" before immediately going back to scrolling and swiping. Swiping right a lot, it would seem.

I shifted in my seat, trying to relieve the numbness on one side of my ass and push it to the other. My gun dug uncomfortably into my hip, and I readjusted my cell phone so the barrel wouldn't shatter the screen.

Cavanaugh watched me do this, pausing his annoying kissy face like he had suddenly discovered something of interest. His lips unpuckered and formed into a disturbing sort of ear-to-ear smile. I paid it no mind, but the sudden change in tactic was curious. Some prisoners kept to themselves. Others begged to be let go. Prisoners like Stuart were hellbent on tormenting you until you slipped. Whether it was to cause an opening or just for the satisfaction of goading was beyond me.

Stuart started mouthing words.

It was easy to ignore him at first, just simply avoid looking at his face. If I could just keep my gaze on his shackles and straight jacket, I could track his activity until we arrived at our destination. I was fine for a few minutes, and would've *stayed* fine if my ego didn't get the best of me. After all, every bull wants to be challenged. I looked at his face and tried my best to make out what he was saying through his slow lip-synching. I expected something like "rent-a-cop" or "pussy" but what I deciphered was nothing along those lines. No jab or provoking insult. Just two words said plainly over and over.

"Yellow Ball."

I became instantly anxious. My guts felt like they were melting together, and I got the sudden urge to throw open the back door and run as far away from the van as I could. I can't really put the feeling into words. It felt like death itself. Like I was being forced to watch someone get hit by a car, but the car was still a block away, gaining in the distance.

He had my attention now, and he knew it. I looked at Webber, who was still glued to his phone. Cavanaugh sat and waited, smug and wrapped in his straight jacket with his eyebrows raised like he had moved a chess piece and was awaiting my turn.

I started to sweat, and my breathing felt uncontrolled and labored. His prying eyes made me self conscious, and painfully aware of the things near me.

The tight fit of my body armor.

The heavy weight of the gun in its holster.

The lodged shape of the phone in my pocket.

I tried to look away from Cavanaugh, but every time I broke eye contact, I could hear those two words like he was speaking inside my head. Yellow Ball. Yellow Ball. Yellow Ball. His arrogance only frustrated me, and I couldn't understand how it was getting to me so suddenly. I had been on so many transport jobs with all shapes and sizes, and *this* dweeb was getting under my skin?

My face and ears were getting hot. It was hard to breathe in the armor, like someone was sitting on my chest. Despite my discomfort, I reminded myself of the important rule stressed by the Commissioner.

Do not, under any circumstances, remove your earplugs.

Cavanaugh took a deep breath and mouthed the two words again. *Yellow Ball.*

I pinched the ends of each ear plug and pulled them out, letting in the sound of the bumpy road and the van's engine. Cavanaugh smiled.

"You say something to me, punk?" I said, quieter than I expected.

Webber didn't hear. It was just me and the prisoner now.

Cavanaugh said nothing for a moment, and I could see his pupils shifting as they rapidly stared into each of my eyes individually. He was calm, collected. When he finally spoke, it was hushed and gentle.

"Do you think the bones of a child taste different than the bones of an adult?"

There was something icy about his words. It made me sick to my stomach.

"What did you just say?" I asked, a little louder.

"Their bones. I've never tried cannibalism, but I've always wondered if it would taste differently."

"You best keep your mouth shut for the rest of the ride, or we're gonna have a fuckin' problem. They said nothing about the condition we had to deliver you in," I said, seething. Having given my warning, I started to return them to my ears.

"Scary," Cavanaugh *tsked,* and tilted his head forward, "but tell me. Was it a spontaneous gift, or did she pick it out herself?" he asked.

"I don't know what you're talking about."

"Sure, sure. What do you think their last thoughts are, as they're dying? Do they ask for Mommy? Or do they ask for *God?*"

The words raked down my back like ice. I thought of the gun, and how much better I would feel if it was in my hand.

"Shut your fucking mouth, or I'll knock all of your teeth out. I'm sure they'd like that where you're going. Very beneficial." As I leaned forward, the prisoner clicked his tongue.

"Cute. Just put it all on the table. Big strong man like yourself. How many have you preached the same threat? Is that what 'does it' for you?" he hissed. "Funny story. I once asked a man to pull out his own teeth. One by one. He cried and sobbed and there was so much blood, but he still did it. Best part is, he still had enough strength to strangle the *DoorDash* driver when she dropped off the food I was going to eat in front of him."

"Sure, sure," I said, looking at Webber. He was still distracted, slightly turned and hunched over his phone. I went to nudge him when the prisoner spoke again, and even though I didn't want to, I listened.

"Is it weird that I feel more pity for fish? A dog will follow you loyally to its own demise, but fish, fish *know*. You can see it in their eyes, swimming around as you pour them into the blender. Like they knew their owners would betray them in the long run."

I looked away. The earplugs were rolling away on the vibrating floor. One of them stopped against Webber's boot. He didn't notice, and the prisoner was still talking.

"It would be so easy. Probably kicking it around right now. Right in the front yard, right under Mommy's nose. You think you could get there in time? *I don't know, really.* Scoop her right up. Like she was never there. You think she'd know the difference between cereal and thumbtacks? Do you think she'd care?"

My blood was boiling. My hand squeezed, suddenly feeling heavy.

"I'd kill you," was all I could say.

"Would you? Or would you join for breakfast?"

"You're fuckin' sick. You know that?"

"Yeah, I'm sick alright. Sick of being in these restraints. I think I've hung around here long enough. It was interesting to see the government dogs scramble in their attempt to control me. The whole time, thinking they *had* me. It's hilarious, isn't it? They're so sure of themselves. Just a bunch of people looking to collect a check. Like you. Not professional in the least. You couldn't even keep the plugs in."

I stared at him, grinding my teeth together so hard it hurt. He smirked at me briefly, before turning to Webber.

He had finally looked up from his phone.

"Did you remove your hearing protection?" he asked, immediately alarmed.

His look of confusion was reduced to a malformed rupture of gore as his visor shattered in a spray of red. The gunshot was deafening, ringing off the inside of the van. The gun in my hand was smoking, the large, ejected casing bouncing off the floor.

"Oh god, what the fuck—" was all I could muster, before the van slammed on its brakes. I was thrown into the still bleeding corpse of Webber, struggling to stay upright as his body rag-dolled into mine. The eviscerated melon that remained for a head leaked profusely under the helmet, splashing at my armor in hot bursts. My boots slipped under the spatter, and as I tried to regain my composure, Cavanaugh remained perfectly in place in his harness. Webber's smartphone screen shattered as it landed face down.

"Oh my, what have you done? Those guns just *go off* don't they?" he taunted.

"You son of a bitch!" I spat, whipping the gun around. I shot him twice, center mass, the gun barking loudly with each squeeze of the trigger. Each blast more deafening than the last. I looked to see both of my shots had missed; one shattering his shackles, the other blasting the hinge that held the strap over his chest. The gun was aiming on its own.

Once the van stopped, I heard the sounds of the drivers throwing their doors open from the outside. Cavanaugh laughed and stood from his seat, shaking the restraints off awkwardly from the confines of his straight jacket.

"What!? How did you... how?" was all I could say. I pointed the large gun at him, but couldn't seem to squeeze the trigger. I couldn't seem to do anything.

"Here's the deal. When your buddies open that door, they're going to hold their fire. Instead of restraining me, one is going to see how many long sticks he can fit in his throats until he... passes away. The other is going to be so kind to remove this jacket, right before he chooses the same makeover you gave your friend."

"Bullshit. They'll stop you," I said, wanting to grab and restrain him but unable to find the will. My body simply refused to respond. Cavanaugh crouched next to me and leaned forward to whisper in my ear. The shouting outside was getting louder, but I couldn't make out what they were saying. Through the ringing in my ears, all I could hear was the prisoner.

"Or they won't. Tell me, your wife and child, do you think they would miss you if I took them? Do you think they would hear you if you spoke to them? Do you think they would reach out to you if you were running after them? Would they cry for help, or would they smile and wave? Think about *that* when you grab that fire extinguisher over there."

I looked at the red can fastened to the wall as the voices boomed outside the door. Cavanaugh leaned in closer, his breath hot in my ear.

"I'm sure you'll find the fine line between consciousness and concussion. And when you wake up, use that cell phone of yours and call for backup. Let them know what happened. *Remind them of their fear for me.*"

With that, Cavanaugh stood and faced the door. I dropped my gun and shuffled to the extinguisher, looking sadly at Webber as I freed the extinguisher from its housing. The prisoner faced the doors as the shouts reached their peak outside the vehicle, like he was about to walk onto a stage. I removed my helmet and laid on the floor, blood soaking into my suit as I held the extinguisher above my head. I told myself I looked that way so I could watch him go, but I knew I did it to better aim for my temple. With a farewell, Cavanaugh looked at me with one last smirk, before facing the doors ahead of him, just in time for them to fly open. As sunlight spilled in around his silhouette, I pulled the extinguisher down as hard as I could.

It was dusk when I awoke. My vision collected through the haze of neon pink, and I tried to remember where I was. A throbbing pressed on the inside of my skull and my ears rang. I tried to get to my feet, slipping as I steadied myself. Through the light of the setting sun, I saw the blood-soaked floor, and the slumped corpse of Webber against the wall of the van.

It came back slowly: the prisoner, the earplugs, the gunshot.

I looked at the fire extinguisher lying on its side, and the echoing words that followed.

Let them know what happened.

I shambled out of the van and jumped out, feeling the crunch of gravel under my boots. We were on a dirt road, heavy forestation lining each side of the path. The van had skidded to a stop on the shoulder in the middle of nowhere. The dizziness faded in and out as I squinted at the sun that poked through the trees. My legs were shaking, and as I tried to get them under control, I found myself vomiting instead. Through the pounding in my head and convulsing of my guts, I saw the first corpse in the road.

It was laying on its side, its face unrecognizable through the gore that splattered the inside of the visor. The top of the helmet was exploded outward, a collection of flies swarming the trail of gory matter that followed the gunshot. The gun was still clutched in their hand.

Opposite the gunshot victim was a second body, almost posed for display. The corpse was on its knees, head held back like they were yelling at the sky. Protruding from their mouth was a cluster of misshapen sticks. Some of them larger and more jagged than the others, each of them looked to fit impossibly in the horribly stretched mouth.

Between the two bodies was a folded red prison jumpsuit and a discarded straight jacket.

Remind them of their fear for me.

I felt for my phone, deciding it was time to call the police. My hands were shaking, and it took me several tries to properly hit the power button. When the screen finally lit up, I could only stare at the screen with sobering clarity.

The lock screen was a picture of my daughter, her joyous smile captured mid laugh. Held tight in her arms was a bright yellow ball.

Rainbow Road

Everybody has that story they tell. The memory hangs out in the backseat of your mind, waiting for the right moment to chip in the group and share your childhood fear. The first time you were scared, the first time you felt *real* fear. By the time you tell the story, you almost forgot it had even happened. Maybe it was just a fever dream you had as a child, maybe the circumstances were fabricated by your adolescent imagination. Even though you doubt it even happened, the memory still lingers, held dearer than what should've been your cherished moments when you were younger. When you think back, you don't remember the first time you tied your shoes, or the first basketball hoop you made, you think of that story. It's there waiting, almost as if it has unfinished business with you, like you're not allowed to move on from it yet. And you tell the story, with a big smile on your face, the ones around you laughing so hard they ugly cry, because your experience was so real and relatable, it could've happened to them just as easily as it happened to you. Once you've shared it, you feel better, and the memory retreats back to its den, hibernating until the stars align and it can torment you once more.

I was at work when the opportunity presented itself. The night shift was over, and we were all in the locker room, exchanging thick uniforms and heavy boots for crocs and basketball shorts. Terry was telling a story about his fear of rats, his face a half grin as he struggled to get through it without laughing. I was on the bench unlacing my boots.

"Dude, I had been looking for this fucking rat for weeks. I would always see it out of the corner of my eye, the little bastard scurrying around when I was trying to sleep. Turns out it had made a nest in the box spring. I had been sleeping on it, dude," Terry says, shivering as he thought back.

The other guys laughed; a cackling chorus of grown men amused by someone else's demise. I laughed as well; Terry was well known for his fear of rodents and was heckled about it constantly. They went back and forth over the details as I kicked off my boots. How did they deal with it? Did they burn the mattress? Did he let it sleep there forever? As the laughter dies down, I think of my story, and wonder if I should tell it. At first I shiver at the thought, but before I know it I'm grinning and dying to let it out.

The old memory resurfaces like a shark from the deep.

A story that happened twenty-three years ago.

A story about a beaver.

"Alright, I got one. Terry, you'll especially like this," I say, standing up.

The guys listen, still wiping the tears from the rat in Terry's mattress. It's been so long since I've thought of the beaver, and the details flood in as I picture it in my head.

"Alright, so this was a really long time ago, when I was a kid. I think I was five or six? Anyway, I used to live in this trailer park, over on rainbow road. That one over there, by the highway." I vaguely point north as I close my locker. There are a few interjections before the story continues.

"Wait, *rainbow* road?"

"Oh yeah, I know that place."

"My aunt used to live there."

"You used to live in *the cans,* Jay? Over by 94?" Terry asked.

"Yeah, long time ago. Been ages," I say and resume the story.

"Anyway, it was in the summer back in the 90s, and we were all playing outside, not shit to do. There was nothing but trailers and a long line of mailboxes. We were all poor and there was no playground to play at, so most of the time all the kids would just group up and we would walk around and play with rocks and shit. We would walk around all day, and our parents didn't care as long as we didn't go by the highway. They were always worried about a car hitting us," I say, and in my mind I can hear the sounds of cars passing by.

"So, there's like five of us, playing by this trailer that didn't have anyone living in it, and all of a sudden one of the kids just freezes and says 'Uh, what is that?' We all look, and sitting on the porch of the trailer is this big fuckin' beaver, just staring at us," I say, the beaver's black eyes and teeth clear in my mind. I shudder at the thought of it.

The guys laugh, and Terry visibly cringes.

"So, we're all frozen there, all of us too scared to move. We had never seen one before. We're all terrified at this beaver, and it's just staring us down, and we're just waiting for it to rush us. Like it was going to eat our bones or something. Real scary shit. Anyway, there's this girl standing next to me, I think her name was Kirsten? She whispers to me and says 'Go get your mom, we'll stay here'. My house was the closest, only two trailers away. So I run home, thinking this beaver is gonna chase me, like it's some kind of horror movie or something. And I run and tell my mom, and she starts yelling about us playing by the highway, and the whole time I'm just scared shitless this beaver was gonna eat my friends by the time we got back."

"No shit? What happened? Did it attack you guys?" One of the guys says, and I laugh.

"No, my mom grabbed a broom and we went back and she pretty much shooed it off. But I still can't shake the look that beaver gave us. We really thought it was gonna eat us. Fuckin' hate beavers, dude." I finish the story, and they all laugh, all except Terry, who looks like he found something new to add to his list of rodent fears.

I chuckle to myself at the thought of the memory, feeling a bit of the weight lift from my mind. Like a shred of the trauma has healed. After some brief shit talking, we all punch out and leave the building, everyone walking to their cars with their heads held high, now that the day's work is done. I wave goodbye and get in my car. As I watch the other guys pull away and drive off, I find myself sitting there in silence, pondering the story I told.

I think of the beaver story, with its nasty buck teeth and black eyes. I think of how funny it is looking back, and I hear the laughter of the guys in my head. The longer I think about it, the more the laughter fades away, and the more I hear screams instead. I think of the story, suddenly feeling guilty, wondering why I said it in the first place. Maybe after all this time, I'm just trying to make myself feel better.

In my head, the memory unravels.

I think of the story, and how it's a lie.

There is no beaver.

There never was.

I lean my head on the steering wheel. I hadn't thought of it in so long; I was sure I could leave it in the past. I hear the screams, my own and those of the other children. I think of the unexplainable memory pushed so far in the back of my mind.

Kirsten was my first crush. I remember her freckled face and short hair, and a little red ball cap she would always wear. Everyone thought she looked like a boy, but I thought she was pretty, even though I really didn't know the meaning of the word. She lived across the park in a yellow trailer and would always come over to play when all the kids got together. There were five of us and only a few of us had bikes, so if we all wanted to play together, we would usually walk around and play with sticks and stuff like that. Sometimes we'd play tag or red rover, but that day we found ourselves just walking around bored. The trailer park was an oval formation, the mobile homes placed in a loop with a circular road in the middle. It was surrounded by trees, except for the side I lived on that was tucked into a hill that the highway was built on.

It was nice outside that day. Our parents booted all of us out of the house so we could enjoy the weather and so they could have some peace and quiet. They only had two rules: don't talk to strangers, and don't go near the highway. The park wasn't fenced off or anything, and you could hear cars and trucks flying past all day long. We were walking the road in a little group, doing laps without any real plan. We continued like this for a while, every time passing each other's houses and telling jokes, sometimes nagging our parents if we could come in yet.

Two trailers down from mine, was the only vacant lot in the park. Nobody lived there as far as we knew. The driveway was always empty, with a concrete slab in place of a trailer. The backyard consisted of an uphill climb through the trees that led straight to the highway. It was silly, but between the emptiness of the vacant trailer and the sounds of the highway, it felt like that specific lot was separate from the rest of the park. I don't know if it was the shade from the overgrown trees, the layers of old pine needles on the ground, or the dead sticks scattered about the unkempt yard. There was always something about it, like it was in its own little bubble.

That's when the dares started.

On that particular boring day, one of the kids had the idea that for every lap we took around the park, one of us would have to step foot on the lot. The mini barren zone always gave us the willies, and the thought of pushing the boundaries of the scary property gave us all a shot of rebellious adrenaline. At first I thought it was scary, and I was worried about getting into trouble. But when I saw Kirsten perk up giddily, I decided to play along so I could impress her. Whatever I could do to seem cool and make her smile.

It felt like we were doing something *bad,* and the excitement of who would go the furthest would hurry us along as we walked each lap around the park. We would take turns, each lap one of us would walk into the driveway, the next would go up and touch one of the sticks, etc. I remember on one of my turns I crept into the yard behind the little driveway and sprinted back, comically yelling like something was chasing me all the way back to the road. Looking back, it was immature, but it felt like the unexplainable gloom was always trying to nip at your heels.

Hours passed as we repeated the cycle. A lap around the park, then one of us running in. There, toward the end, we were jogging around the park, all of us excited to take our next turn. As time went on, kids would get called to come back home, and the group began to dwindle. We started to push faster, each of us paranoid to be the next kid to be walking away from the fun with our head hung low as the others laughed. Before we knew it, almost everyone had gone home.

Everyone except Kirsten and I.

I remember it being my turn next, and the both of us running back to do one more stunt. The sun was starting to set, and we knew any minute our parents would call us. I remember running alongside her, sweating and gasping for breath as the laps tired our legs. Kirsten huffed and laughed as she ran, holding the bill of her ball cap so it wouldn't fly off. This one would be the craziest, I thought. It was my chance to really impress her. I would go into the woods this time, maybe even close to the highway. When we came to the driveway, however, we both stopped. Our smiles faded, and the fun seemed to fizzle away in an instant.

There was an old rundown trailer on the vacant lot, like it had appeared out of thin air. The dingy green paint was peeling, and the porch looked like it was about to collapse. The drapes in the windows were nicotine-stained and ratty, barely concealing the complete darkness within. As I watched, the front door creaked open slightly. From the darkness within, a groaning whisper escaped.

No lights on inside. No car in the driveway.

"What the…" I looked at Kirsten for validation, but she wasn't even looking at the trailer.

She was looking at a woman in the yard.

It was then I noticed her, off towards the trees. She was standing with her back turned, and even though we couldn't see her face, we knew something was horribly wrong. Once white clothes were heavily stained and ripped up, fitting awkwardly on her frame. One of her legs was bent backwards, and one of her arms was missing, a heavy drizzle of blood oozing from the stump. Despite how mangled she was, she stood perfectly still.

We just stood there for a time, both of us silently gawking at her. The air was chilly, like a temperature drop before a bad storm. Kirsten looked at me, the color drained from her face. Without a word, both of us looked in the direction of our homes.

To see which one was closest to run to.

When we looked back in the direction of the woman, we noticed she had silently moved closer. Her back was still turned, but we could see the damage clearer. Horribly road-rashed muscle, black streaks on her clothing from the combination of tires and asphalt.

"What do we do?" Kirsten whispered, her voice a whimper.

"I… I don't know," I managed, my bladder suddenly feeling like it was going to burst. I remember my legs shaking "maybe we could—"

Ahead of us, the woman turned. Not in a normal sense, but like she blinked to facing a different direction. Like someone had flipped a paper over while our eyes were closed. The sight of her face provoked a gasp from both of us. I was crying now, filled with the confused fear you have when you wake from a terrible nightmare.

The woman was missing her bottom jaw, and with it, half of her upper face. The only identifiable thing left of her top jaw was a hanging bloody tongue and her two front teeth. A single eye looked at me angrily, the pupil surrounded by the dark splotching of burst blood vessels. No sound emitted from the woman, but seeing the way she stood there frozen in place, I couldn't explain it. Something was just wrong. Horribly wrong.

"Your house is closer. *Run. Get your mom,*" Kirsten whispered, her voice trembling. Her breath came out as fog.

The mangled woman remained in place, but her single eye was looking at Kirsten now. Before our eyes, she blinked forward, three feet closer in Kirsten's direction.

I wanted to reach for her hand, but it seemed so far away. I looked at her freckled face, tears streaming down them as she stood as still as possible.

"B-but…" I whimpered, and the mangled woman blinked again. A few more feet, facing my direction. Without a single sound, the eye glared angrily at me. I sobbed as she grew closer once more. Her eye dilated in response to my noise, and her only remaining hand twitched.

"Just *go!*" Kirsten's shout echoed across the park, rustling birds from the trees.

I turned and ran, my shoes skipping down the sidewalk. I couldn't breathe. I looked over my shoulder, the terrified look on Kirsten's face as the woman shifted closer burning itself into my memory. Even as she drew closer to her, Kirsten kept her eyes on me, weeping silently as she watched me go.

As she made sure I could get away.

My house was only a few trailers away, but I felt like I was running across town. My legs were weak, my thoughts raced. The further I got from that yard, the warmer it seemed to get. The sun began to feel hot, but my blood was still cold. I tried to focus on the patio door to my home, where my mom would be inside, where I could get her to save us. The adrenaline crawled across me like ice, and I thought just for a moment that everything was going to be okay. It was all just a nightmare. My mom would show up and fix things, just like she did all the other times I had a problem.

By the time I made it to my yard, Kirsten screamed.

The shrill cry of terror and pain made me stumble, and I fell to the ground. I looked behind me frantically, but Kirsten and the woman were gone. All I could see was an empty yard, and I started shaking. I looked to my front door, then back to where I left Kirsten. I didn't know what to do. I thought it would take too much time to get my mom. I shook and sobbed on the ground as my adolescent brain tried to compute the right thing to. I just wanted to help. I just wanted her to be ok. In my fear, I wet myself.

Behind me, Kirsten screamed again. She was getting further away.

I got back on my feet and ran back to the phantom trailer, cursing myself for leaving her alone. We should've just run together. Why didn't we just run together?

"No, no-no-no," I sobbed, my stomach desperately wanting to purge its contents.

My legs begged me to stop, but I pushed them forward. My sneakers scuffed the sidewalk as the hot trail of urine ran down my leg. I ran past the neighbor's lot and rounded the corner of the trailer that shouldn't exist.

When I got to the yard, I couldn't see either of them. The same awful chill returned, and a mist was working its way across the yard. My eyes followed the source, a ghostly fog that was cascading down the porch steps. It was spilling from the trailer, the tiny crack of the door, and the darkness inside. The doorway groaned as the fog billowed out, widening slightly with a creak. The windows started to bleed, and the shutters shriveled like burning plastic. The worst thing of all was what I saw in the trees.

The woman was dragging Kirsten by her arm, painfully whipping her around every time she blinked up the hill.

Dragging her towards the highway.

I screamed for her to stop. The mangled woman paused only for a moment, her destroyed mouth reverberating with what I could only describe as a *snarl*. Kirsten howled in pain as she clawed at the woman, the bruising grip worsening as her helpless hands passed through a seemingly ethereal body. Unnatural and horrible, the mangled woman ascended the hill, every freeze-frame blink bringing them closer to the roaring traffic.

I ran after them. I made it halfway across the yard before my foot caught something, sending me face first into the foggy ground. My palms slapped the ground, softening the fall on something rough and sharp. I tried to get up, but something grabbed at my ankle, winding tight like rope as I tried to shake it free. Kirsten's screaming got weaker the further she got from me. The fog dispersed as I thrashed to be free, and through it saw no grass at all. The canvas of pine needles and leaves was replaced by hundreds, *thousands* of dead birds. I looked behind me and shouted for help, hoping to see my mom, or one of the neighbors rushing to help. I saw nothing but an empty street and twisting vines wrapping around my ankles.

When I turned back to the hill, Kirsten was holding on to a tree, trying to resist the mangled woman's grip. Her fingers clung to the bark, and her sneakers formed jagged ruts in the earth. This slowed the woman for a moment, but she retaliated by breaking Kirsten's wrist. The wet snap followed by the worst sound I have ever heard.

I want to say I broke free. Sometimes when I dream I break free from the vines, and I make it through the fog. Other times "grown-ups" show up, and everything is ok. Sometimes Kirsten has the strength to free herself, and we get away together. And sometimes there is no mangled woman at all, it's only a beaver. In reality, the true ending can never be denied, the version where my scream can only join hers.

Scream as I reach helplessly, and the mangled woman makes it to the road.

I watch as the truck takes them, an impact so forceful and sudden they simply blink away, leaving nothing but streaks on the highway, and a hat on the wind that matched the color.

The fog recedes into the trailer, like a movie being rewound.

The blood seeps back into the glass, and the curtains unshrivel.

The warmth returns and the parents flock outside, mortified as they press me for answers. In time my screaming fades, replaced by the howling of sirens in the distance.

I look up from the steering wheel and dry my tears. The parking lot is empty, and everyone else has left work except me. I think of the images in my head, the weeping eyes I can't unsee. Cries I can't seem to forget.

When I start my car and shift out of park, I think about the years that have passed by. I think of how I never really spoke to my friends again after that day, and how everyone seemed to chalk it up to two kids who were never supposed to play by the highway. The park seemed to fall apart after that, Kirsten's parents moving first with my family to follow. I heard some sort of mass exodus followed; a tiny little park reduced to nothing but a memory. Another traffic accident, another poor child lost.

Tonight, instead of taking my usual route, I took a detour. I take the expressway until I see a road, one so ignored and unkempt you wouldn't know it was there if it wasn't for the reflecting green sign. A sign faded and almost illegible with age. A sign that reads "Rainbow Road."

I turn onto the winding path, one that feels more like the entrance to a cemetery than a backroad. My car rolls over broken pavement and traverses potholes until I see something in the distance, the only landmark in the otherwise empty place that has been consumed by weeds and overgrowth.

As I approach the line of old rusted mailboxes, I slow down. Ahead is the concrete circle, but there are no homes. Only a loop that's been slowly swallowed by the forest surrounding it. My headlights cut through the unnatural dark, the special kind that engulfs in the middle of nowhere. I think of a hot summer day, and a bunch of bored kids with nothing to do. Letting my car idly crawl, I pull into the loop and survey my surroundings.

On Rainbow Road, there are no mobile units to be seen. Each passing slab of the empty lot looks like a gravestone, a gritty reminder of young little lives that will be forever changed. I pass by Kirsten's old lot and think of her freckled face. The way she laughed, and the way she would roll her eyes when I made stupid jokes. I pass by the old lots of my friends' houses and wonder where they're at in the world. I pass by the lot where my home used to be and think of my mother. A time before the therapy I went through, a time before she started talking less and less.

Driving past the old vacant lot, I see no mangled woman and no green trailer. Only the lights of cars flying down the highway on the hill beyond. I look at this one longer, expecting to see something more, something of meaning. I look over the weathered surface of its foundation, years of rain slowly chipping away at the concrete. The grass that has overtaken the driveway, the thin layer of gravel reclaimed by the earth. I stare into the trees; I look at every wicked branch in the night. I search for those twisted limbs and malformed face and wonder if it's hiding somewhere in there. I listen for screams and find cicadas instead. Nothing but empty lots, overgrown grass, and fleeing rodents.

When I reach the end of the circle, I see the exit and stop. I see the winding road, and how it's been so long since I've been here. How I'll have no reason to come back. I let off the brake and keep turning left, going over the same vacant spaces again, but this time I think of the good times. I think of every dare that didn't end in tragedy. I think of every boring summer day where we climbed trees or played tag. I think of every smile Kirsten made and how it would give me butterflies in my stomach. When I reach the end of the circle, I decide to go again, my head filled with laughter and smiles, the kind no longer thought by a late-twenties man. When that one's finished it leads to another, and another, each passing tree and remembered back yard spawning memories long buried under the suffering and loss long ago. Memories deserving remembrance. I kept on the loop for a while, holding the same angle on the wheel as I drove in a circle into the late hours of the night. I thought of many memories, reliving them like they were yesterday. Until something changed.

The flashing strobe was blinding and unexpected, and part of me wondered how I didn't even see it coming in the first place. The squad car must have followed me with its lights off for a while, and I was none the wiser. I pulled my car over, right in front of where my old house used to be.

Putting it in park, I sighed as he ran my plates. The cop took their time, both of our engines running idly in the middle of nowhere. When they finally emerged from their car, I had my license and registration ready. I rolled down the window in time to see an old officer, headlights illuminating a mustached face, white with age. When I offered my paperwork, he waved it off with a question.

"What are you doing out here this time of night, kid? Gettin' high? Gettin' drunk?" he asked impatiently as he looked inside my car.

"No. Just visiting a friend, I guess," I said, and he blinked at me.

"Very funny. You know how many times I get called out here? Look, you kids come out here, screwing around, shootin' up, causing trouble where there's no reason for it. I thought maybe after they set fire to the last trailer out here and we leveled it with the dozer, that would be the end of it. But now you're here, driving circles until dispatch picks it up. There ain't nothin' out here, kid. Either you're lying, or you got the wrong address," he said sternly, his frown curving his mustache.

"She passed away a long time ago, she was hit by a truck. On the highway," I said, and there was an immediate sadness in his eyes.

"I'm sorry to hear that," he said, and collected himself. "That was a long time ago, but I remember it clearly. I was first on the scene. Terrible, terrible thing. The family brought flowers out here for years... and after everyone moved away, they were the last people who came by that weren't trying to cause trouble. But after a while, they stopped coming. Now this place is just an overgrown hole," he said solemnly, trailing off.

I thought of the family visiting each year, and the thought of long-wilted flowers deeply saddened me. I looked around the park as the officer collected himself, looking over the empty lots until my eyes rested on that particular one two doors down from mine. I felt the icy chill crawl over me again, but the officer's voice pulled me away.

"You… you're that boy. I never thought I'd see you again, let alone recognize you."

"Yeah. I haven't been here since it happened. Felt like I had to stop by," I said, peering through the lights at him.

"Well, I'm sorry I gave you such a rough time. And I'm sorry about your friend. People like to come out here and cause trouble. The park was never the same after that, and once everyone moved out, it was a hot spot for squatters and the like for a while. It's private property, and the owner calls and raises hell every time he sees people out here. I understand you're paying respects, but I'm gonna have to ask you to leave. I'll follow you out," he said, and started to leave.

Without much to say, I just nodded and rolled up my window. The officer started walking away, and I watched his silhouette shrink in the side mirror as he made his way to his car. When he reached the door he stopped, his hand pausing as he reached for the handle. After a moment, he turned around and started walking back.

I waited for the mustached face to come into view and rolled the window down again.

"Hey, kid?" he asked, his brow furrowing a little.

"Yeah?" I said. The air was feeling chillier, a light fog rolling over the road. The sight of it made me sick to my stomach.

"Back then. When the accident happened, and I arrived on the scene… you kept saying the same things over and over. 'Green trailer. Lady in the woods.'" he said, leaning on the door.

"I remember," I say, but I'm not looking at him anymore. My eyes are held ahead.

"Are you sure that's what you saw? Are you sure that's what happened?" he asked, and I could feel him studying my face.

"I'm positive. No doubt in my mind. Why?" I ask, looking to the side of the road, to the darkness beyond the headlights.

"When we arrived, there was no trailer. There wasn't any woman in the woods, either. Asked every resident in the park, nobody saw anything. We searched for miles, thinking maybe you were right, and someone had fled the scene. Even got a helicopter."

"Did you find anyone?" I said, gripping the steering wheel.

"Nobody."

"Ah." In the dark I trace the faint outline of something ahead, rectangular.

"But here's the thing. After talking to all the neighbors, we spoke to the landlord. When we mentioned what you said you saw, he turned white. Almost fainted. Said it was impossible. Said he had been running the park for over twenty years, and in all that time, there had only been one green trailer. In the 80s," he said, and paused to chew his lip.

"A young couple used to live there. Pretty young woman, with a drunk for a husband. Whenever he wasn't sunk in a bottle, he was getting into drugs. Always late with rent. Always yelling and screaming at each other. He said sometimes when they fought, he would beat her up pretty bad. She would walk around the loop, waiting for her husband to calm down or fall asleep, said she would ask for help from the neighbors, knocking on doors as she went. They helped at first, but it happened a lot, they said. But she would always go back home. They would make up, and things would quiet for a while. But it would always get bad again. Back then, it was a different time. Police didn't do much to help her, I'm afraid. After a while, they stopped taking her calls. Not long after that, the neighbors stopped helping altogether. It was just a thing that happened."

The fog started to get thicker, but the officer didn't seem to notice.

"One night, after an especially bad fight, he beat her up real bad and left. Took the car and left her there. Landlord said she came out eventually. Limping, her face all swollen. Mumbling his name as she walked the loop in the middle of the night. Waiting for him to come back, I guess. But he never did. And she kept walking, even after everyone put their lights out for the night. When morning came, she was gone."

Through the fog I could see the outline of windows in the rectangular shape, and the dark structure of a porch.

"Police found her on the highway. Hit and run. Nobody knows if it was grief taking hold, or if she was just trying to catch a ride into town. Afterward, they pulled the trailer from that lot, and never put another one on it. Never allowed another green one, either."

I thought of Kirsten's scream and the floating ball cap.

"Look, kid, I don't know what you saw that day. But I'm sorry. About the whole thing. And I'm sorry you lost your friend," the officer said, and patted his hand on the hood awkwardly.

"Do you see it now?" I asked, pointing forward.

The officer raised his eyebrows and looked into the distance. I watched as his face softened with worry, and his eyes narrowed on what lay ahead. Without a word, he grabbed his flashlight and aimed it in the yard. With a faint 'click' the beam cut through the dark, and he panned it slowly around the property.

I watched it shine over the fog, and shine on a familiar, dingy green paint.

Ratty, stained drapes.

And a mangled figure at the end of the yard.

"I don't see anything, kid," he said, and shut off his flashlight.

I looked into the darkness, transfixed by what I knew was still standing there.

"Me neither. Sorry for causing trouble. You have a good night, officer," I said, and started rolling up my window.

He looked like he wanted to stop me, but in the end he let me go. I drove past the empty lots and rusty mailboxes, keeping my eyes forward until I was through the winding road that led out of the park. I didn't realize I was holding my breath until I was turning back onto the main roads. Once I was out, the icy feeling withered away, and I was welcomed by the comfort of green traffic lights.

As I left the park behind me, I released my grip on the wheel and felt the tension in my shoulders melt away. I sighed exhaustedly, keeping my foot on the gas until I made it to the cloverleaf that led me here. I took the ramp quickly, knowing the highway would overlook the park and ultimately take me home. I don't know why I took that way, whether it was just me being defiant, or maybe I just felt like I had to. Or maybe, inside the safety of my car, I thought I would be alright.

Merging onto the highway, I sped onto the overlook and could see the empty park in its wooded sanctuary. Below, I could see the slow-moving headlights of the officer leaving.

The fog and trailer were gone, and with it, the mangled woman.

I returned my eyes to the road, just in time to see a hitch-hiker walking on the shoulder. They walked slowly, leisurely kicking rocks as they went. As I approached, they stopped and looked at me, slowly waving as I rapidly approached.

It was a little girl, with a freckled face and a red ball cap.

When I checked the rear-view mirror, she was gone.

THE SWAN

I remember the day we met; seeing her sitting in the front yard alone, eyeing the moving truck curiously as she fidgeted with a dirty stuffed animal, a little head of long blonde hair blowing in the wind. In a strange way I think of it as a destined friendship, despite the two of us being doomed children in the middle of nowhere. It was the day I moved in with my grandmother; an unfortunate fresh start on the outskirts of town, far away from a normal life and even further from the empty house left behind after the death of my parents. My grandmother, long widowed by the loss of my grandfather, took me in with what I assumed as a child was "welcomed and loving, but perhaps reluctantly unprepared arms". I would later learn that my grandmother was simultaneously serving as next *and* last of kin.

After getting the bleak tour of my grandmother's cluttered house, she showed me to where I would start staying, a small room that laid bare save for a single bed and antique dresser. I only had a few boxes of things left to my name, ones the movers had stacked in the middle of the room to already clutter the only neat room in the house. I remember my grandmother telling me two things before leaving me to unpack alone:

"You're very handsome, you look just like your grandfather."

"Drunk driving is a sin, and whoever robbed you of your parents is rotting in hell."

And with that, she left me in the incredibly dim room to make me something to eat. I remember just sitting on my bed and looking at the boxes, unsure if it mattered to actually open them. Losing your parents at seven years old has a habit of making you painfully aware and dull. In the days of hushed adult whispers leading up to moving out of town, I contemplated the purpose of my continued existence in the absence of my parents. With every-thing feeling so dark, I didn't see the point of opening the boxes or doing anything at all. That was until I heard something hit my window.

For a while, I just stared at the window, dumbfounded. There was nothing to do in her house, which seemed packed wall-to-wall with collectibles, and a cabinet full of bottles that my grandfather had collected. No video games, no toys. From my sunken perch on the bed I watched the window, wondering if I had actually heard the noise or just imagined it. Soon the sound happened again, in the form of a rock hitting the window. When I gathered the cour-age to saunter over and look, I could see the girl from next door. She froze when I saw her, one hand poised to throw another pebble, the other holding the stuffed animal in the crook of her arm. When I opened it, she dropped the pebble and came over, standing on her tippy toes to introduce herself.

"My name's Penny. Why are you here?" she asked shyly, bouncing on her toes.

"I just moved in. My parents died," I said, mostly mumbling.

"I'm sorry. My mommy ran away when I was a baby. You wanna be friends?"

I didn't understand the bruises on her arms or why she had them. I didn't understand how dark and empty the world suddenly became, and why I still had to be a part of it. I didn't understand a lot when I was younger, but there was one thing I clearly under-stood.

Penny and I would, in fact, be friends.

It took me a while to come out of my shell, but I never fully made it back out. I didn't talk very much, something Penny accepted quickly. Neither of us spoke much, really. I remember we would play in her yard most of the time with whatever toys we had, with the understanding that I would *never* mistreat her stuffed animal. Despite it being dirty and ripped in places, Penny held it close at all times, no matter what we were doing.

"It's a swan," Penny would say, "my mommy gave it to me before she ran away."

It didn't look much like a swan, years of wear making it look more like a tired seagull. But Penny swore it was a swan, so I took her word for it. I remember asking why her mother left, one of the first sentences spoken to her. She just shrugged and looked at the ground for a while, chewing her lip and holding the little swan close. Minutes would go by with her lost in thought, and I would just sit there and wait for her. Then she would perk up all of a sudden and ask to play tag or hide-and-seek. We would play day in and day out, usually until my grandmother called me for dinner. Penny would frown and watch me go, and I always felt bad for leaving. I would check on her during dinner, and she would just be sitting on her porch with her swan, or sometimes tossing rocks into the creek that made up half our backyards. I didn't know why she never liked being inside her house, and every time I mentioned her daddy she didn't want to talk about it.

Penny's daddy didn't come out of the house much. Whenever he did, it was usually to yell at Penny for being outside, although he always talked slowly, and didn't make sense most of the time. He would always be tired, and he would always be angry. It would be years before I understood that her daddy was a drunk, and that he liked to beat on her.

Things like that have a habit of sitting on the back burner when you are little. I mentioned the bruises to my grandmother, and she said we shouldn't talk about it, that it was *their* business. Penny didn't want to talk about it either, so I pretended not to see them. In retrospect, I think my grandmother knew and *wanted* to help, she just didn't know how. She would do things to try and make it better every once in a while, like invite her over for dinner when her father was asleep, or bring her sweets discreetly when she had been baking. I remember on an especially bad day Penny had a busted lip, and my grandmother said something like, "He's all she's got. Sometimes you just have to hang in until things get better." There was something so sad about how she said it, and I could tell she was trying not to cry. I remember it feeling sad and gray for a long time, but the sadness wouldn't be so bad if I could see my grandmother and Penny smile.

In my bleak home in the middle of nowhere, I decided if they were happy with how things were, maybe I could learn to be happy too.

As the years passed, things started to get better. A little. When I opened up a bit more, I started calling my grandmother "Gran" which seemed to make her happy. Gran didn't speak of my grandfather much beyond the fact he enjoyed collecting rare bottles of whiskey. He never drank them, which didn't make much sense to me. Gran said some people collected strange things, and she was just thankful he didn't collect guns instead. Even though he had passed years ago, she still kept the cabinet clean and dusted. I would spend nights looking at the old bottles, trying to imagine my grandfather holding them when I read the label.

Penny and I became great friends, a friendship that lasted even after we started going to school. We would ride the bus together, an old rickety shuttle that would take us to a school I didn't much care for. It's not because I didn't have my old friends there anymore, but because the other kids weren't interested in being our friends. Penny and I were the same age as all the other kids, but they just treated us *differently*. I would often hear them whisper nasty things to each other, sometimes about Penny, sometimes about me.

They would often whisper of the marks and bruises Penny seemed to have; the ones I had gotten used to not acknowledging. They would talk about how she wore the same clothes a lot, and how often they were dirty.

They would talk about how I didn't have a mom and dad, and sometimes speculate over what happened to them. Sometimes they would say I killed them; other times they would say they didn't love me anymore because I was "bad".

The teachers would hush and scold them, but they would always say something again. They would always leave us out of activities and pretend they didn't see us. In time I found I hated school, but as long as the two of us could play together once we got home, everything would be alright. At the end of every gloomy day we had each other.

The older I got, the more I came to terms with the loss of my parents. The void they left behind never truly filled. But Gran did her best to raise me and be there for me. Some days were worse than others, and Penny had a habit of picking up on it and finding ways to cheer me up. In return I was always there for her when she needed me, although I wasn't as good at noticing. Penny would always let me know, however, in the form of a pebble hitting my window. We would sneak out some nights, something that proved easy with how early Gran always went to bed, and how drunk Penny's father always was.

We would tiptoe through the shallow creek and duck under the trees that grew along it, keeping quiet until we reached the cornfield that started at the end of our property. The corn would stretch for miles over the hills, but before that was a tiny patch that never sprouted like it should. It was our little secret spot, a nice place where we could lay down and look at the stars and hear the cicadas chirp. Our own little paradise, away from the things that reminded us of how bad it was; Me, her, and her stuffed swan.

Laying down in the squashed and malformed cornstalks, we would talk about our dreams.

I would tell her about my dreams where there was no car accident, and everything was full of color again. Penny would listen, propped up on her elbow with a little smile, holding her sad-seagull-looking stuffed animal close, and smiling as I talked. In that moment, I could lift the weight on my shoulders and let some semblance of light in. I could talk to her in a way I couldn't with Gran, with her mutual understanding of a parent blinking out of sight. I would speak of my dreams, and when I was finished, she would touch my arm and say, "That was lovely," in her adolescent country accent. I would roll over and wait as she looked at the stars, snuggling her stuffed animal that looked sadder and sadder as time moved on. She would close her eyes and think for a moment, putting together the full memory she always managed to recollect. When she opened them, I remembered seeing the reflection of the moon in her eyes, her little globes wide and marveling at the shining sky above.

Penny would tell me how she dreamt of being a swan.

It was a dream she had often, one I would get to know and love more every time she told it. She would tell me she dreamt of dancing among the stars as a swan, spreading her wings and flying across the sky. Up above would be a world free of pain and suffering, a world full of light that would shine so brightly it would erase the pain of everything you'd been through. In her dream she could stretch her legs and run as far away as she wanted, feeling the wind on her feathers as she soared across the sky. She said that in her dream, if she flew far enough, she would find her mother.

I watch her tell her story, the reflection of the stars glinting in her eyes. She would look happy, and the smile she wore while telling her story would put me at ease, and momentarily dull the feeling of loss and longing for days to come. It didn't matter how rough things were at school, or how empty it felt at home. I would think of Penny the Swan, and I would feel better.

Just as sleep would try and take me, Penny would help me up and tell me it was time to go home. Together, we would duck back under the trees and mind our footing through the creek, hoping we could creep back home just as soundlessly as we had left.

Things continued as normal into middle school. I wasn't interested in having other friends. Whenever I had finished my schoolwork, I took to books rather than socializing. Talking to others wasn't something I was particularly good at, and even if I was good at conversation, we didn't have anything in common. Gran didn't have a lot of money, so I was out of touch with whatever video game or movie craze everyone seemed to chat about.

As Penny grew older, she learned to embrace her independence at home and spent a lot of time taking better care of herself and her home. Her clothes were much cleaner, and she spent a lot of time keeping her long hair straight and untangled. Gran did whatever she could to make sure she had essentials like toothbrushes and a decent conditioner, and whenever she bought clothes for me, she always tried to sneak in something for her as well.

The school counselors knew what was happening at home, and sometimes reached out and made some attempt to address the issue. Penny's father would get better for a time, the bruises would stop, and things would feel better. But it never lasted long, and after a while, I supposed they stopped seeing the bruises like I once did. Maybe it was easier for them.

When things were especially bad, I would hear the pebble hit my window. We would go to our secret spot and talk of our dreams, the one thing that would always reset things for a time. But as I got older, I dreamed of my parents less, and thought more of Penny finding another home. One where things weren't so bad all the time.

Penny still talked of the same dream, her dream of being a swan. It still held the same radiance as it always did, but it made me feel different when I heard it. Now when she told it, I wished somehow it could come true.

The summer after I turned thirteen, things started to change.

It was a hot day in July, and I had just finished mowing the yard for Gran. It was the first nice day after a long string of rain, and the creek had gone up above knee level for the first time in years. Penny was hanging out in the grass, drawing a picture of the sad-looking swan stuffed animal. She still carried it around from time to time, but it was hardly recognizable and falling apart. The eyes were barely holding on, and the fur had shed so much in spots it was bald.

It was sweltering out, and Gran suggested we swim in the creek since we didn't have a sprinkler or anything. It was something we hadn't done since we were little.

"Last one there is a rotten egg!" Penny yelled, leaving her swan and drawings in the yard.

Penny didn't have a swimsuit, so we both went in with our clothes on. The water was freezing, so we took turns splashing each other and running away. Gran watched from the top of the hill, laughing as we trounced through the creek. Penny was wearing shorts and one of her father's old T-shirts, one so long her knees would catch on it in the water. It would slow her down when she fought with it, so I would always be able to get away. We went back and forth for a while, splashing and jumping until Gran called from atop the hill and said she was going to go back inside to make us some lemonade.

When Gran was gone, Penny told me to turn around and cover my eyes. I teased her about it, thinking she would use the opportunity to try and get the jump on me. She swore she wouldn't cheat, and after going back and forth I sighed and did as she asked.

Behind me I heard her messing with something, giggling in between the sounds of her straining with something. After a wet *plap* on the water, she told me to turn around and open them. I lowered my hands and turned around to see she had taken off her shirt.

I had never *really* looked at a girl before, let alone see or even know what a bra was. And Penny used my awkward double take to her advantage.

"See if you can outrun me now," she said, before bolting through the water.

Penny tackled me before I could get away, sending us both into the chilly water. We rolled and flailed, splashing each other through bouts of laughter. Penny tried to hold me under the water and I tried to escape, taking turns as the water murked beneath us. We went back and forth, wrestling and laughing until we collapsed from exhaustion, both of us gasping and giggling on our butts in the water.

I don't know if it was the special glint in her eyes or the curve of her smile, but it felt different, like a jar of fireflies had been released in my stomach. Penny scrunched her face and pulled her knees to her chest, suddenly looking embarrassed.

"What?" she said, blushing as she looked away and wiped the long matted strands from her face. She looked at the hill and froze, the color draining just as quickly as it arrived. I could then hear the footsteps.

On the hill was her father, his glazed eyes holding a dead stare.

"It's not, we were just—" Penny stammered, scrambling for her discarded shirt.

Penny's father yanked her out of the creek by her hair, dragging her up the hill as she screamed and kicked. I wanted to stop him, but I was scared, and he was much bigger than me.

"You're a whore, just like your mother! You want to run away? Just like *she* did?" he shouted in her ear, holding her up with a fistful of hair.

When Penny didn't answer, he only got angrier. He tried instigating more, but Penny stayed quiet, sobbing softly as she reached for her yanked hair. He looked around angrily, eyes wild as he sought someone else to inflict his rage upon. At first he looked at me, but was distracted when he saw the stack of papers. With a scowl he let her go, and shambled over to the drawings, grabbing all of them in crinkled handfuls. He stared at the pictures of swans, looking over each one with his puffy eyes. Without a word he ripped them to pieces, scattering them to the wind as Penny cried on the ground. Just when I thought his tantrum was finished, he saw the stuffed animal, and snatched it up with a grunt.

Penny begged him to stop, but it only seemed to fuel his rage. He twisted the stuffed swan's head until it tore, then pulled it apart until the stuffing scattered across the yard. When she tried to stop him, he slapped her, a vicious echo that seemed to carry for miles.

I remember Gran coming out of the house and dropping the lemonade, pleading with Penny's father that we were just kids. He and Gran shouted at each other, and in the end, Gran sat and started crying. I remember looking at Penny for a moment, and feeling guilty that I had looked at her like I did. I didn't understand what her father meant when he said those things to her, but I felt like it was my fault. Like maybe if I didn't look at her like I did, maybe she wouldn't have gotten in trouble.

After he dragged Penny into the house and slammed the door shut, he yelled at her for a while. I wished there was something I could do. I remember getting out of the creek, and Gran just sitting there saying "I'm sorry, I'm sorry," over and over, rocking back and forth. I didn't understand why she was sorry. I didn't understand any of it.

I spent the rest of the afternoon staring out my window, looking at Penny's house. In my hands was the torn up stuffed animal, mangled and deflated beyond recognition. The pictures had all blown away before I could grab them; the wind growing fierce as the sunshine turned to an ugly overcast gray. By the time the yelling had subsided it started to rain, and I found myself looking through the downpour at Penny's window, hoping she was alright. Looking at her house gave me a terrible feeling, a dread that I couldn't describe. I was used to the way things were for Penny, but for some reason, this time felt worse.

When my eyes grew too heavy, I curled up on my bed. I looked at the stuffed swan as I drifted off to sleep, praying that somewhere in the noise of the storm, I would hear the sound of a pebble hitting the glass.

Hours later, I found my prayer had been answered. I opened my eyes to the soft *tink* of the pebble, the familiar chime that found me even through the barrage of rain and wind. I sat up immediately, throwing off the covers and grabbing the stuffed swan to meet Penny at the window. I could see her through the glass, a pale silhouette through the film of spattering rain. I opened the window and was hit by a chilly gust that sucked the warmth from my room.

I motioned for Penny quietly, and she hurried over, holding a hand up against the pelting mist. Her nightgown was soaked, and her hair was matted and tangled. She leaned against the window shivering; her hands trembled on the windowsill.

"Penny! Are you alright? I was so worried..." I started to whisper but stopped. Something was wrong, the way she was looking down, the way her bottom lip trembled. Her cheery perseverance was gone, and in its place, a cold and broken shell. I reached for her and she flinched away, shuddering against the storm as she hugged herself. I waited for her to say something, but I got my answer when she looked up.

The left side of her face had been horribly beaten. Her left eye was swollen shut, accompanied by a dark purple bruising that went from the top of her cheek to the corner of her mouth. I felt the tears immediately, along with the sudden sickening pull in my stomach.

"Penny, no—" My whisper was hushed by a clammy finger, and a feigned smile.

"It's okay. It doesn't hurt much. Not anymore," she said, but her eyes told a different story.

I looked past her to the storm outside, unable to see the creek through the stormy night.

"Are you sure you want to go to our spot? I don't think we'll be able to see the stars. You want to just come inside?" I asked, but she shook her head.

"*No.* There's something I want to show you. We'll be able to see, I'm sure. But I need you to do me a favor first. I don't have much time. It'll be worth it, I promise," she said, and I nodded.

Penny told me she needed a bottle of whiskey from my grandfather's cabinet. She told me she felt bad for asking, but it was the only way to buy enough time for us to get away. She said it was important, and she would only have one chance to do it. I agreed, wanting to do whatever I could to help her.

Penny hid at the window as I crept away, glancing back to her house nervously as I disappeared down the hall. I didn't know what time it was, but I knew it was late. I tiptoed down the hall, the sounds of a late-night game show coming in clearer as I drew near. Gran had a habit of falling asleep while watching television, and I hoped the storm hadn't woken her.

I peeked into the living room to see her asleep, the television's glow flickering as she snored softly in her recliner. As quietly as I could, I walked in front of the screen towards my grandfather's collectible cabinet. I opened it slowly, keeping an eye on Gran as its squeaking blended with the applause of someone winning a grand prize. I grabbed the highest one I could reach, the weight of the bottle feeling dirty in my hands.

I closed the cabinet, and Gran mumbled as the program went to commercial. After stirring under her blanket, the dry rasp of snoring continued. She was sound asleep. I tucked it under my shirt, feeling guilty.

I snuck back to my room and anxiously closed the door behind me. I was sick with worry and scared to find Penny's father looking in when I went back to the window. Instead I saw nothing, only the occasional flash of lightning illuminating the black outside.

An empty yard, glistening in the rain.

"Penny?" I whispered, creeping up to the window. I poked my head outside, holding both the whiskey and the torn stuffed animal.

Droplets pelted my face as I looked around, my stomach twisting as I saw nothing but wet grass.

"I'm here."

I jumped as Penny came up beside me, still shivering in her soaked nightgown. I asked her if she wanted a blanket or something, but she shook her head. I handed the bottle to her and she took it, cradling it like a glass baby. She looked down at the bottle in sadness, her untouched eye lingering on the bottle before she turned back to me. I held the stuffed animal out next.

Penny looked at the broken swan, her lip trembling into a frown as the rain hit it.

"I don't need it anymore," she said, and managed a faint smile, "thank you for helping me. I shouldn't be long. You should bundle up, it's cold out here," she said and kissed me on the cheek. I stood there dumbfounded.

"You're the best friend I've ever had," she said, and scurried back to her house. After she slinked through the back door, I still felt the cross press of the kiss on my cheek. I looked at the little swan in my hand, feeling a whirlwind of emotions within me.

I didn't know what was happening, or how I was supposed to feel about it.

I shut the window, set the swan on my dresser, and started putting on warmer clothes.

Outside, the storm pressed on. I pulled on jeans and a sweatshirt, occasionally looking out my window to Penny's house. Her house stood eerily silent in the storm, and with no light inside it was impossible to know what was going on. I got some boots from the closet, thinking they would be better walking through the rain. After I put them on, I got in bed and covered myself in a blanket while I waited for Penny to return.

I laid in the dark for a while, listening to the patter of rain. I thought of Penny and the kiss she gave me. I thought of her father, and the wild look in his eyes. I thought of Gran, and how she took me in. After a while, I thought of my parents, and how it was harder to see their faces as time went on. As I busied myself with thoughts, the rain settled down to a drizzle, and the thunder was getting farther and farther apart. The wind no longer rattled the siding, and soon, an agitated peace settled in.

And with that, a pebble.

Penny was waiting by the window when I got there, still in the same damp nightgown. She looked tired and cold but determined.

She held a finger to her lips before I could say anything, then nodded and climbed out the window. She took my hand and led me to the back yard, her bare feet and my boots squishing in the wet grass. Her grip was cold but fierce, but she looked back with a smile that assured me everything would be okay.

The storm was fading, and on the horizon the dawn fought to poke through the gloom.

Together we went down the hill leading to the creek, holding each other up each time the earth slid beneath us. The creek was rushing from the rain, but Penny didn't let it slow her down. She was focused, pushing through steadily as I held on tight. My boots sucked at the mud, but I kept up, sucking in a breath as the cold water passed by my legs like ice.

We made it through, both of us huffing with excited exhaustion. As I caught my breath, she let go of my hand and ducked into the trees that led to our secret spot. I looked back at our houses, the mental noise of the pain they brought fading the further we got away.

When I ducked in, Penny had already reached the edge of the woods. She motioned for me to follow and disappeared into the corn. I followed quickly, clumsy soaked boots trudging through with every step. I tried to keep my focus ahead, watching the corn get closer and closer, trying to keep up. With the faint light of dawn, I noticed something in the mud beneath me. It didn't make sense at first, but the longer I looked, I started to notice a pattern.

Two sets of bare feet were imprinted in the mud. Two facing in the direction of our houses, two facing the cornfield. A single smear drug between them. The path led all the way to our secret spot.

Once I reached the corn, I saw a single patch of disturbed stalks. Some of them had been flattened or broken, a path the smear ran directly through. On the other side of the corn, I could see the outline of Penny waiting patiently. As I waved my way through the stalks, I started to hear something. Like an incoherent mumbling. It got louder the closer I got; the mumbling turning into the groaning, then mumbling again.

When I made it to the secret spot, Penny was there. She walked over silently and took my hand and smiled, pulling me into a hug with both arms. She was still cold, but she wasn't shivering anymore. I had never hugged her before, and it was then I realized how thin she actually was. Like she was sick.

She rested her head on my shoulder for a while, and for a moment we just held each other in the peaceful dawn. She looked up at me and smiled, half of her face beaming, the other unable to. She touched my face, running her thumb over my cheek softly before looking to the sky.

Above, the stars were shining, brighter than ever before.

"Thank you for coming with me. Thank you for letting me show you," she said, and it was then I saw the wriggling shape behind her.

On the ground was Penny's father, writhing on the ground. Lodged in his mouth was the bottle of whiskey, a heavy wrap of duct-tape keeping it in place. The bottle was empty.

She stepped out of the way so I could see. Her smile faded to a blank slate of indifference. I looked at her father in surprise, instinctively stepping away from him. Penny held my hand tight and kept me by her side.

Her father tried to struggle but couldn't, his unfocused eyes lolling at the sky as he fought against makeshift restraints of clothing and belts. Dribbles of vomit caked his face, and he seemed caught in a constant state of heavy gasping. Through the gasps were attempts at words, each of them heavily slurred and muffled by the lodged bottle. Before long, my gaze was pulled away from him, *behind* him.

The wide mass stirred in front of the corn; a shape almost concealed by the haze of the leaving nightfall. It moved with the sound of an ocean wave, its size expanding on each side, until I could see long elegant feathers fan out like daggers. A long neck rose from its body, curving and extending until it towered above. A head the size of my body looked directly at me, then started leaning toward me. A neon glow burst from the horizon, painting the shape as it encroached toward me.

The giant swan stood with stark brilliance, its ballerina shape menacing and pure. Pitch-black eyes narrowed on me, its massive and elegant beak poised and ready to stab me through the chest. I looked up at it helplessly, squeezing Penny's hand as I resisted the urge to let my bladder go. The beak kept reaching toward me, and when it was almost close enough to touch, it stopped.

Penny reached out and placed her hand on the beak, and the colossal bird froze. It turned to her slowly, and she stepped forward to rest her head against the feathers on its neck. The animosity faded away, and the swan relaxed. It leaned into Penny's embrace, and above the stars glimmered in the static above. There was a deep humming in the swan's breast, and Penny smiled.

Before I could relax, the swan looked back at me, and softly prodded me in the chest with its beak. I looked and Penny and she nodded, and with a trembling hand I reached to pet its neck. Each feather soft as the finest silk, but brimming with electrical energy. Like I was touching a battery. When I looked into its eyes, I felt like it was looking into my soul. When the swan was done with me, there was a deep hum. Then it craned its head to look at Penny's father.

The man lay miserably on the ground, still mumbling through his vomit. He tried to look around, but there was an absence in his eyes. Each thrash was confused and belligerent. Resisting without knowing why. He didn't see the swan. Even when it came for him.

The beak parted as it reached his torso, then clamped down slowly like a vise. The father screamed as it pinched together, breaking the restraints and peeling his flesh effortlessly. The swan's bite took everything with it, ripping layers of skin and muscle and leaving an exposed chest cavity in its wake. It reared back and swallowed the viscera; the mass sliding down its tube of a neck. I wanted to run. I looked at Penny and gasped.

Penny's mouth was open wide, her jaws struggling as she bared her teeth. It kept opening until her jaw broke, a terrible wet crunch that brought tears to my eyes. She was looking at me, a single tear falling before her eye *disappeared,* buried under folds as her face scrunched and folded together, making way for what was forcing itself out of her throat.

A long bill, blood-stained and burnt orange, kept protruding until it crowned a head. Penny's head separated to accommodate the expunging mass, and I watched in horror as her body tore vertically, and a pair of stained wings stretched from the remnants of her shoulders. The strings of the nightgown snapped, revealing a feathery breast speckled with red.

I held on until there was nothing left to hang on to, and could only watch as short, paddled feet stepped out of the gore. The swan that burst from Penny walked awkwardly at first, but after a few steps, balanced on newfound feet. It looked up and the giant swan, who nodded from up above.

Penny's father was still trying to scream, but his strength was fading. His chest was a mess of flayed pectoral muscle, shifting organs, and a beating heart struggling to stay inside its ruined containment. I watched as the baby swan walked over to him, its dark eyes looking down thoughtfully.

Right before it dug into his chest.

The beak was sharp, separating the tissue as it rooted around. Penny's father thrashed weakly, unable to defend himself. When the beak found his heart, it pinched and ripped it free, holding it up triumphantly before rearing back and dropping it down its throat. Arterial spray scattered in all directions, staining feathers and corn alike.

When the baby was finished, it backed away from the corpse, the bulge of the heart still working its way down the throat. The giant swan reached down and gave an affectionate embrace. The sun burst through the tree line, and tantalizing pink and orange painted the sky. They stood there like sculptures, like masterpieces from carved diamonds that reflected the light of the sun.

It was beautiful.

When they were done, the swans looked at each other, then looked at me. The smaller one looked back at the mother and stood awkwardly, shuffling on its paddled feet. The mother *scoffed* and nudged the baby over to me. It walked hesitantly at first, but eventually approached, its wings held bent in front of it. The mother turned and scooped up the rest of the father, gathering him up in one large, delicate bite.

I looked at the small swan, then looked at what remained of Penny. Whatever was left was fading into the grass, withering away like ash on a campfire. I looked at the remains, feeling a ball in my throat and a heaviness in my chest. The swan reached out a wing and blocked my view of it, its dark eyes looking upset. It exhaled through its nasal passages in a way that felt... *sympathetic.*

I reached out for it, and it leaned against me, its long neck resting on my shoulder as its wings stretched out and wrapped around me. Through the blood and feathers, I felt the embrace of Penny, a kind soul meant for a better world. The swan whistled softly and I started to cry, throat-aching sobs I couldn't hold back. The swan hummed softly, swaying with me. We stood like this until my tears ran dry, and the swan pulled away to rejoin its mother. I wiped my eyes and watched her go, the haze of the sun lifting the weight of the pain I had gotten so used to ignoring.

Together they stretched their wings, thousands of feathers casting shadows over the corn. And with one grand flap, they were gone.

Ever since she was a kid, Penny dreamed of being a swan. It was a dream she had often, one I would get to know and love more every time she told it. She would tell me she dreamt of dancing among the stars, spreading her wings and flying across the sky. Up above would be a world free of pain and suffering, a world full of light that would shine so brightly it would erase the pain of everything she'd been through.

I'm older now, and things are much better than they used to be. I learned to have another family, one that won't have to know the pain of a broken home, and don't have to wonder if they belong. Sometimes I go out at night and look up at the stars. I think of Penny the Swan, and if I look hard enough, I can see her flying with her mother.

THE BLACK UNICORN

"As long as you don't have a bad trip, you'll be fine."

Aubryn said as I looked at the gummy she handed me. The edible looked nothing like I thought it would; just a lightly colored, sugar-coated disc. It certainly didn't look like something to be excited about.

"What is it again?" I said, keeping it in my hand as I looked at myself in the mirror. I had never worn "goth" clothes before, and so far my first impression consisted of *tight*.

"An edible, duh. You know what it is. We've been over this already. Something to help you loosen up. So you're not such a prude," Aubryn said, joining me in the mirror. She raised her skirt with a finger and flashed one of her long legs, the one that was tattooed entirely black. I looked at her reflection, subconsciously tugging at the bottom of my corset. My skirt seemed too short; my boots too high. Meanwhile, Aubryn looked like a natural countess.

"How do I look? It feels so... weird," I said, looking at the combination of fishnets, chains, and black eyeliner. I had never dressed goth before, and everything I was wearing had come from Aubryn's closet.

"Frumpy," Aubryn said, flipping her hair. I frowned, and she started to laugh.

"Only joking, darling. Embrace it, it'll be fun. Come on, our Uber is here. We're gonna be late." She shouldered her purse and headed for the door as I gawked at myself some more. I felt ridiculous, like I had dressed like a clown for a children's birthday party. In my hand, the edible was getting sticky.

"Are you sure about this? It seems like a little *much," I said*, holding the gummy out. Aubryn responded by popping one of her own in her mouth.

"Ted was a *pig,* he cheated on you. You need to get out and have fun, they're really light doses. Just a nudge in the right direction. Come *on*, girl. Give the *True Crime* a rest. Let's get out and live a little," she said, opening the door to my apartment and waiting.

A sigh left my lips as she opened the door. I looked at the melting gummy and reluctantly put it in my mouth. Aubryn cheered as I chewed it, swinging her purse around to celebrate. It tasted stale, the sugar-coat failing to mask the greasy consistency once you bit into it.

Downstairs the Uber was waiting, a little hatchback idling at the apartment curb. The driver, a younger man, got out and held open the backseat door. He tried to feign his surprise at our outfits and failed miserably. I got in first, while Aubryn stared awkwardly at the driver.

"What, never seen a real woman before?" she said, leaning forward and moving her shawl to expose the swell of her bust. The driver took the opportunity to check his phone awkwardly, and she sighed and climbed in slowly.

"Fuckin' shoes," she said, as the driver closed the door behind her.

"How long does it take to kick in?" I asked sheepishly as we settled in.

"I don't know. Not long, hopefully. It's different for every-body, I guess," she said, getting a mirror from her purse and checking her eyeliner.

"Wait? I thought you said you tried them before!" I yelled. Aubryn paused, and her reflection in the tiny mirror slowly looked at me.

"I lied," she said.

I called her a whore, and she shrugged.

"Look, I took one too. We're in this together," she said, and with a delicate stroke, ran the dark eyeliner pencil around.

I leaned my head against the window, watching the cars kick up mist as they passed. It had rained all morning, hopefully the end of a long string of storms. I thought of Ted, and how just a week ago, I never would've dreamed of going out dressed head to toe in such extreme clothing. We would usually spend Fridays snuggled up on the couch, watching horror movies on whatever streaming service. Maybe even open a bottle of wine. That was until two weeks ago, when I found out he was sleeping with *two* different coworkers. Now I was off to some sort of nightclub that… traveled around?

"What are you ladies doing tonight?" The driver asked coolly.

"I'm lookin' to get *fucked,*" Aubryn blurted, snapping the mirror shut. The driver glanced at her in the rear-view for a second before returning his eyes to the road.

"You said the club moved around? Like a circus?" I asked out loud, mostly at her.

"Yeah. Only sleazier, and they, like, set up shop in abandoned buildings." Aubryn moved on to lipstick while I imagined a sweaty local bar, except decorated with leather and chains.

"Is that even legal? How did you even hear about it?" I asked.

"Saw something about it online. I've seen them mentioned before, this is just the first time they've been in the area. Thought it might be fun," she said, pursing in her lipstick.

"What's it called again? The club I mean."

"*The Black Unicorn,*" said Aubryn, in a spooky voice.

"Wow. Edgy."

The driver quietly drove as we talked. It seemed to get darker the further we got, streetlamps thinning until there were nothing but dark roads. We had gone into the "rougher" part of town, the side I wasn't very familiar with. By the time I didn't recognize the surroundings at all, he started to slow down. Without a word he pulled up to the sidewalk and stopped, putting it in park and unbuckling. We looked around confused, seeing only a liquor store and a rent-a-tux shop with its lights out for the night. There was no club to be found.

"Uh, what are you doing?" asked Aubryn, reaching into her purse, where she was well known for carrying bear-mace.

"We've reached the destination," said the driver, opening his door.

"Bullshit," I said, but he just sighed and pointed to the phone mounted on the dash. The GPS signaled we had arrived.

"But there's no club, just the liquor st—" Aubryn started, but the driver cut her off.

"Must be down *there,* " he said, pointing to the right.

Wedged narrowly between both stores was an alley, completely dark aside from the tint of red light at the end. It looked like somewhere you went to be intentionally kidnapped.

"You're kidding," I said.

"Look, I just put in the address and drive there. This is where it said to go. Unless you want to pay for a ride home, I don't know what to tell ya," said the driver, looking back at us.

Aubryn and I exchanged looks, and after a moment of silence, the driver got out and opened the door for us.

"You sure about this?" I said before getting out.

Aubryn looked down the alley for a moment, before shrugging again.

"I'm sure it'll be fine. Anything happens, I'll mace 'em," she said, and got out. I reluctantly followed.

Once the drive was paid, we took a deep breath and headed down the alley. It was dark and creepy as fuck, our heels clacking as we entered the darkness. The red light got brighter, and soon we heard the *thrum* of bass.

"If we're getting human-trafficked, I swear," I said, trying not to sound nervous.

"It's actually pretty cool," Aubryn said, one hand still stuffed in her purse.

The beat got louder with every step, and I could make out a muffled industrial tune. We looked for some kind of sign, but there was nothing but damp brick on either side. At the end of the alley was an abrupt turn, and when we rounded the corner we both jumped.

A man was leaning against the wall, almost blending into the red glow. He was wearing a mesh top and a kilt, his face obscured by a goat mask. There was an opening in the goat's mouth, where he was busy dragging off a vape rig. As we approached cautiously, he exhaled a cloud, one that wafted up and caught the light of the red lamp.

"IDs please," was all he said, his combat boots scuffing the concrete.

We both awkwardly fished for our licenses, and I suddenly felt *very* out of my element. The man waited patiently, the loud bass thumping down the alley. Behind him was a metal door, one that had been crudely spray-painted black. Blue eyes scanned each I.D. from behind the goat mask. After a moment, he handed them back.

"Cool. Welcome to The Black Unicorn," he said, and reached for the door.

He yanked it open and motioned inside, the music blasting through the doorway. The inside was pitch black, with a strobe light firing non-stop.

"Your edible kick in yet?" I asked Aubryn, suddenly feeling anxious.

"Not yet," she said, biting her lip as she eyed the doorway, the strobe light reflecting in her eyes.

I looked back down the alley at the empty street. The driver had already pulled away.

"Come on, let's go," Aubryn said, already pulling me with her. Once we were in, the doorman shut the door behind us, mumbling something like "have a good time."

We were in some kind of coat room, several leather and fur jackets lining the walls in the tiny space. The strobe came from the ceiling, an aggressive flash that both made me excited and anxious. I looked at Aubryn, her features blinking in rapid stills. After a silent agreement to keep our stuff on us, we headed into the next room that appeared to be the bar.

The strobe faded to a bright neon glow, one accented by a living cloud fed by a fog machine. Overhead was a dancing blacklight, multiple beams cutting through red hue. We waded through the crimson mist in time to see dozens of heads lift and look at us. The patrons of The Black Unicorn eyed us for a moment, most with indifference, others with curiosity. There were people of all shapes and sizes, each donning their own combination of lace, leather, and ink. Sculpted muscle wrapped in tight latex, and seductive curves in nothing but body paint and pasties. Piercings in every imaginable place, each glinting in the swirl of blacklight that filled the room.

"Where do we sit?" I asked, wincing at the music's volume. Aubryn motioned to the counter, where there appeared to be open seats.

We made our way to the bar. Aubryn led, weaving through the crowd. Some looked at her hungrily, others scoffed. A scrawny man wearing a plague doctor mask playfully reached out with a cane, and she ignored it.

I couldn't help but take in the room around me, half-marveling, half-intimidated at the intensity of everything around us. At one table a heavy-set man wearing nothing but a leather vest was setting fire to shot glasses, while someone in a clown costume cut up fine white lines. Another woman was resting her chin on her hands calmly, while a man in a devil mask steadily dug into her back with a tattoo gun. The devil mask looked up for a moment and nodded, before returning to his work at hand. In the very back, it looked like someone was receiving a blowjob.

Aubryn and I sat at the counter, me holding my purse close while she looked around. There was a kindling magic in her eyes, and part of me wondered if it was just the edible kicking in. She looked from one table to another, aweing at the company. I wished I had shared her sense of wonder. Whereas she looked like she was at home, my gut was telling me to run for the door.

"What should we get to drink?" she said, looking behind the bar. I shrugged and looked for a paper menu, and discovered there wasn't one. A large chalkboard "menu" sat between the shelves of liquor, scribbled writing reflecting in the blacklight. There were a bunch of your household beer names, followed by a long list of cocktails I hadn't heard of. At the top of the list in large capital letters, it read: SPECIAL. Standing next to the board was a burly man in a Hawaiian shirt, thick forearms flexing as he shook a tumbler.

"Two specials, please!" Aubryn said, leaning over the bar. The bartender nodded, uncapping the tumbler and pouring the contents into a glass in front of him.

"What's in the special?" I asked, and she shrugged. My look of contempt only made her laugh.

"Come *on,* girl, relax. We made it! It doesn't look that bad. It looks fun, doesn't it? And there *are* other girls here. It's not just a sausagefest," she said, nudging me with her boot.

I looked at the other girls in their risqué outfits and immaculate make-up, each of them smiling in one way or another, even the girl on a leash. There was something special about the confidence everyone seemed to have. It didn't matter what getup they had, they fucking owned it.

"I suppose it's pretty cool," I said, and Aubryn started to clap with excitement.

"See? I told…" She trailed off, her eyes focusing on something across the room. I turned in my stool to see what she was looking at.

Across the room there was a man leaning against the wall, returning her gaze. He was shirtless, a harness stretched over rippling pale muscle. His hands were in pockets of his slacks, smoke dancing from the cigarette in his lips.

"Oh my..." Aubryn said, reaching down to hike up some of her skirt, showing off her tattooed leg. The cherry on the man's cigarette started to glow, and without a word he started heading over.

"Are you kidding me? Already?" I said, aggravated. We had just gotten a seat, and she was already trying to slip away.

"Don't worry dear, I'm sure it won't take long. They never do," she said, shouldering her purse.

The man came over and put the cigarette out in one of the many ashtrays on the bar, taking the time to show off the tautness of the straps across his chest. He looked at Aubryn for a moment, a long uncomfortable stare that she returned. I held my purse closer to me, and without a word he walked away, to the back. In the direction of the bathrooms.

"Don't leave without me!" She said, giving me a look of fake apology before eagerly following.

You bitch.

I watched them go, the *thrum* of the bass rattling my ears. This wasn't the first time something like this happened, and it wouldn't be the last. She would usually stick around for the drink first.

I slouched on the stool, the tightness of the corset suddenly feeling exhausting. Through the noise of the goth bar, I thought of being at home, on the couch with some True Crime. I yawned and rubbed my eyes, immediately feeling the sting of the makeup. I had forgotten about the heavy eyeliner. I cursed and grabbed a napkin off the counter, wondering how much I had smudged it.

Ahead of me, the bartender set down two martini glasses, each filled with a jet-black liquid. Sticking out of each glass was an olive on a toothpick. *The specials,* a first round apparently on me.

"How much?" I asked, cupping my hand to my mouth so he could hear.

"Twenty," he said, leaning on his elbow.

I got a bill out of my purse and he took it, shoving it in his pocket before walking away. Sitting alone I looked at the drinks, wondering if they were even safe to consume.

I looked towards the back of the club, to the little neon signs labeled "guys" and "girls". The hallway was empty, save for the two mohawked individuals intertwining their tongues in the shadow. There was an uproar of laughter behind me, and I looked to see one of the women with a shaved head was riding a guy like a horse, walking on his hands and knees as she hit him with a trotter. The table behind them laughed and clapped, barely audible through the music. The rider whipped him again, and he whinnied and turned around, giving me full view of his junk confined in his speedo. The back of each thigh was tattooed, cursive letters that read *"Pretty Please"*.

I grabbed my martini glass and downed it, immediately wincing. The mixture started with bitters and a punch of alcohol, one that burned hot as it flew to my stomach. A sour tail blended everything together… and it actually wasn't that bad. I coughed against the strength of the drink, feeling the heat in my face immediately.

I arched my back on the stool, feeling a gradual lift of stress. Maybe this place wasn't so bad after all. I looked at the empty glass, wishing there was more in it. Behind me, I heard another *snap* from the trotter. The music changed to something harder, with more bass and electricity. The light show reflected the intensity. My foot seemed to tap on its own. In the rift of pleasant, hard relaxation, I felt my phone vibrate through my purse. I dug it out and unlocked it, the brightness from the screen stinging my retinas. I expected it to be Aubryn.

It was a text from Ted. I locked my phone, tossed it back in the bag, and grabbed Aubryn's drink. It went down even smoother than mine. I exhaled heavily, feeling the rush of the heat as I set the glass down. I propped myself up on my elbows, resting my chin on my fists as I looked around the bar.

Hiding in the array lights and fog was art on every wall, pictures of paint that popped with every strobe. A shibari-tied woman in barbed wire. A large deer with gore hanging from its antlers. A masked man wielding a chainsaw. I followed each piece curiously, watching them pop in the flashing lights. My eyes rested on one, a framed canvas much bigger than the others.

A goddess sitting on a throne, atop a mountain of corpses. She was covered head to heel in tight leather, accentuating her bust along with long, curvy legs. A cattle prod was clutched in her grasp, arcs of lightning traveling across her arm. Her head was that of a unicorn's but painted black.

Behind me, I heard another crack of the trotter. Much louder than the last.

I pushed off the counter, my limbs feeling suddenly heavier. I turned to see the *Pretty Please* and its rider, but saw nothing besides an empty floor. The two of them were gone.

What?

I knew I hadn't imagined it. I looked at the group that had laughed at the spectacle, only to find their table empty. Their drinks had vanished from their table as well, multiple empties replaced by a single glass of scotch. Behind the glass was a man in a suit, sitting straight and staring right at me through a pair of round, wire-framed sunglasses.

I rubbed my eyes again, only to feel the makeup punish again. Through the sting I squinted at the man, who was now raising his glass as if to toast me. There was a crack in his face, almost like a scar that ran through the center of his forehead down to the wrinkled folds of his neck. He raised the glass to his lips, and promptly dumped the drink all over himself, as if deliberately.

I looked around to see if anyone else had seen it, but nobody else was paying attention. In fact, nobody else seemed to be doing anything. Everyone seemed frozen, stuck in whatever pose they left off in, but *wrong*.

The man in the leather vest that lit the shots was slumped in his chair, drool oozing over several empty shot glasses. The clown's fine lines were smeared and scattered, blood leaking from his big red nose with his head reared back in his chair. The woman getting the tattoo had collapsed face down and with limp limbs weakly laid across the table. Behind her the devil mask mercilessly continued his art, red splatters coating the gun as he worked furiously. Something had changed. Something wasn't right.

I turned to the bartender for help, my reaction slowed and distorted as I searched for the man in the Hawaiian shirt. I found him standing behind me, blue eyes focused as taut hands ran the cloth over a glass.

The music kept getting louder, and I had to shout to get his attention.

"E-excuse me! Do you see that… do you see that man over there?!" I asked with a hiccup. I swallowed hard, each muscle requiring greater effort to respond. Everything felt slowed down.

He looked at me with annoyance, pausing his task. He leaned in slowly, staring maliciously through the sporadic strobe.

"Have you ever been slapped so hard, it knocks your fuckin' teeth out?" he said, just loud enough to hear. He stared at me intently, his pupils large and pulsing. A smirk crawled over his bearded face, and the blackness of his pupils burst, scurrying away like skittering roaches.

I recoiled from the bartender, who only laughed and continued polishing the glass.

What the fuck?

My head was swimming. I looked to the back of the club towards the restrooms, where Aubryn had disappeared. The neons for the bathrooms were flickering weakly, burning out. In a panic, I dug into my purse for my phone. With clumsy hands I pulled it out, almost dropping it. I hit the power button, only to get the same black screen.

My phone was dead.

I tried again and again, and when that didn't work, I held the button to restart it. It did nothing, just a useless brick in my hand. I put it away and looked at the man across the bar. He nodded with a smile and slowly took off his sunglasses. I felt a sick sort of tunnel vision in his direction, like I couldn't look away. He let his sunglasses fall, a soundless gesture that was lost to the music. The bass slammed my ears, and the lights focused on him. I looked at the scar on his forehead, the seam between his face that was starting to bleed.

It wasn't a scar. It was a zipper.

The man pinched the zipper flap and started pulling, separating the bleeding teeth as it ran down his nose and over his mouth, continuing down his neck. The zipper tore through the collar of his shirt and burst the buttons of his jacket, a red stain that grew the longer he pulled. His face went slack, the skin loosening as his hand disappeared under the table out of view. The skin began to part, something dark writhing within.

The music stopped, and from the face came a hand.

Deep red dripped from the hand as it reached out, a visceral slime that splashed over the empty glass and onto the table. Inky black and covered in latex, it grabbed one side of the face and pushed, making way for another. Together the hands pulled the face apart, peeling it back as it made way for a head. The husk of skin buckled and slacked as another face pushed through, a gimp mask with its eyes and mouth zipped shut. The new limbs shone in the frantic strobe, slapping wetly as it found its balance on the tabletop.

I couldn't breathe. I looked around for help, only to see the same frozen scene from before. Only the devil artist continued to move, the gun *whirring* and digging, blood splashing the wicked mask. The gimp suited man was crawling over the table now, oily drool seeping from every limb. As the limp skinsuit fell away to the floor behind it, the gimp man looked at me, an indescribable animosity radiating from its expressionless, synched-up face. With the sound of tearing meat, the lips started to part, the metal stitching bleeding as a high-pitched scream blasted from its mouth. It sounded like nails on a chalkboard.

I stumbled out of the stool, nearly falling as my feet touched the floor. My legs felt like gelatin, a mixture of fear and the booze making my knees weak. Each step was awkward and poorly placed, the platform boots working against me as I bounded for the bathroom. I needed to get Aubryn and get the fuck out of there. Behind me the gimp man shrieked, but I didn't dare look back. I heard it leap from the tabletop, a rapid squelching echoing as it fought to chase me.

The strobe rapidly fired, and I could only see the ground in front of me moving in flashing bursts, like an old film. Each frozen slide brought me closer to the bathroom doors, and I focused on the dying neon lights. Just as I heard the gimp gaining, I shoved through the door of the girls' restroom and threw myself against it, forcing it shut. I was so worried about keeping the gimp out I didn't realize the lights were off until I stood alone in the dark.

There was an electrical *pop*, then the lights flickered on. After a few blinks it stayed on, the starkness of the tile blinding in the sudden illumination. I shielded my eyes against the fluorescents, expecting to feel the impact of the gimp on the other side. But the door remained still, and I closed my eyes as I caught my breath. Each heavy breath was restricted by my corset, and I wished badly to tear it off. My vision felt delayed, like my brain was comprehending a second behind what my eyes took in.

The wet sounds of smacking lips made me open them again. Before me was Aubryn and the man in the harness, intertwined in a fit of standing lust. They stood like they were on strings, both of them leaning and groping without proper footing. Aubryn had one leg hooked around the back of his, her back arched and arms posed like a marionette. The man moved his hands slowly, one moving a strap off her shoulder to expose a pierced breast, the other disappearing between her legs and under her dress. I could hear the labored breaths and sensual moans in my head, so loud it rattled my brain and gave me goosebumps. The lights flickered again, and the man noticed me.

The man looked first, his eyes swirling pits of black. He smiled at me for a moment, before turning back to Aubryn, running his lips over her neck as she leaned back. He let his hand run over her breast before squeezing it hard. Aubryn winced against his touch and opened her eyes to see me.

Her eyes were bleeding. My mind fought to calibrate the sight, and I released what was streaming down was what was *left* of them.

I screamed.

"Go on without me dear. *nnjəss ᗝon ᴍɐnƚ ƚo ᴍɐlɔy"* Aubryn said, her voice fading away.

Oh god—

The man squeezed until his hand shook, the other still hidden under her dress. The skin around his grip started to bruise, and with a sickening *tear* he ripped the breast from her torso. Aubryn's lips parted with an exasperated breath, even as the bare tissue beneath was exposed. Even as he sank his teeth into her neck and pulled a chunk of flesh with it. The spatter of blood on the tile crisp and hot in my ears.

Oh god, oh fuck, fuckfuckfu—

I pulled on the door, her bleeding tears guilting me as I fought to get away. I yanked on the door but it was locked, locked from the outside, the deadbolt rattling every time I pulled on the knob. The far side of the bathroom started to dissolve, smearing like an Alkeseltzer tablet in water, twirling to a focal point in the center of the back wall. Like a black hole.

"Let me out! LET ME OUT! FuuuUUUCꓘ Ⱡ∈Ť ɱ∈ ØUŤ!" I screamed, the echo of my own voice distorting as the words were being sucked away. The door wouldn't budge.

The sight of the man peeling her was pixelating and drifting away, spaghettifying as the spherical void pulled them into it. The room was fading into nothing. The door unlocked, and I looked back to see Aubryn reach for me. I left her.

As soon as I was on the other side, I fell immediately to the floor. Pain scrawled like lightning across my limbs as my elbows and knees took the blow, the long platform boots feeling like clubby, awkward extensions. I touched my elbows and felt the warm stickiness of blood. The tile floor had been replaced with a crude metal grating, one that stretched into darkness on both sides. High above, a lightbulb came to life, the familiar red glow returning. The ceiling seemed to stretch higher than I thought possible. Gasping for breath and hugging myself, I frantically looked around me. The goth bar was gone.

In its place, a long, singular hallway.

"Help!" I shouted, an echo that bounced infinitely on both sides.

One by one red bulbs blinked on, each to the deafening sound of a hammer drop. I flinched against each one until they were so far away the noise felt like an afterthought.

"HĒLLO?" I called weakly, my words muffling under the weight of the dominating silence.

Nothing seemed to matter, so I walked.

I chose right, for no particular reason.

My footsteps were loud on the grated floor. The air was heavy and musty, growing thicker with every clumsy step. There was a buzzing in the air, like a string of bug zappers strung together. I could hear screams in the distance through the buzzing, both of pleasure and pain. Dozens of them, hundreds. Every climaxing cry melted to an anguished scream of torment, blending together in a loop. The longer it went on the less I could differentiate between the two, until it droned into a repetitive song suffocating euphoria. The darkness seemed to move around me, shadowy tendrils whipping for my attention. I flinched against their grasp at first, ducking away every time one stretched towards me. But the longer I pressed on, and the more my eyes adjusted, I realized they weren't reaching for me. They were pointing *down.*

Beneath the grate was a sea of bodies, bloody and rotting as far as the hallway stretched. A trench of blood and skin and leather, thousands of faces petrified in a scream. Their eyes followed me as I walked, each clanking footstep drawing a new set that traced me. Hollow and soulless they watched, beady pupils that begged for help but lacked the strength to ask. I wanted to help them but I couldn't, they were so far away and I didn't know how to—

My boot struck something solid. I was so busy with what was below I hadn't been looking ahead. Sprawled across the grate was a body, pants around their ankles, a bloated belly poking through a leather vest. Charred burn marks lined his chest and stomach, trailing all the way down below the waist. I looked away from their flaccid member, drawn to the mess above their shoulders. The face was obliterated, large seeping holes punched all the way through their skull, and despite the heavy bruising on their neck, their last expression appeared to be… in awe.

I stepped around the man's body, only to find another soon after. A polka-dotted costume ripped open at the waist, and a clown face caved in at the center. The corpses continued on forming a trail, a trail of bloody breadcrumbs across the grating.

A couple with mohawks was sprawled in the same fashion, as was the woman with the shaved head. Stepping over them I could hear the crackle of electricity, followed by strenuous groans. The eyes below followed me as I approached, two shifting figures coming into focus through the darkness. Between the electricity and pained groans was the occasional suck of breath, one of relief and desperation. Above another lightbulb flashed, the same tired glow raining from above.

An exposed man in a speedo was suspended in the air, gasping for air as a cattle prod was run repeatedly into his abdomen. A single hand held him against the wall, squeezing tight as he struggled against the shock treatment. Each time the prod let up he breathed the same hushed word.

Please. Please.

Pretty Please.

A woman held him against the wall, elbow-length gloves glinting in the light above. She was easily a foot taller than him, holding him up like a writhing peasant in an unbreakable grip. Long legs with spiked platform boots stood defiantly as he squirmed in pain, wrapped in climbing leather that accented the feminine curve of hips. A tight corset covered everything but her full breasts. Dual piercings of a star and moon unified by a silver chain hung from her nipples.

The dominatrix held the cattle prod into his stomach, staring intently as he struggled. Glowing pentacle eyes, burning from the head of a black unicorn. The man seized and frothed at the mouth, the veins in his neck taut as he clenched his teeth. She worked the prod methodically, piercings jingling with every thrash. When she finally let off, he let out an exasperated sigh. I watched as the man finished, an exhilarated and exhausted climax she welcomed by further squeezing his neck and rearing back her head.

"Thank… you—"

The Black Unicorn rammed her head forward, driving her spiral horn through his left eye socket with wall-shaking force. Contorted limbs went limp, plucked away from the edge of pleasure into the crush of death. She withdrew the horn and rammed it through again, his lolling head smashing into the wall repeatedly as she crushed teeth and bone. Once the decimation was complete, she tossed him aside and ran a slick black glove over her corset. An exhalation of smoke billowed from her nostrils as she spread her fingers, admiring the gory strands.

I started to back away, stumbling over the corpses behind me. The Black Unicorn looked up from her fingers, blazing star eyes settling on me. She curled her hand into a fist, the dark fluids oozing as she squeezed. An electrical snap followed, arcing across the forked tip of the cattle prod.

"No! Please!" I shouted, knowing it was useless. She stepped forward, her wicked heel crunching the skull of her latest specimen.

I climbed to my feet and ran, the heavy platforms bounding loudly on the grated floor. Behind me The Black Unicorn whinnied, an excited cry that taunted me as I ran. The bulbs passed overhead, the red and black fade passing as I ran as hard as I could. I could hear her taking her time, bones snapping against metal with each delicate step.

I kept running, the many eyes below watching in silence, following in silence. But each step only brought more darkness, the same repetitive glow passing. She whinnied again, and her steps became faster, loud metallic bangs joining the chorus of my panicked sprint.

clang CLANG clang CLANG clang CLANG clang CLANG

My chest heaved with every breath, my desperate will to live fueling as I ran harder than I had in years. The muscles in my legs strained and pulled, fighting against the awkwardness of the long boots. Despite the screaming in my joints and the burn in my lungs, I pushed as hard as I could.

Ahead, the darkness parted, a shining beam of light in the form of sliding doors. At the end of the seemingly endless corridor was an elevator, bland paint and tile beckoning safety. I pushed toward the light, each lunge more punishing than the last. Behind me The Black Unicorn screamed, and the heavy steps turned to the drum of hooves. I heard the *buzz* of the cattle prod nipping at my heels.

I leapt into the elevator, hitting the back of the cab so hard I felt it rock on its cables. I looked back at the dominatrix. Her long, elegant legs had bent back into wicked hind limbs, sparks flying off the floor as she rushed toward me.

I hit every button in the elevator and watched painfully as it waited to close. With an audible *ding* the doors receded, slowly closing on the madness that engulfed me. I sat helplessly against the wall, tears streaming as the bright pentacle eyes stared me down. Just as they closed she slammed into them; the metal warped against her halted momentum.

I hugged my knees to my chest, and the car began to move.

I didn't know where, and at this point, I didn't care.

I sobbed for a while, the floating sensation of the elevator bringing me an odd sense of peace as we traveled to the unknown destination. It was over, at least for now. I rested my chin on my wiped my eyes, feeling the burn of makeup once again. Through my blurred vision I saw droplets hit the floor, little red specks in front of the toes of my boots.

I glanced up and saw one of the ceiling tiles being scooted over, revealing a dark crevice. Through the darkness poked the gimp, his bleeding zipper mouth parting in a scream. I looked away and shielded my face in denial, just in time to hear the winnie and see the spiral horn burst through the elevator doors.

Through the sickening swirl of black I heard a voice, snarky and loud. Red light faded in and out, followed by an annoying strobe. My head felt heavy, tossing side to side along with limbs that failed to respond. Jerky movements, unfocused steps. The loud latch of metal, then the red glow again.

"Get back! Get the *fuck away* from her! I'll fuckin' mace you, swear to God."

I opened my eyes to see a man with a goat mask, hands up in surrender. Aubryn was shouldering my weight, a task that seemed to be going downhill quickly. I felt myself rocketing towards the ground.

"What the fuck, what is happenuuuuuuuGH—"

I threw up violently, haunted by the sounds of my stomach contents hitting the pavement. I heaved until there was nothing left, then looked up to see Aubryn holding the bear mace, along with a very surprised goat bouncer. We were back in the alley, outside of the bar. The bouncer mumbled something like "alright, sheesh" and retreated back inside, closing the door behind him.

"Girl, what the fuck happened?" Aubryn said crouching down, still clutching the mace. She rubbed a hand on my shoulder, and I shrugged her off.

"You said *go on without you,*" I mocked, my memory coming and going in broken, painful fragments.

"*What?* I said 'don't leave without me'. I wasn't even gone that long," she said, her eyes softening.

"I, I don't know," I mumbled, still spitting vomit. Bitters and bile burned my throat.

"I was only gone *ten minutes.* I came back, and you were passed out at the bar! What, five, *six* drinks?" she exclaimed, digging out her phone.

"No… no, that's not right," I said, trying to get up. My head throbbed with every heartbeat.

"I thought you were fuckin' dead. What happened in there? Are you okay?" she asked, making an effort to comfort me while she held the phone to her ear.

"How strong… were those edibles?" I asked angrily, wiping my mouth.

Aubryn paused, her mouth open in confusion.

"Honey, they weren't edibles. They were *vitamins.* I was just trying to loosen you up. I'll get us a ride, let's just get the fuck out of here," she said, and started speaking into the phone, stepping away.

I got up and looked at the metal door, the *thrum* of music dull on the other side. I heard laughter through the bass, and the familiar snap of a trotter hitting skin. The laughter kept on, even as Aubryn arranged a ride, and walked me down the alley.

A car arrived minutes later, and she helped me in, apologizing repeatedly as we got buckled. I rested my head against the window, my head full of fog and lights and discomfort. The driver put the car in gear and started pulling back on to the street.

"You ladies have fun tonight?" he asked, angling the mirror to see us.

As Aubryn flirted with the driver, I couldn't help but look back at the club, watching the red glow as we pulled away. Just as it was out of sight, the lights went out, leaving nothing but a dark alley.

LYING AWAKE

I used to sleep soundly at night. I used to come home after a hard day, shower, and snuggle up in the blankets. With the buffeting of a box fan and the hum of an air conditioner, I would lull to sleep each night, fading out of consciousness until my alarms woke me the next day. I didn't stress over sounds in the night. I didn't toss and turn at the unexpected wind and rain, or the flash of lightning in a thunderstorm. No matter how trying my day was, no matter how long the hours. I would find sleep quickly and eagerly, ready to face the challenge of the next day. That was, until two days ago.

Two nights, staring at the ceiling. Wondering if I locked my door, wondering if *everyone* did.

Even if I did, would it matter?

Every time I close my eyes, I think it'll be standing in the doorway of my bedroom. I swear I can hear its breathing, labored and heavy with mucus. I feel the heat of its snarl on my neck, and I hear the drag of its claws on the bed sheets.

When I open my eyes, there's nothing there.

I *know* it's there.

Waiting.

My name is Lisa Regan, and I'm a police officer in the town of Dyer Falls. What I saw two days ago will forever haunt me, as long as I live.

Dyer Falls used to be a quiet, small town. I thought for a while that the town was perhaps too quiet, although that is every cop's dream. But nothing ever seemed to really happen in my town, save for the occasional speeding ticket or fender bender. Being a cop in this town almost felt like a redundancy, the highlight of the week consisting of cattle getting out, or someone having a little too much on a night out. After academy training and staying in shape and studying to effectively do my job… it all kind of felt like it was for nothing.

Until that girl went missing and was ultimately found dead in the river. It was a catastrophic event in a town where the only deceased are from old age. Even though the "Car Salesman" case was solved almost open and shut, something seemed to change in town after that. Like something had torn in the fabric of our close-knit reality. People kept more to themselves, and the warm welcome of our town was replaced by an eerie chill we couldn't shake.

The girl in the river was only the beginning, the struck match to light a kindling paranoia that would only grow in the following year. Once the gloom had settled in, it never left. Like it was there to stay. Whenever it would get quiet again, there would be something disturbing around the corner. Something else to headline the paper, to remind us the normalcy wasn't coming back.

A man burned up in his car, along with a murdered cat. Unexplained sightings all over town, from the woods at night to busy places in broad daylight. Mysterious lights in the woods. Overdoses on deadly drugs, ones that were not only untraceable, but untestable. Reports of something lurking close by. The calls became so frequent, even reports of internet ghosts didn't seem that far off. People began to disappear, without rhyme or reason.

Some left photographs behind. Others left their cars on the side of the road, the engine still running. Each case runs cold, just as soon as it happens. While these things seem unrelated when you lay the reports out, you can't help but feel like someone is punishing this town.

The calls of unexplained sightings keep coming. The missing persons fliers are piling up. Our police force is small, and we're spreading incredibly thin. We're all trying to do our part and assure the community that they're safe. Every shift we look up at the sky, and we can *feel* the dark cloud. How can they believe what we tell them when we don't believe it ourselves? At the start of every morning or late-night shift, we wait for the call, for the case that will break us.

Two days ago, I received my call. I'm telling you the story because I hope… no, I *need* someone to believe me.

A vague report of trespassing in the middle of the day, around 5p.m. Some kids playing around on private property. It was something that happened all the time; teenagers looking for a secret place to drink, smoke, and fool around. The only strange thing was that I was called to a location I'd never been to before. It was on a long stretch on County Line Road, a long, wooded portion that was nothing but trees and overgrowth as far as I knew. There was no road marker.

I arrived on the scene, pulling my car onto a barely visible gravel drive in the tree line. The path was blocked by posts and a heavy chain, a simple yet effective barrier that kept my cruiser from going forward. I radioed that I had arrived and would have to proceed on foot.

"10-4," dispatch responded, the chirp of my radio echoing.

I stepped out of the vehicle and traversed the chain, keeping my eyes ahead of me. The path led to a small clearing, and what appeared to be an abandoned barn. If I was lucky, it was just kids sneaking off for some cigarettes, but it boggled me how they had gotten in the middle of nowhere without a car. There wasn't anyone in sight; nothing but tall swaying grass and derelict barn that seemed to be standing solely out of spite. It was apparent whoever owned this property didn't take care of it, and it looked like no one had set foot anywhere near here in a long time.

From a distance, the barn looked ready to collapse at any moment. Not only did it *look* like it didn't belong, the faded gray paint of the outside and the weathered shingles almost seemed rejected by the thriving green grass around it.

I worked my way towards the clearing slowly, keeping an eye open for the suspected teenagers as I approached. I couldn't smell weed or cigarette smoke, and the closer I got the more I thought it was just a false alarm. The tall grass surrounding the barn blew freely, and I couldn't find any depressions in the grass wherever I looked. I kept looking at the barn in the clearing, the long-faded and peeling structure standing like a sore in the middle of its lush surroundings. Just seeing it made me uncomfortable. It looked just like the kind of "kill house" you'd see in Hollywood cinema.

I checked the perimeter around the barn, the cool breeze picking up as I walked around it. The building itself seemed to radiate cold, and the air around it felt… electrical. Something about it felt wrong. The only thing I could hear was the whistle of wind through the cracks of wood. I pressed my face to the wall and peeked in. Old farming tools hung within, each covered in the heavy rust of neglect. Through the haze of dust particles and shadows, I saw a cellar door.

Something nudged my foot, and I jumped. I looked down and saw a cat sitting silently at my feet. Its eyes were green and piercing, its fur a distortion of white, black, and orange. It looked up at me and meowed, the wind rustling its fur.

"What are you doing out here, little guy?" I asked and reached down to pet it. It didn't look pleased to see me here and didn't make any effort to greet me. Across its neck was a collar, with a little silver trinket that read COOPER.

I reached for it, but he backed away. He looked in the direction of my car, then looked back at me. Another meow, this time much slower. His eyes bore into me with an intensity I can't explain. Like there's fire burning in them. The air started to feel chilly, and I felt myself shiver. The cat looked towards my car again, a guttural groan seething from the tips of exposed fangs. The wind picked up, and with it, the stench of death.

It wasn't until then my eyes noticed something in the thick of the trees behind him, a slow realization of details coming together. It looked just like red at first, but as I focused on it, I started to see the limbs… and their lack of skin.

It was a pile of body parts, torsos and limbs stacked like a bonfire.

In front of me, the cat started to hiss. It reared back, teeth bared as its fur stood on end. I reached for my gun and felt the sickening realization that he wasn't looking at me. He was looking behind me. I heard a single footstep, followed by a grunt. Before I could draw, something knocked me on the back of my head, and my world turned black.

I wake to the stench of dirt in my nostrils. My entire right side aches, and I feel like I've been tossed off a cliff. Aftershocks of an unconscious impact rattle deep into my bones, and a delirious panic begins to kindle. I struggle to open my eyes, and my officer instincts fight to ignite. My body tries to obey, each attempt like a failed generator cold start. The gears *want* to turn, but there's a miscommunication.

It's dark, and I'm punished when I open my eyes. All I can see is the absence of light. I try to sit up, my limbs reluctant to obey. The ground feels damp and uneven as I try to push off of it. My head is heavy, and moving it provokes more pain. After several attempts, the best I can manage is sitting. The weight of gravity is nauseating. In the darkness I spin, trying to recollect something other than this. I reach behind my head and feel the dried stickiness of blood. Feeling the consistency on my fingertips brings static in my mind, and I find myself vomiting. My head lulls as I toss it to the side, and my ears are assaulted by the sounds of splashing bile. In the hangover of retching, I have a moment of clarity and recall the aching stiffness around my waist.

My belt. The flashlight, the gun.

I feel the cylindrical shape on my hip and draw the flashlight. There's something loose jingling around inside. I press the button, and the flashlight produces a flickering, fading beam. The light hurts, but I command myself to take in what I see in jarring, erratic bursts.

I'm in what looks like a dugout tunnel. To my left is an old metal ladder, and I follow it up to the ceiling. The shaft to the exit goes up at least twenty feet. Three details stand out miserably, erasing any hope the flashlight seemed to bring.

Halfway up the shaft, the ladder is mangled horribly, twisted steel that would be impossible to climb. Hanging from the top portion of the ladder is my radio, out of reach. The top of the ladder passage is blocked off by what looks like a wooden door. My conclusion is that I was tossed down here, and it's a miracle I didn't break my neck in the fall or gore myself on the broken ladder.

The flashlight is dying, and I abandon what's above to see what's ahead. I swing the flashlight to my right and only get a second before what I see is burned into my mind, even after the light dies. The dugout tunnel continues in a straight corridor, but ahead the dirt is covered in mutilated body parts.

I smack the flashlight in desperation and get nothing except the haunting reminder of what lies ahead. My only hope for escape is further *in*. My legs shake as I climb to my feet, my aching body protesting every movement. My steps are hesitant at first, my knees wobbling under the weight of my ailments.

Albeit blindly, I navigate the walls of gore. Bones and pulp crunch under my boots as I feel my way forward, and every noise makes me sink further inside myself. Despite the growing chill, the stench of hot roadkill still remains.

I do not know how I got here, or why I trudge forward.

I try to use my phone as light, but I can't get it to respond to my finger. The apps open and close rapidly on their own, and the flashlight doesn't work. The signal bars jump from one to four, each lighting individually. I try to reset it, but when I hold the power button, it fails to turn back on.

In my hand is the shaking weight of my Glock 22, feeling heavy and worthless in the dark. I can't even recall when I pulled it from its holster. I point it ahead of me as I walk, my finger twitching on the trigger.

My eyes adjust to the darkness, although I plead with them not to. Gaining insight into my surroundings only leads to a further delve into the insanity. Empty sockets, sinewy jaw bones. My mind tries to piece it together, the reason for the plastered butchery, but produces no answers.

Ahead a tune softly plays, a murmur of direction beyond the meat. In the end I followed it. Not because I want to, but for lack of an alternative. The path behind holds the same darkness as in front of me.

I try not to think of the textures my boot soles communicate, but my thoughts refuse the coddling. I feel them poking through the spongy mass I trudge. I think they're marbles or Legos, but I know they're *teeth*.

The thought makes me stumble and I slip, my hands grabbing desperately for something to save me. My fingers hook into a rod-like structure, and my face is stopped inches from the mess that is the floor. My grasp starts to slip, and I correct myself. When I withdraw my hand, a substance follows, stringy and warm.

A ribcage.

I try to scream, and my gut wishes violently to vomit. The end result is the perpetual half-suck of breath, an open-mouthed gasping that continues even after I'm moving again.

The longer I walk, the more I learn of my surroundings. It's not a hallway or a corridor but a *tunnel*, something that had been carved out of the earth before getting redecorated with human remains. I think I'm descending. The putrid cool of the passage is growing colder. My breath disperses into fog and I start to shiver.

There's a fork in the tunnel. The left leads to more darkness, and to the right is light. I struggle to make sense of it, the little glimmer outline of a rectangle. It's a door, framed impossibly into the walls of the cave. The sight doesn't give me hope, just a foreboding drone the longer I look at it. Like it's trying to signal or tell me something.

Like I'm going to die.

I approach the door. The tune is louder, an old song scratching on a record player. I can hear a loud *thwacking* coming from within, like a blade burying in a block. I think I know what I'll find, but my hand finds its way to the knob anyway.

When I open the door, the first thing I see is the large figure standing in the center of the room. Its body is broad, bulging muscles donning an apron glisten from a dingy overhead lamp. The music drones on as he works, a tired record spinning on an ancient player in the corner. Sharp wicked tools hang from the walls, each stained with evidence of heavy use. Hand-crank augers, scythes, hammers. The butchered bodies of dozens litter the room, coagulating streams trickling to a large floor drain.

I watch the large blade cleave flesh, separating an arm from its shoulder. From what's left of it, I can see it's a woman and recently deceased, steam rising from the freshly pooled blood. Piercing eyes from what I think is a pig look down and admires its work, one of its beefy hands playing in the arterial spray. Its tongue laps like a panting dog, the curve of its smile unnatural and grotesque. Its twisted snout sniffs the air, catching a scent that makes it look up at me.

Behind the Pig Man, the music stops. He looks up at me and cocks his head, moving like an animated nightmare. Its smile widens, and one of his pointed ears twitches.

I want to hide, but it's too late.

I want to run, but there's nowhere to go.

I want to scream, but I can only watch.

Watch as it squeals.

Academy training specifies two shots, center mass. I give him four. The gun barks in my hands, my grip slipping against the gore on my fingers. The rounds punch through its gut, .40 S&W Hollow points ripping through the surface, only to be halted. Like his insides were solid.

The bullets only seem to agitate him. He groans loudly and grabs the body on the table by its throat. He squeezes it angrily, a hand the size of my head closing around the windpipe until the dead woman's eyes bleed. He hefts the mutilated body over his head, and with a loud squeal, he throws it at me. As the corpse rockets towards me I slam the door, and as the body crashes into, I can hear him flipping the table out of his way.

A second later, the large cleaver bursts through the door, sending splinters as it chops through effortlessly. I raise the gun and retaliate, firing rounds through the wood to slow him down. He shrieks as I shoot him, swinging wildly before retracting his arm. His other one comes next, punching another hole through, this time with a meat-hook. It nearly grazes my face, the door crumbling as he reaches as far as he can. The door barely holds him off, and I light him up again, peppering him until the gun runs dry. Even as a bullet digs a trench through one of his eyes, he does not stop.

I turn to run, ejecting the mag and replacing it as he breaks through the door. Despite the many wounds, the Pig Man doesn't seem to be slowing down. Fear bleeds into my adrenaline as I hear him squeal, an unnatural cry that seems more excited as he gives chase. I'm faster at first, but his heavy footsteps crush through the floor's gore as I slip. My hands shake as I rack the slide on the Glock.

I take off opposite of the butchering room, into more tunneling I can barely see through. My eyes adjust to the dark, but not enough to see every jagged bone, every strip of slippery meat. I hear his footsteps gaining, and I turn to fire. The muzzle flashes illuminate the horror he is, and I watch him approach with every consecutive gunshot. Even as the rounds smack into his chest he raises the cleaver, so high it drags on the ceiling. With a grunt he brings the blade down, and I feel the wind from the swing as I throw myself against the wall. The cleaver buries into the floor, kicking up a spray of gore and dirt. I raise the gun and point at his face.

The Pig Man reaches out and grabs the gun, his thick fingers immediately engulfing both the firearm and my hands. I pull the trigger and miss, catching a glimpse of his grin as he lifts me off the ground, my fingers threatening to break. He lets go and slams me into the wall with his head, his skull acting as a battery ram that knocks the wind out of me and crushes my breasts against my chest. I fall to the ground, losing my grip on the gun and slipping in the gore beneath us. My gasp for air is met with a colossal boot on my stomach.

His squeal is loud and echoes through the tunnel as he watches me struggle. He leaves the cleaver stuck in the ground and holds up the meat hook, running his long tongue over the bend in the steel. I try to crawl away, pawing the dark gore in search of the handgun. My fingers graze a human skull, a severed foot, *other* fingers. I try to get away, but his beefy hand grabs the back of my neck and yanks me upward.

Through gasping breath I kick and try to scream, trying to do anything in my power to avoid the meat hook. The Pig Man lets me struggle, a barely human chuckle chattering his crooked teeth. His breath is rancid, a metallic stench of death and decay. I see my end coming, in the form of the sticky hook he drags across my face as he savors what comes next. As he toys with me, I desperately feel my belt for something, anything, to help me.

Empty holsters-handcuffs-taser-mace. MACE.

As the Pig Man stares at me with its remaining eye, I raise the can of mace and empty it into his fucking eyeball. The Pig Man howls against the pepper spray, jerking his face side to side to avoid the mist as I hold the button down. I cough and hack against the spray, my eyes tearing as I exhaust the can. When it's spent, I shove the empty can in his eye, lodging it into the fissure left behind by the bullet. The squeals are broken, almost robotic. The Pig Man swings wildly and lets me go, the hook catching and ripping the meat plastered to the walls as he tries to dislodge the can. I stumble to my feet and run, drawing the taser as I try to get away. I know he won't be slowed for long. The tunnel moves in a blur around me as I run, my breath slowly returning.

Another fork. I go left. I want to wipe my eyes from the spray residue, but my hands are covered in blood. Behind me, the Pig Man squeals angrily.

Another fork. Right. There's no logic behind my direction, only a further descent into the underground madness. I squeeze the taser so hard it hurts. Beneath my feet I start to feel traction. Squinting against the dark, I see the gore is thinning, giving way to metal. The squeals behind recedes further away, angrier the longer he can't find me. The smell of roadkill fades, replaced by oil and grease. My boots meet a solid surface, and I'm able to run without worry of slipping. Just as the squeals become a whisper, the tunnel opens up, wider and taller until I find myself in a vast open space. Machines and metal scrap litter the floor in piles, cracks of light coming from above.

"HELP! HELP ME!" I scream, afraid to stop for too long. My voice reverberates endlessly. I look around the massive room, my surroundings starting to make sense.

It's like a factory, but *tainted.*

I look for an exit but it's so dark, everything blanketed by the shadows of the machinery. I want to hide, but I don't know where he won't find me. I find myself looking aimlessly, the taser pointed in front of me.

I hear the throwing of a switch, and the room explodes with light.

An orange glow floods from above, and the machines around me roar to life. I see the Pig Man against the wall, throwing one lever after another, each adding more deafening noise. Gears turn, pistons engage, and hydraulic lines jerk with the flow of fluid. Geysers of steam shoot from crags in the machines. I look around at the spinning blades, flattening rolls, and grinders. Each is caked with the remnants of human flesh. Shredders chew at gnarled bones, and rotting limbs are blended into paste. Beneath my feet, the diamond plate floor is stained with the fluids of a thousand victims.

In the noise and flashing lights stands the Pig Man, his eye blood-shot and irritated. His mouth is frothing, his face is bleeding. Despite his condition his smile curls, and I see a bulky circular saw in his grip. With a loud squeal he pulls the ripcord, and the saw roars to life with the other machines. Instead of rushing towards me, he slinks away. I hear him rev the saw, but with the barrage of noise I can't hear from where.

Trembling, I duck into the machinery as well, crouching under a table of spinning conveyor rolls. I crawl quickly to the other side, weaving in between machines that seem impossibly built in this hellscape. Concrete is fused with steel in a way that doesn't make sense. Pipes jut from the floor randomly, welded together almost artistically. Like everything is patched together from someone's imagination.

Somewhere the saw revs, and I duck into the workings of another machine to hide. I crawl around beams and weave past rubber hoses, occasionally looking behind me to make sure he isn't following. Shadows dance from the lights above, a disorienting pattern that makes me dizzy. My chest and stomach hurt, and the smog billowing in the room makes me want to gag. I look frantically for some form of safety, but behind every metal cranny is just an extension of the same industrial nightmare. The beams started getting closer together, forcing me to crawl ahead in a narrow path. I no longer had room to turn around, and suddenly I felt a twinge of claustrophobia curling around me.

Behind me the saw screams.

I look back and see the Pig Man, the angry eye staring as he ducks into the small passage. The circular saw arcs off the ground, sparks flying off the floor as he tries to duck under after me. I panic and crawl faster, a primal fear spreading as I think of the saw tearing through my flesh.

The Pig Man squealed, the *ynnnynnnynn* of the saw getting closer as I drug myself along. My elbows knock against the floor and I bump my head off the low ceiling, the passage slowly feeling like a funneling prison. The walls get tighter and the light starts to fade, and before I know it I'm at a dead end, a cold wall suddenly cutting me off.

"No, no, nonono—" I look behind me to see the Pig Man was only fifteen feet away, baring his teeth as he drew closer. I pound against the wall in desperation and feel it give. The passage is cut off by a large toolbox, the wheels rusted and locked in place.

"Move, damn you!" I shout, pushing the box as hard as I could. It budges slowly, wheels squeaking in spite. I hear him getting closer, but I don't dare to look back. I try to shove it again, this time throwing my shoulder into it with everything I have. The wheels break free, only to catch an inch later. The box tips over, tools spilling in a loud crash as the drawers empty all over the floor. I hurry over it, just as I feel the vibration of the saw eating at the floor behind me. I roll over it painfully, sockets and wrenches skittering around as I crawl to my feet. I feel a rush of relief as I get out of there, only for my stomach to sink like quicksand.

The area ahead was just a twenty-by-twenty open square, completely cut off by concrete walls. Chains hung with hooked ends hung from the ceiling, inches above my head. I had backed myself into a corner. There was nowhere else to go.

I turn to see the Pig Man emerge from the passage, his bulky frame squeezing out awkwardly. He's holding the saw lazily, the same excited smile. This was the end of the line, and he knew it. The only way out is back through him.

I look at the floor, at the scattered tools spilled from the tool chest. I holster the taser and pick up the biggest thing I could find: a large open-ended wrench the length of my arm.

"Fuck you," I shout, hefting the wrench in both hands. "You want it so bad, come get it, you fucking *pig!*"

The Pig Man pauses for a moment and lowers the saw. He tilts his head curiously.

"Come on!" I yell, ready to swing.

His smile widens, and he looks away from me at the blinking button on the wall next to him. He lifts a meaty finger and presses it.

The floor beneath me rumbles, and a glaring red spotlight shines from above. Between my feet the floor started to separate, and an ear-splitting roar erupting from below. Beneath me is a pit, and at the bottom, the biggest shredder I have ever seen.

The floor disappears, and the Pig laughs. I drop the wrench and grab on to the chains above, holding on for dear life as the toolbox falls below. The teeth chew at the toolbox, hammers and screwdrivers bending under the immense force of the shredder. It struggles at the momentary clog, only to speed up and clear itself like a garbage disposal. I scream as I flail in the air, and the Pig Man revs his saw once more, swinging wildly to knock me down. Sparks fly and the chains ripple, the spinning blade of the saw only inches away.

I sway on the chain, kicking away every time he swings. I grabbed on to another, but every time I move I dangle further out of control. My grip is slipping, and he will reach me eventually. I have to make a choice: the saw, or the shredder.

I look below at the spinning teeth and wonder if I would even feel it.

The Pig Man swings again, this time aiming for the chains above me. One of the chains is ripped from my hand, and I almost fall. He revs it up again and opens his mouth, a savage scream rippling from it.

Dangling from one hand, I draw the taser and fire.

The electrodes shoot across the pit, crackling barbs sticking into the back of his throat. The Pig Man seizes uncontrollably, contorting hands dropping the saw to the depths below. He bites down on the wires, drool flying as the current shocks him over and over. I yank the tether and he loses his balance, his feet twitching as he tries to stay on the platform. Through the shock he reaches for me, his remaining eye glaring angrily, even as I chuck the taser into the pit.

The shredder sucks in the wires, then yanks the Pig Man with it. I watch him tumble after, stumbling through the air until he fed the gears himself, shoulder first. They eat at him greedily, the motors struggling as they chew at his body. Skin and muscle torn away with bloody bites, the shredder burning up as it reveals what lay beneath. Under the hide of the Pig Man is a skeleton of nuts and bolts, pistons and cogs. The shredder eats away at him slowly, sucking in his feet and hands, grinding away at his snout.

The Pig stares up at me as it consumes him, a look of burning hatred from below even after the floor begins to return and seal off the pit. The shutters close and I return my feet to the floor, legs shaking from the thought of what remains in the pit underneath it. I duck back into the passage I came from, the machines groaning and winding down.

When I return to the entrance of the tainted factory, there's an explosion, like a bomb going off. The walls shake and the floor quakes, and from the dark depths of the factory comes an ear-piercing scream.

The squeal of a thousand angry pigs.

The back of the room erupts, a detonation of blood and steel from the shredder pit. The machines peel apart and vacuum to the epicenter of the sound, scrap and bloody bone coming together in a jigsaw puzzle of metal viscera. The squeals get louder as the mass grows, an enormous snout and pointed ears taking shape in a sanguinary replica. The head turned towards me, and a jagged grin peels through the wreckage. A long arm made of jagged metal reaches towards me, the fingertips consisting of various spinning drill bits.

I run back into the tunnel, the Pig's song booming behind me. The sound of slithering steel grinds throughout the factory, and I hear something converging on me from multiple directions. I push on, tired legs traversing the steel floor that slowly recedes back into sticky gore. The tunnel forks, and I weave blindly, the angry metallic cry following wherever I go. Left, right, left, straight.

My lungs burn, my feet slip. I feel the darkness rapidly approaching, a squelching slither along with a single thumping drag. I hear the Pig consume the tunnel behind me, filling the void like a tidal wave of blood and machine. I take another left and the tunnel just keeps going, a deeper descent into an endless stretch of plastered guts and darkness. I keep running, keep pushing, but I can no longer see where I go. I run until all I have left is the slithering behind me and the sounds of my own tired squishing steps. Like I'm running in place.

A bright white light, shining like heaven. The beam cuts through the darkness and starts to strobe, slowly rounding the corner into an unseen fork in the darkness. A corridor I would've passed blindly otherwise. I bound towards it and turn sharply, my boots sliding as I clumsily right myself. The light continues to flash and I follow, mustering every ounce of energy I have left as I pursue it. My legs start to burn and I realize I'm climbing an incline, the slippery texture fading away to clammy dirt the higher I climb. The light waits for me at the top of the hill, and behind it, I can see what looks like an exit. An end to the tunnel.

Behind me, the squeal shatters the air, an angry cry of malevolence that seems to worsen the closer it gets. It nips at my heels with its drilling fingers, but I keep my eyes forward, focusing on the light ahead and the widening exit behind it.

The ground rumbles and the walls start to cave in, the weight of my pursuer trembling the earth as it gets closer. The squeals rattle my ears but I keep going, my legs shaking as I fight to climb my way out. The tunnel is collapsing.

Ahead the light flickers, and in its wake, stands a cat. The sight of him brings back an epiphany of memories, a trespass call to a derelict barn, and a dark cellar within.

A calico cat named Cooper.

When I catch up, the cat runs alongside me, looking back curiously before diving through a hole overgrown by weeds. I break through shortly after, tumbling to a stop in the overgrowth, exhausted and defeated. The last thing I see in the tunnel is the face of the Pig Man, skin stretched over a frame so large it takes up the entirety of the passage. I long claw reaching for me, pointy augers of metal and bone. The ceiling collapses, and the squeals fade away, like I'm waking from a bad dream.

I lean back against a tree, staring at the knoll I just came out of. With the entrance collapsed, it looks like it was never even there. My blood-stained uniform and the agony in my body assures me otherwise.

Above, the sun is setting. I hear a soft purr and see Cooper sitting next to me, his piercing eyes reflecting the haze of the sunset. I sit there for a moment and stroke his fur, something he seems to momentarily allow. He doesn't lean into my pets; he doesn't look away from the sun. The only thing he manages is the same low purring.

When I catch my breath, I dig my phone from the mess that is my pants pocket. Not only am I surprised when it lights up, it's acting normally, and I actually have service. I hear something in the distance and look up just in time to see a car pass. Not twenty feet from me is the highway, although where in town I'm not sure.

I climb to my feet and dial the number for the station, holding the phone to my ear as I head toward the road. When they answer, I start to explain myself in exhausted, broken sentences.

I look back at the trees, and Cooper is gone.

***

I'm telling you this story simply because… nobody believes me. My fellow officers give their support and have been there for me since, but I can see the doubt in their eyes when I speak up.

You see, we went back to the derelict barn on County Line Road. We found my car where I left it, parked in a little patch of grass on the shoulder. Everything is there as I left it, no signs of tampering, no evidence of theft.

But there's no road leading to the property, no chained-off drive. There's no abandoned property. No derelict barn. No signs of recent activity or presence in the slightest. Just an undisturbed forest that goes on for miles.

I even led them back to where they found me on the side of the road. There's no caved-in tunnel, no mysterious cat, no signs of me even being there; aside from my bruises and ruined uniform. No Pig Man, no nothing.

They've given me time off, time to "collect myself" before coming back to the station and making a proper statement. I also have to undergo a mental evaluation to ensure I'm fit to return to duty.

I suppose I should be thankful. Thankful to be alive, thankful that I made it out.

But every night, I'm left lying awake. I think of that pig and the things I saw down there. I think of how he wouldn't die, and the machinery that writhes underneath his flesh. I think of all the bones I found down there, how many victims he's claimed. The ones he used to decorate the tunnels with gore.

Tunnels that stretch under this entire fucking town.

I lay in bed at night, and I can hear him squeal. I close the windows and lock the doors, but I *know* he's still there. I *know* he won't stop.

I'm telling you this just in case nobody ever hears from me again. I *will* go looking for him. I'll find another tunnel. Someone has to. I just hope he doesn't find me first.

AUTHOR'S NOTE

In 2012, I read Anansi's *Goatman*. I had just finished high-school and was no stranger to horror, having grown up watching scary movies and playing games like *Resident Evil* and *Silent Hill*. But there was something especially disturbing about the tale, and it was my first exposure to internet/creepypasta styled horror. *Goatman* would continue to be referenced as a legend between me and my brother, always remembering the unexplained encounter in the woods when we looked into the backyard. This was years before I even knew of Reddit Nosleep, and even longer before I would start writing online.

I started writing for Reddit in July of 2021, when a friend suggested I try and reach a more available, immediate audience. I had written short stories before, long third-person scenarios every few years or so, but never really did anything with them. When I built up enough confidence writing flash fiction in a sub called r/ShortScaryScaries, it was then suggested I try and post some stories to r/Nosleep, the biggest horror writing sub on Reddit. Writing in only first-person and obeying a long list of guidelines for a post to not get removed felt "yucky" to me at the time (it still does), but I wanted to give it a shot and see if people would enjoy the longer kind of stories I was used to writing, as well as find some sort of validation from the crowd that reads lots of it. *Car Salesman* was the first of these stories, and the start of me taking myself seriously as a writer.

Here we are. Twenty stories, three years later. Starting with a grumpy man in a dealership parking lot, to an underground dwelling pig demon, who loves to decorate his abode with the flesh of those traveling the streets at night. Some of these stories were written in forty-five minutes, others in months. Some were easy, and some were a complete nightmare. But I love every one of them, and wouldn't change a thing about them. The characters I've developed and the monsters I've created will forever live on for me and my family, much like the Goatman my brother and I talked about when we were teenagers. Except instead of Goatman, I have a guiding light named Cooper, and a certain tall unicorn dominatrix. I hope you enjoyed these unusual stories, as much as I enjoyed creating them.

Before I go, I would like to take an opportunity to thank those who helped me not only through my first year as a serious writer, but those who helped me through the process of writing each of these stories in this collection.

First and foremost, I would like to thank my son. He's not old enough to read this yet, but he's the reason I made this collection in the first place. He loves all things scary, and is always on the lookout for the next big scary thing to draw in his sketchpad. He came up with the name Braxton, and has doodled hundreds of pictures of the monsters from this book, from the hell-deer from *Watch For Deer* to The Paper Mache Man himself. He's a wonderful kid, and the best gift a parent could ask for. I love you bud. Sorry so many of these took so long.

Secondly, I would like to thank my wife. She has read *every single one* of my stories, edits them, and helps me fix them when they are garbage. She roots for me when the going is good, and picks me up when things are far from it. She listens to every story idea, and helps me find the pieces when they struggle to fit. And endures conversation of the entire independent writing process. It can be a bit of a broken record sometimes. Love you sweetie. Thanks for carrying the weight every time I spend hours typing in front of the screen.

Next, I would like to thank my friends and family for their undying support, and for believing in me. Thank you for pushing me along and taking the time to listen to me ramble the same shit every time you see me. Sorry I'm always busy. I love you all.

I would also like to thank those I've met along the way in the online writing community, **N. Lamar, Jacob Early, Ryan Major, Jessie Langley, Kenichi Himura, Travis Brown, Estelle Sim, Jordan Grupe, G.C. Clarke, Damian Kane, Rafael Marmol, T.W. Grim, R.M. Staniforth, Grant Hinton, Blair Daniels,**

Rene Rehn, Victor Sweetser, Rebecca Levine, Chris Hicks, and Tors-Anders Ulven. You are all wonderful people.

Special thank you to **Velox Books**, for breathing new life into this collection. Looking forward to more projects on the horizon.

Lastly, I would like to thank **you, the reader,** for taking a chance on this horror collection. I hope you enjoyed these stories, and I hope to entertain you in the future. If this isn't the first book you've read by me, it's good to see you again. Thank you for enjoying more of my nonsense.

Until next time,
Jesse Pullins

MORE CHILLS FROM VELOX BOOKS

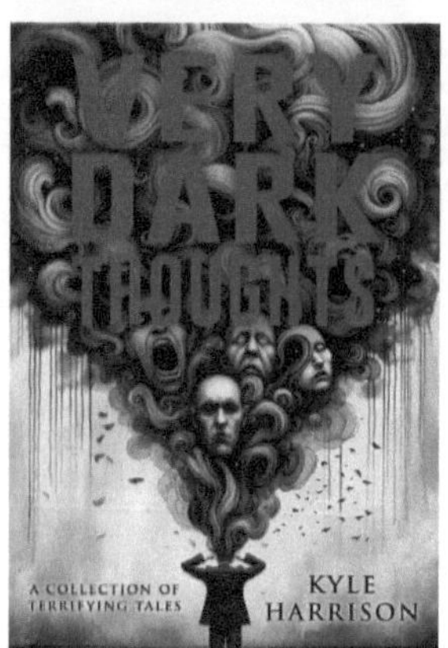

MORE CHILLS FROM VELOX BOOKS

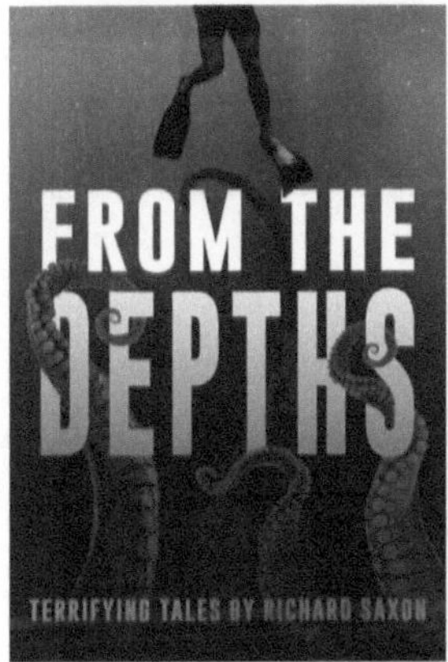